The Garden of Little Rose

Suzanne Snow writes contemporary, romantic and uplifting fiction with a strong sense of setting and community connecting the lives of her characters. Previously, she worked in financial services and was a stay-at-home mum before retraining as a horticulturist and planting re-designed gardens.

Living in Lancashire and appreciating the landscape around her always provides inspiration and when she's not writing or spending time with her family, she can usually be found in a garden or reading.

Also by Suzanne Snow

Welcome to Thorndale

The Cottage of New Beginnings
The Garden of Little Rose

SUZANNE SNOW

The Garden of Little Rose

CANELO

First published in the United Kingdom in 2021 by

Canelo
31 Helen Road
Oxford OX2 0DF
United Kingdom

A CIP catalogue record for this book is available from the British Library.

Print ISBN 978 1 80032 291 2
Ebook ISBN 978 1 80032 119 9

Printed and bound in Great Britain by Clays Ltd, Elcograf S.p.A.

2

To my mum Irene, a gardener

Chapter One

When all three of them were last together, they had talked of sunlit Tuscan villas beneath glittering blue skies and evenings spent lingering over moonlit dinners, catching up with one another as they contemplated the future and celebrated their past. But on a miserable early April afternoon, instead of exploring the galleries and cafes of Florence, Flora Stewart was in the front passenger seat of a creaky old Jeep, rattling along a single-track road around an island off the west coast of Scotland, where she and her two closest friends were to spend the weekend.

'How much further?' Sophie grumbled from the back seat, leaning forwards to peer at the map balanced on Flora's knee. Flora had been relieved to discover it in the glovebox after they had lost any trace of phone signal some miles back, and she was confident now that they were heading in the right direction.

'I would've bought a TomTom if I'd known we'd have to navigate the old-fashioned way. I had no idea you could still buy maps on paper.' Sophie shuddered as she glanced through the dirty window of the Jeep, another deep puddle sending muddy water flying over the glass. 'Clearly modern civilisation has yet to discover this island. Are you absolutely certain we'll have access to reliable Wi-Fi?'

Flora laughed and grabbed her seat with both hands to steady herself as the car sped over another hidden rut in the road, looking sideways at Mel.

'Sorry!' Mel raised her voice as she jumped on the clutch to change down a gear and the Jeep lurched in response. 'We can't all live in luxury in London like you, Soph. Of course there's Wi-Fi, but I'm not planning to be staring at my iPad all weekend. Anyway, stop complaining – both of you were up for this hotel when I found it. You know I've always loved the Hebrides.'

'But that was before you suggested Florence,' Sophie reminded Mel. 'I get few enough chances to escape the family, and slumming it in Scotland wasn't top of my list.'

Mel laughed, pushing her glasses up into her hair as a feeble sun disappeared back behind the clouds churning overhead. The view began to fade once more, hiding the landscape from their sight. 'Come on, it's five-star! With a spa *and* a hot tub in the garden.'

'And you're expecting to use it?' Sophie was incredulous. She huddled deeper into her chic navy coat and tugged on leather gloves, now that her phone was tucked away in her bag. 'Have you actually been looking outside whilst you're driving? I won't be going outdoors at all this weekend; I didn't pack thermals or my waders.'

It was impossible not to laugh, as another shower of hail landed on the roof, making conversation difficult but not impossible, and even Sophie started to giggle. Flora reached for the unreliable heater and turned it up, trying to generate a bit more warmth in the noisy old car.

'The hotel's on the Atlantic side.' Mel glanced across at the map, still dangling precariously on Flora's lap. 'Apparently, this is one of only two proper roads around the whole island; the rest are just farm tracks leading to the crofts and other houses. And the population is so small that just one person used to drive the ambulance, bus and taxi, all in the same vehicle. He was the postmaster and local police officer as well. How romantic.'

'There's nothing romantic about that,' Flora pointed out. 'It's called practicalities. Most people here probably had more than one job back in the day. And you're getting married soon, Mel. Feeling romantic about everything will pass and you'll be back to normal.'

'Hope not,' Mel answered, slowing down again to let another vehicle pass them on the single-track road. 'I quite like it, Flora, even if you don't.'

Flora glanced at Mel then and her face suddenly became alive with mischief. 'Forget the hot tub, Mel – I dare you to swim in the sea. That's what you get for bringing us to some out-of-the-way island instead of Italy.'

'What!' Mel screeched, meeting Flora's laughing expression with eyes that widened in horror and dawning realisation. 'No way! Just because we've always dared each other doesn't mean we have to carry on! We're grown-ups now, with careers and homes and partners… and stuff.'

'Don't be ridiculous, Mel,' Sophie piped up eagerly, leaning forwards to perch herself between the two front seats. 'Coming away this weekend is all about enjoying ourselves and forgetting our responsibilities. Daring each other is exactly what we should be doing. I think the sea is a brilliant idea: the waters are supposed to be warmed by the Gulf Stream. You've always liked wild swimming.'

'In the summer, not in April… in the Hebrides! Well, in that case, Sophie Williams, I dare you to wear flat shoes all weekend. Even at dinner.'

Tiny – hardly more than five feet – Sophie always wore heels, and Flora grinned as she glanced in the rear-view mirror and met her friend's look of horror.

'But I've only brought one pair of ballet flats to wear to the spa,' Sophie wailed. 'I'll look ridiculous wearing the same shoes all weekend. Absolutely not.'

'Fine,' Mel told her airily. 'Then I'm not going in the sea. Sorted.'

'If I wear them at dinner tonight, then you'd better swim before we go home, Mel.' Sophie looked at Flora crossly. 'You started this,' she told her through gritted teeth. 'And seeing as you're now single and without a date for the wedding, we dare you to find one before the weekend's over.'

It was Flora's turn to be alarmed now, and her eyes widened in dismay as she understood the challenge Sophie had laid down. 'Are you crazy? Up here? Where do you suppose I'll find a suitable, single man who's likely to turn up in Ripon on the right day? No, thank you, I'm more than happy to go to the wedding on my own.'

Sophie shrugged, unconcerned. 'Doesn't matter if you don't – the point is to try. A dare's a dare, and I'm up for it… if you two are?'

'Fine,' Flora said breezily, convinced that the opportunity would never arise, as she reached for the map slipping off her knees. 'Mel?'

Mel nodded, meeting Sophie's now cheerful gaze in the mirror. 'Okay. If you absolutely insist.' The clouds parted for a few moments as she turned the Jeep onto a wide driveway, flanked by green lawns and beautifully planted borders filled with shrubs offering early-season colour. 'See, Sophie? The map worked. We're here.'

Flora stretched sleepy limbs; it seemed a long time since she had left home this morning. They had spent a merry evening in her little house near Thorndale, in Yorkshire, miles from the island but still closer than either of her friend's homes. She was hungry, but dinner could wait until she had had a long, hot bath, and she drew in a breath as the driveway swung to the right and the hotel was gradually revealed. Mel pounded the brake pedal for what seemed like forever until the Jeep lurched to a halt, and Flora heard gravel scattering beneath the wheels.

'Wish you'd washed it,' Sophie told Mel, as she shoved her door open and climbed out, staring warily at the churning sky above them. 'Surely you didn't need to bring half the farm with you?'

'No point,' Mel grinned at Sophie as she joined her on the drive. 'Look at the state of it now.'

Flora unwound herself from the car, as Sophie continued to grumble, knowing that her muttering was only the result of having a young child not yet sleeping through. Also, Sophie had been hoping for Italian sun and was instead facing the vagaries of the Scottish weather. The ferry had been delayed and they were all feeling tired. But then Flora's smile widened, as she turned around and stared with pleasure at the building.

'Wow. It's beautiful, Mel.'

A glorious house stood before them: a magnificent baronial tower topped with turrets and curious gabled corners stretching behind the main building, revealing a grand entrance beneath. The Saltire flag of Scotland flew high above one turret, battered by the wind into twisted strips. It was impossible for Flora to see more of the garden, as another sharp shower of hail came raining down on them and they grabbed their bags from the car as a porter hurried out to meet them.

'Sorry about the weather, ladies,' he called cheerily, reaching for their luggage and tucking it underneath his arms with ease. 'Welcome to the island of Alana. Come on in and have a dram to warm you up. It's forecast to be better tomorrow.'

Through her work in garden restoration, Flora was used to old properties and their history, but this was her first experience of the Scottish baronial style and, once inside the huge main hall, she was captivated. The grandeur of the curved oak staircase soaring to the first floor and the cleverly positioned antiques perfectly emphasised the hotel's period design, whilst the warmth and seclusion suggested modern luxuries yet to be discovered. To her left a few guests were relaxing on comfortable chairs in the drawing room, quietly chatting as they enjoyed afternoon tea before a crackling log fire. Flora shivered in her short-sleeved top, whilst Mel checked them all in. It had been much warmer back at home this morning, as well as sunny and bright. The porter stood ready with their bags and, once they were finished with the receptionist, Flora and Sophie followed him upstairs, while Mel dashed ahead.

'Here we are.' The porter paused halfway along a wide corridor on the first floor and unlocked a big, wooden door with a card he produced from his waistcoat pocket. 'Have you remembered that all of our rooms are named after Hebridean islands? Miss Grainger is here in Iona; Mrs

Williams is next door in Skye and Miss Stewart is just across the way in Islay.'

'Could've been worse.' Sophie grabbed Flora's arm, as Mel stepped out of sight with a merry wave. 'At least it's not Muck!'

Sophie disappeared into her room, and Flora choked back a laugh as the porter opened the door to Islay. Once he was gone, smiling his thanks for the tip she had given him, Flora looked around in delight. The room was beautiful and she absorbed the details as she slowly turned around. Damson and gold highlighted every feature, from the cosy chair in front of an oak writing desk to a deep, striped sofa and luxurious curtains draped around a pair of wide windows. She stepped past a queen-sized bed to catch a glimpse of the garden, but rain was still battering the glass and it was impossible to see far through the mist outside. She hovered at the window until there was a knock at her door, which was immediately flung open.

'Shall we meet in an hour for afternoon tea?' Mel crashed in, hurrying as always and optimistically, in Flora's opinion, brandishing a bikini. 'I'm going in the hot tub; Sophie's already in pyjamas and I know you want to have a bath. But I'm sure you can't wait to get outside. Have you brought your gloves?'

'Not this time.' Flora turned away from the window and crossed to her suitcase on its stand to begin unpacking. 'But I won't need them for exploring. Even I'm not planning to get my hands dirty this weekend.'

As soon as Mel was gone, Flora slipped her shoes off and headed into the bathroom. Long hot baths had become a rarity since she had moved into a cottage on the estate where she worked. She could manage with a shower, even if the uncertain nature of the plumbing in her little house meant that sometimes it was like standing beneath a dripping tap and at others like torrential rain. She couldn't wait to climb into the inviting spa bath and linger for as long as possible. She turned on the taps and poured in a generous dollop of water-lily bath lotion.

Mel's official hen night had been two weeks ago, when they had spent a happy weekend with friends in London, enjoying a macaron-and-martini experience before brunch the next day. But this weekend was just for the three of them. Their friendship went back so long that Flora had almost forgotten there had been a time in her life when she hadn't been friends with the other two. They had met in the first term at secondary school, when friendships were harder to come by, bound together by being day girls instead of boarders, and therefore excluded from the tea-and-toast rituals after classes and evenings spent poring over prep. When she was fifteen, Sophie and Mel had provided loving support and a lifeline to normality after it had taken Flora months to recover from glandular fever and the pneumonia which had followed. Her friends had also offered endless comfort and shelter after devastating loss and the shocking discovery which had followed two years ago, and Flora loved them dearly.

But before meeting up with them again, she wanted to be alone for a while. As they had been leaving Flora's cottage this morning, Mel had explained that her fiancé's best man, David, who also happened to be Flora's ex-boyfriend, was planning to bring his new girlfriend to the wedding. Flora wanted time to think about it but, as she undressed and climbed into the hot water, she knew it didn't really matter. She stretched languidly as she imagined how she would feel, seeing him with someone else. It would be strange, certainly, but more like seeing an old friend than a boyfriend she still desired.

Somewhere during the past couple of years – Flora couldn't even pinpoint when – they had slipped from an easy pleasure in one another's company into a steady familiarity that meant each weekend missed or date postponed had mattered less whenever it happened. As they both became preoccupied with their different careers, when they did meet, they went to the same places, ate the same things and quickly forgot that they weren't yet required to slide into middle-aged contentment. So, David would perform his duties at the wedding with a new partner at his side and Flora would wish them well, even if she couldn't quite shake off the feeling of disappointment that she would be without a date of her own – she was resolutely ignoring the dare her friends had set her in the car.

In the end they didn't manage afternoon tea. Sophie stayed in her room, Mel got chatting to another guest in the hot tub, despite the rain, and Flora fell asleep in the bath. When they did finally meet, they raided the minibars and opened a bottle of champagne, piling into Flora's room to get ready for dinner. Mel was dressed first, changed into trousers and a green tunic that emphasised her short, red hair and green eyes. She hated high heels and it was still up for debate whether she would wear flat shoes to her wedding, instead of the beautiful vintage sandals that Sophie was begging her to consider. Sophie had got hair and make-up down to a fine art and was quickly ready in a navy jersey dress perfectly complemented by her sharply layered blonde bob and blue eyes.

She was wearing silver scalloped, Chloé ballet flats and her smile was ironic when Mel complimented her with a smirk.

Flora took her time getting ready. Her appearance counted for little in her work as a garden historian, where her hands were often rummaging in soil and her face exposed to every kind of weather. For this evening she had chosen narrow black trousers and a lacy, primrose ruffle camisole top that flattered the tone of her skin and lifted the outfit from simple to stylish. At five feet eight she didn't really need heels, but she stepped into black stilettos, hoping that their unfamiliarity wouldn't trip her up. She scooped her long brunette hair into an elegant ponytail and slid tinted lip gloss across her mouth.

'You look gorgeous,' Mel told her as she topped up their champagne flutes, discarding the empty bottle in its bucket of watery ice. 'Absolutely stunning. David is so going to regret breaking up with you.'

'Thank you, but I don't think he will. And we decided together to separate – you know he wants to get married eventually and that's not for me.' Flora smiled to soften her words, appreciating her friend's comments about her appearance.

'Bet you're glad to be in heels, and not those horrible work pants and steel toecap boots? You've probably forgotten what your own feet look like.'

'Thanks a lot!' Flora gave Mel a glare that was meant to be fierce, but failed. She reached for the last of her champagne instead and emptied the glass. 'I can't deny it's been a while since I dressed up properly. And getting my nails done was a serious incentive to coming here this weekend.'

They made their way downstairs and found seats in the bar, where they watched the waiters expertly mixing drinks before sending them out to the scattered tables filled with guests. Cocktails were ordered and menus passed around as they settled onto stools. Flora changed her mind at the last minute, opting for a non-alcoholic cocktail instead of the martinis that Mel and Sophie had chosen.

'You lightweight!' Ever decisive, Sophie had already made her choice for dinner and she leant forwards to replace the menu on the bar as she looked at Flora crossly. 'It's barely six years ago since you were a student, but you're definitely in danger of becoming an old fart. We haven't come all this way to complain about how old and boring we're getting.'

'Me, boring?' Flora asked her incredulously, as Mel smirked while studying the menu critically with a professional eye. 'I don't have my timetable worked out a month in advance and circulated by email to the rest of the house.'

Sophie was still smiling as she shrugged. With a husband shouldering a high-powered role as an economist at the Treasury and a two-year-old, as well as her own online business, Sophie made sure that everything in her household ran like clockwork. 'So? Eddie's plans often change and it's helpful if we all know what's going on.'

Mel glanced up from her menu and snorted, but Sophie ignored her and carried on. 'Even though David's family were lovely, Flora, you know he would've probably expected you to pick up where his mum left off. He did buy you slippers for your last birthday, didn't he?'

Flora placed her menu on top of Sophie's and reached for her glass. She thought they would have forgotten about that little detail. She knew she ought to have defended David; her friends were making him sound much worse than he actually was.

'Enough.' She held up her hand in protest but couldn't help laughing, too, happy to be with her friends again. 'No more about David. It's definitely over and there's nothing else to say.'

'David's a sweetheart – we all want everything to work out for him,' Sophie still hadn't finished. 'But you let yourself settle for something comfortable and safe, which wasn't surprising after everything that happened with your dad and how it made you feel about trusting someone. No, don't look at me like that! You know it as well as we do. Of course it was shattering, finding out about his other family right after he died.'

'Shattering!' Flora couldn't keep the sharpness from her tone, her mind taking her straight back to those shocking days after her dad's sudden and unexpected death. 'You saw what it was like, Sophie. I hated what it did to Mum, and I don't ever want to let myself be deceived like that.'

'She loved him, Flora, she couldn't help it. She just did.' Sophie reached for her hand to squeeze it. 'She didn't get to choose who she fell in love with, just like the rest of us.'

'Yeah, well, it's not for me. Finding out that your parents' marriage was all one big lie is quite enough to put me off. You know I'm so happy to cheer you both on and wish you every happiness with two lovely men who actually deserve you. And if they ever let you down, then they'll have me to deal with.'

'And we love you for it, Flora, as well as everything else.' Sophie leant back with a smile. 'But let's forget all that for the weekend – it's history. It's time for a bit of fun and you're going to find it here with some hot, gorgeous guy, I'm sure of it. It's not like anything has to come of it.'

Rolling her eyes, Flora took another sip of her drink. A quick glance around the room left her feeling perfectly confident that she wasn't about to find the man of her dreams in here, and the remote, sparsely populated island seemed unequal to Sophie's expectations for the dare. Flora was off the hook.

Chapter Two

After dinner, they headed into the drawing room for coffee, choosing a comfortable sofa near a curved bay window overlooking the garden. The spring days were beginning to lengthen the evenings and dusk had only recently settled into darkness. Sophie sat down next to Mel and Flora settled into a high-backed armchair nearby.

A jumble of mismatched blue and floral printed sofas were clustered together around coffee tables, perfectly complemented by pale lemon wallpaper and a patterned carpet that didn't quite reach the walls. Folding doors to the piano lounge next door were open and Flora heard the sound of Cole Porter drifting across to them. Her mind well remembered the phrasing of the music and she followed it with a practised ease that she thought she had forgotten after she had switched studying music for horticulture. Mel's eyes were trying to close, as she finally began to slow down and relax, and Flora glanced at Sophie, recognising at once the implacable look on her friend's face.

'Ready, Flora? It seems as good a time as any.'

Flora immediately felt worried. 'For what?'

'For your dare! We need to find your plus-one for the wedding.' Sophie was calmly scanning the room for suitable candidates and she lowered her voice. 'There's nobody in here that will do, so it has to be the very next man that enters the room, provided he's alone and appears to be single, of course.'

Flora heaved a sigh but inched forwards until she was perched on the edge of her chair. She couldn't believe how seriously her friend was taking this. From the corner of her eye she saw Mel sit upright with a grin, as she realised what was going on. As Flora slowly stood up, she heard Sophie's splutter of laughter, and her heart sank as she glanced across to the door. An elderly man had sidled in with the help of a walking stick, wearing tartan trousers and a Prince Charlie jacket. Flora heard Mel laugh, too, and she turned around to glare at her. But then she felt Sophie's hand clutching her leg and she swung her gaze back to the door: the elderly man had ambled back out again, and a much younger and taller man had taken his place.

He had paused to greet someone, allowing Flora a moment to study him. He was wearing a simple white shirt and dark grey trousers, which highlighted broad shoulders and long legs. Dark blonde hair was cropped short, and she was near enough to notice stubble covering a determined jaw below a slightly uneven nose that must once have been broken. A brief grin hardly softened his eyes when he nodded at somebody else, and she sensed at once that he was used to getting his own way. Flora could see it in every detail she had already noted, from his brisk handshake to the cool and measured way he studied the room before him.

Sophie gave a strangled squeal and her fingers tightened on her friend's calf. 'Flora, quick, before somebody else snaps him up. He's not wearing a wedding ring. Worth a try, at least.'

Flora found herself putting one foot in front of the other as she walked towards him, nerves spinning wildly. She almost wished he would turn around and leave before she had a chance to speak to him, and yet she already knew that would bring disappointment. He was alone, quietly watching the room, and then Flora was hovering awkwardly beside him, uncomfortably aware that several pairs of eyes were watching.

'Oh hi,' she said, an unexpected glow warming her face when he turned his head. She realised his eyes were almost a slate grey rather than blue, and she was surprised by their impatience as he looked at her. He gave her a brief smile that was more dismissive than polite, the gesture bringing out the fine lines around his mouth. He moved aside to let her pass and looked down at the phone in his hand, swiping abruptly at the screen with an irritated sigh. She caught the subtle scent of his aftershave – cardamom and fresh summer spices – and thought distractedly that he would be perfect for dancing at the wedding, as he was a good four inches taller than her, even in heels.

'I'm really sorry to bother you.' Flora hardly recognised the high squeak of her own voice. He lifted his head, as though surprised that she was still there, and the suggestion of a smile returned when his eyes found hers, before roaming slowly over her face, where her blush still lingered. 'I'm staying here, and I have to ask you a question. My friends, over there—' She waved her arm hazily towards the window, 'They've insisted on a silly dare. We're here on a sort of hen weekend and, basically,

I have to find a plus-one for my friend's wedding in a few weeks.'

'Excuse me?' His confusion was reflected in the sharp reply and slight lifting of his brows, and Flora crashed on desperately.

'Just say no, of course – why wouldn't you? But I had to ask the first man we saw, and it wasn't you… and then it was.' Flora fell silent, all too horribly aware that she was babbling utter nonsense to a gorgeous stranger. 'Sorry, I'm not making any sense,' she muttered quickly. 'Forget it.' She turned away.

'Go on then. Ask me to be your guest. If that's what you were trying to say?'

His voice, with its rich Scottish burr, was deeper than she had expected, full of amusement and warmer than his eyes. She spun around and a few moments dragged by, before she responded, conscious of the air between them vibrating with tension and expectation. She forced herself to stand still, as she spoke quietly.

'Would you like to be my plus-one at my friend's wedding next month?'

The phone in his hand began to vibrate again, but he silenced it without looking at the screen and pushed it into a pocket. His gaze had never left hers throughout their exchange, and Flora felt the atmosphere around her shift, as though she had crossed to a place where the very air was unknown to her.

'I'd love to.'

Completely thrown by his easy and unexpected acceptance, her eyes widened in alarm. 'You don't mean it,' she stammered, and she knew he was enjoying her surprise.

'A simple no would have been fine. I know you won't come – it's a stupid idea.'

'But you invited me. Are you saying you've changed your mind?'

Flora gaped at him and couldn't think of a word to say, couldn't find a response to his confidence and the ridiculousness of what she had done. He waited, his earlier impatience dispelled by his obvious enjoyment of their exchange. She shook her head slowly and he found his phone once again.

'Should we swap numbers? Seeing as we'll probably need to contact one another if I'm to be your guest.'

Flora could never remember her own phone number since she'd changed it a few months ago. Glad of the excuse to have a moment to think, she pointed to the sofa again. 'My phone's over there. Maybe later?'

She turned away, her mind spinning as she tried to imagine what would happen next. Her heel caught in a rug and it was a few seconds before she managed to twist her shoe free. She had no idea if he were still watching, but she could see Mel and Sophie falling about, hardly bothering to conceal their amusement. She stomped over to them, lowered herself into the armchair and reached for her drink.

'Done,' she spluttered, horribly aware that her cheeks were still glowing as she gulped a mouthful of coffee. 'Don't ask, I'm sure you saw everything you need to know. He won't come.' She pushed the cup back onto its saucer with a rattle. 'Have they not brought the whisky yet?' She became suspicious as she saw that Mel was looking serious. 'What? What is it now?'

'I'm sure I've seen him before.' Mel's concentration produced a frown, as she delved into her memory, and Flora's gaze followed the man as he crossed the room to the bar. Flora also noticed nearly all the other women in the room seemed to be looking at him, too, and that made her even crosser. *Wish I'd tried the tartan guy*, she grumbled to herself.

'Well, it doesn't matter,' she said out loud, feeling her pulse gradually slow and her adrenalin begin to retreat to more normal levels. 'We'll all go home on Sunday and then I'll never—' She didn't quite manage to finish her sentence, as Mel shot upright on the sofa and grabbed Flora's arm, a look of satisfaction brightening her expression.

'I've just realised who he is.' Mel was triumphant now the confusion had disappeared and Flora knew she was about to find out, whether she wanted to or not. 'That, Flora, is Mackenzie Jamieson, I'm sure of it. I think his family owns this hotel. Good choice, babe. Just think, if the two of you get together, Sophie and I will be able to come for weekends whenever we like.'

Flora gave a moan of horror, wishing it were already Sunday morning. So, she could never come back to Alana, even if she wanted to, and at this very moment she wished she hadn't come here at all, despite the promise of a whole day in the spa tomorrow. Flora listened as Mel continued the story and her dismay, as well as her reluctant curiosity, grew with every word.

'Apparently, the hotel was opened after the island was sold by the previous owners in a community buyout a few years ago. There was some mention of a serious girlfriend at one time, but it seems he's quite private and nobody's very sure if she's still around.'

'And how on earth do you know all of this?'

'Google, of course. I looked him up when I found the hotel. But the photograph didn't look very recent: he had a beard and his hair was longer. He's gorgeous, though, isn't he?'

Flora was reluctant to admit it, not that she had the chance to speak, as Sophie suddenly squealed urgently. 'He's coming over,' she hissed excitedly, flicking an expert hand through her hair. 'With the drinks.'

Flora barely had time to register Sophie's comment before she became aware that Mackenzie Jamieson had halted beside her chair, and she knew her skin was glowing all over again. From the corner of her eye she glimpsed a long leg, close to her seat, and deliberately watched Mel instead, who was happily smiling up at him.

'Ladies, your whisky. I hope you'll forgive me for choosing for you.' He was looking from Mel to Sophie as he spoke. 'A Macallan ten-year-old single malt, nicely full without being too sweet. Perfect for after dinner.' And then he turned to Flora. 'For you, something different.'

Flora squirmed as he singled her out, wishing he hadn't, and trying to appear calmer than she felt.

'A Lagavulin sixteen-year-old malt – full, smooth and complex. I hope you enjoy it.'

He placed the glasses on the coffee table and Flora noticed at once that he had rolled up the sleeves on his white shirt, revealing powerful arms browned by the sun and covered in softly curling golden hairs. Then she heard him speak again and surprise, as well as simple good manners, forced her to look up at him. Those curious slate-grey eyes were waiting for hers and the atmosphere between them began to simmer once again.

'Here's my card. Text me when it's convenient. I don't want to take up more of your evening, Ms…?'

'Stewart,' she replied coolly. She accepted the card without looking at it. 'Flora Stewart.'

'Flora Stewart.' He repeated it slowly, his eyes locked on hers. She had the impression he was testing the shape of her name, rolling the letters into something that sounded casual and intimate all at once. He bent to collect their empty coffee cups, before straightening up and sweeping his glance across each of them. He gave a quick nod and turned away without another word. Flora stared at his back as he headed off towards the bar with the tray, still astonished by the turn of events.

Sophie leant forwards to mutter, 'I thought you said he wouldn't come?' Her eyes narrowed slyly, curiosity and mischief alive in her expression. 'Because he has just given you his telephone number. Nice work.'

Flora shook her head in vehement protest. 'It was definitely a no. Well, he sort of said yes, but he won't actually come.'

'Whaaat?' Sophie's screech attracted curious glances and Flora tried to shush her furiously. Undeterred, Sophie carried on, her voice only slightly lower. 'What did you two actually say to each other?'

'Thank you, Mr Jamieson.' Mel jumped in, raising her voice quickly before he was lost to them in the groups milling nearby. He paused, still holding the tray and turned around. He nodded at Mel before his measured glance met Flora's flustered one across the people in between them.

'Mac,' he said casually. The sudden grin he gave her was so teasing that Flora wondered if she was imagining the challenge in his eyes. 'My name's Mac. You can send the invitation via the hotel if you like.'

Chapter Three

It was only seven thirty the following morning when Flora slipped through reception and out of the hotel. Mel was most likely fast asleep, and she knew that Sophie intended to spend a few extra hours in bed whilst she was here. As their first treatments in the spa weren't booked until ten o'clock, Flora decided that she could take an hour or so to explore, taming her hair into a ponytail tugged through a baseball cap.

The weather had changed again and instead of rain pelting the hotel and smothering everything in mist, the skies had cleared to reveal a bright sun. Once outside, Flora paused and breathed in the first scent of the day. It smelled of spring and the promise of life emerging from the winter slumber, even later up here than back in Yorkshire. It was absolutely her favourite time of day and most definitely her favourite time of year.

Gravel crunched beneath her feet as she set off and she heard the noisy growl of a delivery van heading around the back of the building, as her gaze took in the beautiful and carefully planted garden surrounding the hotel. But she would explore this later, if time allowed. She wanted to head around the tiny island and make her own discoveries, not those which came presented in a handy leaflet and kept tourists on the beaten track.

From the map she had found in her room, Flora knew that a footpath in front of the hotel eventually widened into a track that wound its way to a pier on the north-eastern side of the island, the furthest point from the ferry. She wasn't expecting to see many people at this hour and she settled into an easy pace, quicker than a stroll but allowing herself enough opportunity to savour the magnificent views all around. She loved walking. It was part of her day job as well as her favourite way to unwind. And since she had given up athletics at a competitive level years ago, when illness had struck and changed the course of her life, it was all the exercise she now took.

The island was stunning, and Flora knew that she was seeing it not quite yet at its best. Having grown up with the beauty of Yorkshire around her, she was used to spectacular landscapes, and working for a heritage charity had only enhanced her love of history. This morning, any attempt at walking purposefully was soon abandoned, as she kept pausing to stare at another mountain in the distance, still topped with snow, or drop to her knees to examine a young plant hidden amongst the bracken, just beginning to unfurl itself from the harshness of winter. She had to dodge free-roaming cattle a couple of times and they ignored her as she passed by.

After almost thirty minutes Flora thought that she must have missed the coastal path to the pier some way back and must now be heading inland instead. Cross with herself, she realised she had also left her phone behind. Ahead, she thought the mountains in the distance were on the mainland and so she carried on, hoping that she might complete a circuit of the entire island if she kept up a good pace.

Ten minutes later, hot and beginning to think she would never find the hotel again, Flora hurried downhill on a rough footpath and saw a house tucked between trees, perched above ground sloping down to a tantalising glimpse of the sea below. She paused to glance at her watch, intending to carry on. But there was still a little time left before she ought to return. She stepped off the footpath and crossed a field, dodging rocks and nervous sheep alarmed by her presence. In places the ground fell away so steeply that she had to grab clumps of heather to steady herself, as she clambered over the craggy terrain. When she reached a low stone wall, she hopped onto it and dropped down on the uneven and weed-filled driveway below. She turned to look properly at the house.

She knew at once it was empty. There were no visible signs of life – no cars, noise or people in sight. It was big but not grand, and from its location near the sea, Flora guessed that it might have been built as a holiday home. A few windows were boarded up and weeds were clinging to the wide slate roof, hanging down over the dirty glass beneath and tapping against the sills as though trying to get in.

Flora was quite certain that she was trespassing so, despite her desire to look closer and perhaps discover a few secrets, she turned around to leave. But then she saw a door. A tatty, faded green door tucked into a wall beside the house and she knew immediately it would lead to the garden. Flora also knew she would have to negotiate clumps of nettles and weeds tangled across the door, but still she lingered.

It'll probably be locked, Flora told herself as she walked towards the door, a sudden swirl of excitement fluttering in her stomach. She reached out and twisted the wobbly iron handle. It wasn't locked and the door creaked eerily but gave no other sign of protest, and she pushed it aside, kicking at the nettles.

She was standing on the edge of a terrace stretching across the back of the entire house, and her heart began to pound as she turned full circle, trying to absorb every detail, as though she would see it only once. Silently, Flora crossed the terrace until she was in the centre, facing the main garden.

A row of yew trees either side of three flights of steps led to more terraces and she carefully planted her feet onto the first one, which was smothered in damp moss and crumbling into pieces. She followed the steps slowly until she reached a weed-filled gap at the bottom of the second terrace and looked up. She was staring at the remains of a formal garden, sweeping down the hill towards a narrow beach beyond the hedge. What must once have been a lawn had disappeared into a sea of grass waving gently in the breeze.

Flora crouched down, pushing her fingers through weeds and soil until she could feel the rough stone beneath. Slowly, she stood up, hardly daring to indulge her exhilaration as she began to realise what she might have stumbled upon. She hovered for a moment, envisaging in her mind how the garden must once have looked, until she caught sight of her watch. She groaned, knowing she ought to return to the hotel and not at all sure that she knew the quickest way back. Reluctant to leave, she turned around and sneaked another peek at her watch, hoping she might have been wrong about the time.

She was certain that there would be other areas of the garden, besides this formal one she had discovered.

She walked carefully back up the terrace and had almost reached the south-east bay window when she heard a thudding noise. She froze as her heart jumped in alarm – there it was again. It sounded like a door banging and she made her way along the uneven terrace as fast as she dared, until her feet found a patch of slippery bittercress. She skidded on it, crashing to the ground with a muffled shriek that she tried to conceal, as her arms flew out to break her fall. She winced as she pushed herself onto her hands and knees, listening for a sound from the house. Nothing. Carefully, she climbed to her feet and crept along the terrace, wondering if unseen eyes were watching her. She had almost reached the drive, when the clatter of a door behind her made her yelp in horrified surprise.

'Hey! Wait!'

She knew that voice and had no intention of waiting. She hurried on, picking up speed as the throbbing in her ankle began to ease, but escape wasn't going to come easily. He was quicker, and seconds later he had caught up and reached for her arm, gently drawing her to a halt.

'Morning. I didn't expect to find you here, Flora Stewart. You're quite some distance from the hotel.' Mac sounded surprised rather than annoyed, but Flora had no desire to make a fool of herself again.

She turned to face him and began to apologise. 'I'm really sorry! I didn't mean to pry.' She withdrew her arm from his hand and continued, 'I was just leaving.'

She hoped the baseball cap was hiding most of her blush from his scrutiny. He was wearing a dark T-shirt and shorts, revealing legs that were exactly as she had imagined: lean, strong and tanned. Sunglasses were tucked into his T-shirt and his chunky work boots were covered in pale dust. The golden blonde stubble was longer, and he seemed totally different from the cool and composed businessman that Flora had met only last night. Inexplicably lost for words at his changed appearance, she couldn't think of anything else to add.

'I don't mind.' He pushed his hands casually into his pockets as he watched her. 'Not many people find their way up here and go wandering around the garden.'

She glanced at her watch. Perfect. She was going to be really late now. Gesturing carelessly across the garden, as though Mel and Sophie were lurking nearby, she explained, 'I should've brought a map. I have to go; I'm meeting my friends and I'm running behind. I am sorry, Mr Jamieson, I should have appreciated this isn't part of the hotel grounds.'

'Mac,' he replied, one shoulder rising to bat away her apology. 'Just Mac. Please don't apologise, it's really not necessary. This is a nice surprise, after meeting you last night.'

Flora ignored that last comment and the flick of pleasure it brought. She had been hoping he'd forgotten their awkward encounter after dinner yesterday, but it was clear he had not. She wasn't about to reveal just how much he had been in her thoughts since then.

'Most of our guests aren't interested in seeing a garden in this sort of state. May I ask why you came here? I saw you from the house and it seemed as though you were searching for something.'

Flora's glance sought out the garden again, trying to tuck a few more details into her memory to take away.

'I found it by accident and couldn't resist exploring.' She turned back to see that Mac was still watching her, and she couldn't look away from the unfamiliar warmth in his expression, as a smile played around his lips. 'Gardens to me are very special places, especially ones that have years of history to offer and so many secrets to tell.'

'Like this one? Even though it's such a mess?'

'Yes. Exactly like this one. I know already that somebody long ago cared very much about it and I can picture in my mind how it might once have looked, planted with different colours and textures, and filled with the sound of people enjoying it.' She felt almost as though she had been here before and understood its stories without ever having learned them.

'I see.' The grin Mac gave her was so sincere that she felt it like a push to her chest. It softened his face immediately, deepening the lines around his mouth, and making him seem more boyish and much less intense. 'May I show you something else, something I think you'd like to see?'

'I can't, I'm already late,' she said helplessly, her feet itching to move and follow him to discover whatever it was he wanted to show her. He was already at the top of the steps and he turned, holding out a hand.

'Sure? It won't take long. Do I have to dare you?'

'I think you just did.' She could use that to excuse her lateness to Mel and Sophie, at least; all three of them always followed through on their dares.

They were both smiling, as she slipped her hand into his and he gripped it tightly while they made their way down the unsafe steps. At the bottom, they began swishing through the wet grass around their legs, like wading through water, and she reluctantly freed her fingers from his.

Meeting a man such as Mac Jamieson and discovering a garden was not at all what Flora had imagined from this weekend. Everything was unexpectedly shifting around her and she wasn't sure how to feel amongst it all. They ducked down beneath low branches at the edge of the remains of the lawn and emerged in a narrow lane. On their left was a stone stable block, clearly abandoned and in a poorer state than the house behind them.

'Is it far?' She reached up to pull a few stray leaves trapped in her long hair. 'Mac, I really don't have time for this.' His name came easily to her lips and she repeated it in her mind.

'No, almost there.' That light, teasing tone again, so different.

He increased the pace now they were free of the wild garden, rushing them down the lane and past a pair of small, roofless cottages. He pushed his way through a tiny gap in a tall, overgrown hedge beside the little houses and reached for her hand again, tugging her gently through behind him. He didn't seem to notice the thistles leaping up around their feet, and finally paused only when they had scrambled through the cottage garden and reached another door, set in a high wall.

She had seen many historic gardens before and knew what would be contained between these walls. The familiar excitement of discovery had returned, and she itched to go inside and explore the old, walled garden for herself. He grinned as he opened the door, letting go of her hand. They looked at each other and she knew that something between them had altered: perhaps he was sharing this forgotten place in a way he hadn't before.

'Go and see.'

She stepped through the door, down three narrow steps, and climbed carefully over more thistles, smashed clay pots and a broken wheelbarrow dumped nearby. She could smell the sea, hear it, but couldn't see it. The view of the water was concealed by the high stone wall and huge yew trees protecting this magical and private area, separate from the formal garden she had already seen. To her left, tumbledown greenhouses leant against the length of the south-facing wall; in front lay the remains of an orchard. Slowly, she made her way around, crushing the nettles spreading across lost paths and pushing past the ivy scrambling up the walls, eating into the stone. Wholly captivated, she slowly turned away from the sound of the sea, her thoughts whirling with possibilities of what had been here before, and when.

Mac was sitting on the steps at the entrance where she had left him, his arms wrapped around his knees, and he shuffled sideways to make room for her. Flora was lost in wonder, and she knew not quite all of it was inspired by the garden. She sat down, their shoulders bumping together, feeling the coolness of the stone through her jeans.

'It's so kind of you to let me look around, Mac. It's a beautiful garden and I think it's very special. Thank you.' Their arms were still pressed together in the narrow space and she heard his short, wry laugh.

'I know that it was once, many years ago.' A quiet sigh followed his words, as he stared at the chaos spread before them. 'Hopefully, it will be again, eventually. There'll be clearance work carried out at some point, but the house and outbuildings are the priority, before their condition deteriorates any further.'

'Are you the architect, then?' Flora had read the details on his card the moment she was alone in her room, stopping short of googling the practice he worked for in Edinburgh.

Of course, this was none of her business, but she waited for his answer, trying to communicate nothing of what she was feeling, beyond casual interest. She couldn't miss the satisfaction in his tone when he replied.

'Yes. And the very happy new owner, too – the sale was completed a few weeks ago.' Mac's expression was jubilant now. 'I've spent a lot of time on the island over the years, and I've known this house and wanted it since I was a boy. It's been empty since I first saw it and I used to sneak in and explore on my own sometimes, dreaming about restoring it before it was too late, and someone came along and demolished it. I still can't quite believe it's actually mine now.'

'How wonderful.' Flora couldn't have hidden the delight in her voice even if she had wanted to, as she realised that this remarkable, secret place would not be forever lost. Their eyes met, and she saw the pleasure that her response had given him. 'May I ask you a question?'

'Another one? Does it have anything to do with a wedding?'

He was laughing and she heard the trace of indignation in her response to his playful reply. 'No!' But she still wanted the answer, so she pressed on. 'Are you able to tell me if the garden was designed by Rupert Lassiter?'

'Who?'

She heard the teasing note in his voice, sure he was looking confused on purpose but not certain why. 'Lassiter was a Victorian architect who specialised in Arts and Crafts designs. I'm sure you know it was a movement that started in the mid-nineteenth century, creating designs that celebrated beauty and simplicity through skilled craftsmanship. I'm not very familiar with Lassiter's work but I do know he practised mostly in Scotland, and I thought this garden might be one of his.'

'Sounds interesting. Thanks for the suggestion.'

Mac stood up, reached for her hand again and pulled her upright, and she felt his quick touch on her back as he guided her through the door. They passed the little cottages, both walking slowly and seemingly reluctant to hurry these last moments together. But there was something she had to say, and Flora paused, halting their progress. 'Would you mind if I offered you some advice?'

'Not at all.'

'Whoever was responsible for the garden has left behind a remarkable legacy and I would only say please don't rush into clearing it all away and starting again. Underneath what's here now, I think there could be lots of original features and it would be worth taking your time to uncover them. I'd expect to find an informal planting style balanced by natural materials in the landscaping, and the way the garden becomes less formal beyond the house is typical of the period.' She shrugged, her glance roving around their surroundings. 'Sorry, I'm not trying to tell you what to do with it – it's your decision, of course. It's just, well, it could be important.'

He was eyeing her curiously as he considered her words. 'I see. You're very welcome to stay and explore, Flora.'

Flora thought about Mac's offer, distracted by the encounter with him and the discovery of the garden, until suddenly she remembered Mel and Sophie – and their plans for the spa. 'I can't,' she replied frantically, half-wishing that she could stay, even as she hurried away from him, back towards the house. 'I really do have to go, I'm very late.'

'Follow the lane to the T-junction and turn right, it's the quickest way back to the hotel,' he called after her, and she resisted the temptation to stop and look at him one more time. 'I'll be here if you can come back tomorrow. I could show you around properly.'

Flora wasn't sure she had heard him correctly, as she raced on and the call of his goodbye drifted into the sound of the sea. But his comment mattered much less than the realisation that bumping into him today had awakened sensations she had discarded during the gradual end of her relationship with David. She barely glanced at the garden as she stumbled back up the broken terrace and pushed through the green door onto the drive, feeling as though she had been to Narnia. She set off at a steady pace, thankful for the first time in years that she'd been a middle-distance runner and not a sprinter.

Chapter Four

It took Flora a good thirty minutes to run back to the hotel, grab a shower and sprint down to the spa in the converted stables in the grounds. She saw that her friends were already in the pool; Mel was bobbing up and down, whilst Sophie swam expert lengths in a perfect crawl. Flora chucked her bag into a locker and two minutes later was in the water with them.

'So sorry,' she called, as she headed towards Mel. Sophie spotted them and powered over, swimming easily past the stragglers in her way. 'I got lost on a walk and then I discovered a garden.' That was as much as she wanted to say for now, at least until she had had an opportunity to do a little research. She also needed another chance to speak with Mac and confirm that it really was the forgotten remains of an early twentieth-century Arts and Crafts design.

'Really?' Sophie stared critically at Flora as she trod water, tipping her head to one side and removing her goggles. 'Just a garden? You're very pink, Flora. Are you sure that's all?'

'I had to run back; I went a bit further than I meant to.' Flora's reply was hurried, and she flipped over so that Sophie couldn't see her face. She didn't want to give her friends an excuse to press her for more information and she certainly had no intention of mentioning the unforeseen meeting with Mac just yet. As she and Sophie had completed their part in the dares, Mel had reluctantly promised to take a short dip in the sea before they left the following morning.

As the day wore on, Flora found it difficult to ignore Mac's invitation to return to the lost garden. By the time she had been exfoliated and massaged, with newly perfect nails and feet that felt transformed after reflexology and a pedicure, she felt like a completely different woman and not the one usually found scrabbling about in borders or potting sheds with tools and a trowel. Champagne had been on offer all day and she had enjoyed more than a glass by the time they returned to their rooms to change for dinner.

Her long, glossy brown hair, naturally highlighted by the sun, was shot through with golden streaks that brought out her blue eyes – *sapphire*, as Sophie insisted on describing them. Flora spent longer than normal applying make-up but kept it simple, finally spraying perfume on her wrists and neck. Sophie appeared, making approving noises, and Flora agreed to let Sophie dry and style her hair, coiling it into thick waves that tumbled halfway down her back.

Once she was alone again, Flora lifted her outfit from the wardrobe: a simple, elegant wrap dress the colour of sapphire – matching her eyes perfectly – that caressed and clung to her body, its hem sitting above her knees. Black slingback heels, a matching clutch and she was ready, anticipating the evening ahead with butterflies in her stomach. She left her room and soon heard the subtle sounds of guests gathering together, as she made her way downstairs.

She crossed the drawing room, spotting Mel and Sophie perched on stools at the bar and already chatting with the handsome waiter.

'Flora! At last, come and try this! Ewan's mixed the most amazing cocktail with coconut vodka and lime, and it's utterly delicious. We've just ordered another one.'

Flora smiled at Sophie's exuberance as she settled onto a stool, her long legs reaching easily to the floor, and took the glass that the young man was already offering and thanked him. Sophie was right: the drink was gorgeous and she sipped it slowly as they chatted together. It wasn't long before their table was ready, and they headed into the dining room.

Flora wasn't sure how she managed to get through dinner without blurting out everything to her friends. They had never kept secrets from one another but what was there to say? That she was surprised by her growing attraction to Mac Jamieson and thrilled by her discovery of the garden? Or that she was certain she'd never see him again after tomorrow, despite the dare? Once the meal was over, and they had ordered coffee and wandered back into the drawing room, she began to feel unsettled, desperate not to let what could easily become a silly crush disrupt her precious weekend with Sophie and Mel. The room was filling up gradually, as guests left their tables; replete and drowsy, they settled down together to chat quietly and enjoy the hotel's understated hospitality.

'Flora? Look who's just arrived.'

Flora heard the glee in Sophie's comment and saw Mac walking across the room to the bar, nodding at people but not pausing to chat. Although he wasn't dressed for dinner, Flora couldn't help noticing how he still turned every head.

'Looks good, doesn't he? Bet he'd scrub up well for a wedding.' Mel laughed at Sophie's observation and they both looked at Flora, testing her reaction.

She tried to watch him with only casual interest but was caught staring when he glanced across to her. His eyes gleamed as he took in her appearance, and she felt a small thrill that seemed to make the rest of the room disappear. He winked – a gesture so simple and sexy, suggesting an intimacy that words never could. But then he turned away, his attention claimed elsewhere, and the moment was gone as quickly as it had come.

'I saw that.' Sophie's perfect eyebrows lifted in suspicion. 'What's going on? Have you seen him again since last night? Have you made plans to bring him to the wedding?'

'No, of course not.' Flora knew she sounded defensive as she altered the truth. She was saved from having to explain further when Mel suddenly burst in the conversation.

'He's coming over, Flora!' Mel didn't bother to try to hide her delight. 'Hello, Mac, how lovely to see you again.'

Flora forced herself to sit still as Mac halted close to her chair and she tried to pretend this wasn't really the moment she had been waiting for all evening, as well as the reason she had allowed Sophie to style her hair. She raised her head, hoping that the wild thudding of her pulse was not obvious to anyone else. The blonde stubble from this morning had gone, revealing smooth skin, and Flora was already imagining how it would feel to touch.

'Hello again. How was your day – did you enjoy the spa?'

She heard the cool note in his voice again: the quiet reserve was back, and she wondered if this was his way of maintaining a professional distance from guests; it was quite unlike the boyish enthusiasm she had discovered earlier. She listened to the rush of Mel's eager chat, content to play no part.

'Oh, it's been a fabulous day, thank you. The honey-and-milk wrap was exquisite – I feel about ten years younger already! And the radiance facial was amazing, exactly what I needed before the madness of a wedding. And look at Flora's hands after her manicure: they're so pretty now; usually she can't quite scrape out all of the soil from underneath her nails.'

Flora stilled as Mac examined her hands and, no doubt, her crossed legs underneath them. She shot Mel a filthy look and her friend ignored it, completely unconcerned.

'And have you explored the island yet?'

Mac was casually addressing all three of them, but Flora was sure the question was meant for her. Clearly, he was trying to find out if her friends knew how she had spent her morning.

'No, I'm afraid not.' Mel gave him another happy look. 'Your spa is just so fantastic there's absolutely no incentive to leave the building, quite frankly. Except perhaps for the hot tub – the view from there is stunning.'

'Flora did,' Sophie pointed out with a wicked smile, looking at Mac from underneath long lashes. 'Disappeared first thing and came rushing back late, all flustered.'

'It was a garden,' Flora answered hastily, trying to make light of her distracted appearance in the swimming pool. 'You know what I'm like in a garden; I lose all track of time.'

'Hmm...'

Flora felt quite sure that Sophie was being deliberately evasive and shot her a scathing look.

'I know you love your job, Flora, but I've never known anyone get so excited over a heap of old plants, even you. Are you quite sure it wasn't something else?'

Flora reached for her cup, as they all waited for a reply she wasn't prepared to offer.

'And what did you think of the garden you found, Flora?' Mac casually tucked a hand on the back of Flora's chair. She felt the lightest touch of his fingers on her hair, reminding her of the feel of her hand in his earlier. She was quiet as a waiter appeared to distribute whisky and offer more coffee. Once he disappeared, Flora gave Mac a truthful answer, unable to disguise her pleasure in the discovery.

'I loved it. I thought it was extraordinary.'

She knew he was pleased by her reply and, once again, something passed just between the two of them. 'Enjoy the rest of your evening, ladies. Please excuse me.' Mac smiled as he turned away.

Flora turned back to her friends after Mac's polite withdrawal, intending to put the latest encounter with him where it belonged: somewhere far from the simple reality of her life. But after he had left, she was still distracted and distant, and couldn't stop thinking about the garden – or Mac. She tried to drag her mind back to the purpose of the weekend as she chatted with her friends, reminding herself that it was about spending precious time with Mel and Sophie before the demands of the wedding claimed their attention. But still, Flora wondered, if she got up very early in the morning, might she just manage another hour in the garden before they had to leave for home?

It's been untouched for years; it could be important, she told herself firmly, ignoring the other reason leaping around in her mind. She thought of her laptop and books back at home, with all the information she needed to confirm her suspicions. Her phone was unreliable at best and she didn't want to borrow Mel's iPad so she could stare at it, doing research, when they should be relaxing together. She sipped her whisky slowly, noticing that it was different from the one Mac had chosen for her last night. They all fell quiet, lost in their own thoughts.

'I know we've had a lazy day,' Mel said sleepily a short while later, nursing her almost empty glass, the alcohol taking effect. 'But I'm really tired. Sorry to be a bore but do you mind if I go to bed?'

'Oh, Mel!' Sophie crossly banged her own empty glass on the table and glared at the bride-to-be, and Flora giggled. 'Surely you can manage just one more drink. I can't bear the thought of going to sleep so early when I can have a lie-in tomorrow. You've no idea what bliss it is to wake up when you feel like it and not have a two-foot toddler landing on your head when you're still dreaming about Jamie Fraser in *Outlander*.'

'A drink upstairs?' Mel said, brightening as another waiter arrived to clear away the empty coffee cups. 'Let's take a bottle up to my room, and you can tell me some more about you and Jamie. Does he always wear a kilt?'

'Except when he doesn't…' Sophie's look was dreamy as she stood up decisively, hands on hips, ready to continue with the evening. 'But your idea's perfect. We can order from room service. Flora?'

Flora nodded, and they left the drawing room and crossed the main hall. For her, the excitement of the evening, its possibilities, had just ended. They were halfway up the wide, thickly carpeted staircase when she heard a voice she recognised.

'Flora? I'm sorry to interrupt. May I speak with you for a moment please?'

'What is it?' Mel gave Flora a gentle push towards Mac. 'Have you not been a good girl and given him your number yet?'

Flora glared at Mel and she heard Sophie's gleeful laugh. 'You go on,' she said casually. 'I'll join you in a minute.'

Mac was waiting at the foot of the stairs, and she was utterly conscious of the way her body responded to the weight of his look as she walked slowly towards him. His shirt was damp and drops of rain were trickling through his hair, and she realised that he must have been outside since they had spoken earlier. He brushed a hand across his face, wiping the wetness away with impatient fingers.

'Thank you for waiting. I apologise for keeping you from your friends; this won't take long.' He pointed to the reception desk. 'Come through, we can talk in there.'

He opened a door behind the desk and waited for her to go through into a small office. Two computer screens perched side by side; above them, a row of closed-circuit television screens discreetly monitored the guests' movements as they made their way to and from the hotel and around reception. Mac propped himself against a desk and pointed to a chair nearby. Flora shook her head, happy to remain standing. She didn't know what he could possibly want with her, certain that the need for privacy had nothing to do with telephone numbers or silly invitations to a stranger's wedding.

'You were right, Flora, this morning. Both the house and garden were designed by Rupert Lassiter.'

Her eyes widened in thrilled surprise, as she realised what he was telling her. Being right mattered much less than stumbling upon the abandoned remains of such an extraordinary garden. So many questions leapt into her mind and she didn't know which to ask first.

'I'm sorry I didn't tell you earlier,' he said sheepishly. 'I knew, of course, that Lassiter was the architect, but I remembered finding this in the house and wanted to share it with you when I confirmed your suspicion.' He reached into a pocket. 'Your understanding of what you saw today and what might still remain astonished me.'

Mac passed her a photograph, his fingers brushing hers. Flora looked at the picture, holding it carefully. Taken from the south lawn and facing the house, the photograph showed the terrace and herbaceous borders in perfect summer glory, filled with plants spilling onto the path and trailing over the stone walls. An older girl and boy, together with two smaller boys, were picnicking on the lawn and Flora instantly understood that the big, old house had once been a much-loved home and not always the silent shell she had seen today. Thoughts and ideas were racing through her mind so quickly that she lifted a hand to her face, as though to help decipher them, and words leapt out in a rush before she could stop them.

'It really was beautiful!' she exclaimed, still holding the photograph. 'Do you have any original drawings left? Or copies of Lassiter's planting plans? Have you thought about professional restoration or contacted any of the relevant associations?'

'Hey, slow down – one question at a time!' Mac lifted his hands in mock protest as he took the photograph from her, his eyes never leaving hers. 'Okay, I'll try and keep it short. Róisín House and its garden, which you saw today, were built in 1908 for the family who had owned the island for generations. There were two children: a son, who married and moved away, and a daughter who lived there with her parents until they died.'

He paused, as a telephone on the desk rang but was quickly silenced by someone unseen in reception. Flora waited for him to continue, impatient to hear more of the island's story.

'When the son died suddenly, not long after his parents, the island fell into dispute between *his* son and the daughter, and there was a court case to resolve ownership and decide whether she could remain at Róisín. When the nephew eventually won and took possession of the island, his aunt was forced to leave, and the house was abandoned until his descendants sold everything thirty years later. I do have Lassiter's original plans for the house and just one of the formal gardens.'

'What a remarkable story. So sad, really.' Flora tried to imagine the people who had loved and lost the house, only to see it abandoned by someone who clearly hadn't cared about its future. She brought the subject back to the original family. 'Who were the children in the photograph, do you think?'

'I'm not sure… probably the son and daughter, and perhaps cousins or friends; it must have been a wonderful place to grow up. I don't know very much about the family who lived in the house; they died so long ago and most of the people who are left on the island don't remember them. I'd like to research their history properly at some point; I've found boxes of personal stuff in the house but haven't had time to go through it yet.'

'Thank you for sharing this with me – I really appreciate it. It's been a privilege to have a glimpse of the garden as it used to be.'

Flora saw a flare of curiosity in Mac's face. 'May I ask you something? Your friends mentioned your job earlier. What is it that you do?'

'I'm an assistant head gardener with the Garden Heritage Trust; my interest has always been in the conservation and restoration of historical gardens.'

'Where are you based?'

Curious, wondering why he wanted this information, she decided to answer him. 'Middlebrook Hall, in Yorkshire. It's a Georgian estate still undergoing restoration, and I'm one of a team of five full-time gardeners.'

'So, you must have lots of experience and qualifications?'

'Some, yes. I joined the Trust two years ago after working in private gardens. I specialised in historic garden management for my horticulture degree and I have a master's in garden and landscape history.'

'Actually,' he said thoughtfully, pushing his hands into his jeans pockets. 'That hardly matters, after what I saw today.' A pause, then he continued. 'Flora, do you think you would—?'

The door from reception sprang open, startling them both. The night porter burst in, clutching a handful of jangling keys and a small case.

'Oh, I'm sorry,' he said awkwardly, looking at Mac and then Flora as rain dripped from his coat onto the floor. 'I didn't realise there was anybody in here.'

'It's fine,' Mac assured him, giving a friendly nod to emphasise his point. 'We were just about to leave.'

The porter held open the door and, once back in the hall, Mac hesitated, seemingly caught by indecision as they faced one another. They were alone, temporarily, the soft murmurings from the drawing room as faint as the evening light.

'I should go,' Flora said, realising with shock that, yet again, she had left her friends' company for Mac's.

'Let me walk you to your room.'

'There's no need, really.' She was already turning away and heading for the stairs. 'Thank you for letting me see the photograph.'

'Flora?'

Flora ignored the crazy impulse to spin around and rush back to him, to discover what it was that he wanted, aware her ability to remain composed when she was with him quickly diminishing.

'Will you come back tomorrow, to the garden? I'd really like to show you around properly.'

This time she did pause, her excitement growing as she thought of exploring the whole garden and making more discoveries. But she feared making a fool of herself again, and squirmed as she remembered the dare, barely twenty-four hours ago, that had led to the flustered invitation to join her at Mel's wedding. She liked her life just the way it was, and she knew that a man such as Mac could disrupt her carefully ordered days in ways she was desperate to avoid.

'I can't.' She swung around, not quite able to disguise the dismay that the decision to refuse him had caused. She had turned down a marvellous opportunity and she hoped he would assume her regret was all because of the lost garden. 'We're leaving in the morning; I should really be with my friends. I don't have time.'

'Of course, I should have realised.' Mac's hand fell away from the banister. 'So… about the wedding?'

'What about it?'

He shrugged. 'Obviously, I don't know the date so I'd have to check my calendar. Does the invite still stand?'

'Why would you even come? It's not like we're friends or anything.'

He grinned. 'I've been to a few weddings in my time but I've never received an invitation quite like yours. You're daring and funny, as well as beautiful. And passionate. I only had to see you in the garden this morning to know that.'

He thought she was beautiful? Daring? Flora felt a rush of pleasure, swiftly followed by alarm. She needed someone she could love and trust with her heart, not a man like Mac, with his confidence and curiosity, that keen gaze unsettling her every time it landed on her. 'You won't know anyone,' she said quickly. 'Why would you want to spend a day with strangers?'

'I know you, Flora, and I've met your friends. My table manners are acceptable, and I can do small talk when I have to. I have a nice suit. And I promise not to step on your feet when we dance – I'm told I'm good at it.'

A sudden image of dancing with him at the wedding popped into Flora's mind: a picture of being in his arms, holding him, her height making it easier for her lips to reach his mouth. She shook her head, trying to send away the tantalising thought. 'This is crazy! The wedding is hundreds of miles away!'

'I have a car. I'm generally punctual.' A wry smile was still there as he countered every argument with a simplicity she couldn't refute. Flora was conscious of the moments ticking by again, her best friends waiting upstairs.

'How do I know you'll come, even if you do receive a proper invitation?'

'Because I'll RSVP, like everyone else.'

'That doesn't mean you'll actually turn up, though.'

'It'd be pretty rude if I didn't.'

She couldn't help it, she was laughing now – the challenge was clear as he pushed her to decide, to follow through on her invitation. She ran up the stairs, turning to see him still waiting at the bottom. She was in no danger, not really. She was leaving tomorrow, and he wouldn't come to the wedding. This was nothing more than teasing banter, playing her at her own game. 'Maybe you should dust off your dancing shoes.' She heard him laugh, as she darted along the corridor to Mel's room.

Chapter Five

They were ready. The carriage was outside, Mel's mother had already cried, and her father was still pacing the sitting room, twisting bits of paper between clammy fingers as he swore he would never make another speech. Flora, Sophie and Eva – Sophie's little daughter – were waiting in the hall of Mel's parents' house, clutching hand-tied bouquets of pale pink roses, as the bride paused halfway down the staircase, holding the train of her exquisite silk and organza gown across one arm.

'Oh, Mel,' Sophie breathed, clinging tightly to Eva's little hand as she gazed at her friend in awe. The little girl was already fidgeting in her miniature bridesmaid dress and new ballet pumps. 'You are absolutely perfect.'

'We should leave now.' Helen, Mel's mother, was already fretful as she called up the stairs to her daughter. 'You really don't want to be late, Melissa. Not today.'

'Oh, Mum!' Mel stood patiently, as Flora deftly rearranged the train of her dress for the hovering photographer. 'It's not like they won't wait.'

Flora stifled a smile and made her way to the front door a few moments later, holding Eva's tiny bouquet. Once they were all settled in the first carriage, with Helen grimly clinging onto her hat, Eva was excited again and keen to play a game of I spy, which mostly involved her telling everybody what she saw and making them guess the answer anyway. Then Flora heard her phone, hidden inside her little satin bag, begin to buzz. She realised she had forgotten to turn it off and reached into the bag to silence it before they were in the church. It was a text, three simple words:

See you there.

Flora read it again and unintentionally dropped the phone onto her lap, barely aware of Sophie's conversation with Helen and Eva's giggles, as the noise seemed to fade into the landscape flashing by. Her pulse began to race as she contemplated the short message, and she picked up the phone again. Another text had already arrived and her gaze flew over the words, which were accompanied by a smiley face.

I said I would.

Flora had waited until she was back home in Yorkshire, away from Mac, before texting her telephone number to him. A polite reply had followed, and she knew that Mel's parents had posted a formal invitation to the hotel a few days later, which had been accepted.

The first image of the garden at Róisín had arrived a couple of days after that and Flora had gasped when she had seen it: a view of a summerhouse, its walls bound with ivy that had gathered the building in its clutches. The broken door was open, a seat inside, faded, dusty, and another one tipped over nearby. She had replied with a *wow* and since then Mac had sent her two more images of his ancient and forgotten garden, each offering a glimpse of its history and calling straight to her soul.

She hadn't returned to the garden on her last morning on the island and the regret still lingered, as she imagined the opportunity to see it once more gone. She had had serious doubts that Mac would actually turn up for the wedding, certain that he was playing games, just as she had been when she had invited him. Until the text moments ago, she had been getting quite anxious about how Mel and her parents would feel when he, surely, left an empty space on his table.

After just ten minutes' steady trot, the church was already coming into view and, along with it, the exhilarating prospect of seeing Mac again. She was already seeking him out amongst the guests making their way to the door, as the horses came to a stop in the quiet country lane beside the beautiful old building.

Some people were turning their heads to observe the bridesmaids' arrival, and Flora could hear the murmurs of appreciation as she carefully stepped from the carriage, holding the skirt of her strapless, lavender satin dress. She was glad she had spent several hours having her nails manicured, make-up applied and her hair swept up into an elegant chignon. She was always dashing outside to the garden and rummaging in soil, often without gloves, but she knew that today she looked beautiful: the fitted dress suited her height and figure perfectly, emphasising a cleavage and curves that were usually hidden inside a polo shirt and gilet.

And then she saw Mac, taller than almost everyone around him, striding towards her through the churchyard. She was surprised that he seemed so pleased to see her, everything else fading away as she watched him approach. A sheer, unfamiliar excitement set fire to her senses as she failed to subdue an answering smile of pure delight.

'Hello, Flora.' Even though she was wearing heels, Mac still had to bend his head to brush her cheek with his mouth when he reached her. 'Great to see you again.'

She had forgotten the sound of his voice and the richness of his Scottish accent. Everything else, she remembered: his height, the breadth of his shoulders, his confidence and that innate ability to turn heads. He was wearing a dark grey suit and white shirt with a pale-blue silk tie, the colours perfectly highlighting his sun-bleached short hair.

'You actually came,' she whispered, still stunned by his appearance. 'I can't believe it.'

'I said I would.' There was amusement in his tone as he watched her, brightening up her day just by being there. 'Didn't you believe me?'

Flora had no time to reply as Sophie dashed over with Eva in tow. 'Mac, you made it – I'm so thrilled.'

She gave Flora a quick wink and Flora rolled her eyes, trying to disguise her pleasure. Mac greeted Sophie cheerfully, and solemnly shook Eva's hand, telling them both that they looked beautiful. Flora tried not to feel put out that he had not included her in the compliment. But when he turned to her again, she saw a glint of approval that he hadn't voiced, and she blushed. Deliberately, she looked away, determined to respond more like her usual cool and considered self. The photographer was already busy capturing each part of the special day, snatching casual and relaxed pictures as the last of the guests arrived, hurrying into church to find seats and settle the youngest children into buggies, hoping for the peace of a nap.

'We'd better go,' Sophie said, as the photographer beckoned them over to the gate. 'Mel must be nearly here.' She threw Flora a mischievous glance. 'I'll stall the photographer for a minute; don't be too long.' She hurried off again, taking Eva with her, easily darting through the churchyard in her heels.

'I'm sorry you don't know anyone else,' Flora said, a note of anxiety in her voice. 'I hope it won't be too awkward for you.'

'I've already met a few people.' Mac sounded perfectly at ease as they slowly followed Sophie towards the photographer. He reached for Flora's arm, steadying her when she faltered on the cobbled path in her high heels. 'I told them the truth; that we met through work, mine at least, and that I'm delighted to be here as your guest.'

Flora pulled her arm away, regretting it almost immediately as she stumbled again, and he caught her quickly.

'You didn't mention the dare?' she hissed, waving half-heartedly at Mel's great-aunt Nora, who was parked on a wooden bench and eating crackers from a plastic bag. 'Please tell me you didn't?'

'Of course I didn't.' He bent down to murmur into her ear, his hand still on her elbow. 'Perhaps I should've said that you bought me at a charity auction.'

'Not sure I could afford you,' she retorted, and he laughed. Flora saw Eva spot her father and run off to him, shrieking excitedly, sending her flowers flying as the photographer snapped each moment. Mac disappeared into the church to find a seat as Mel's carriage arrived, and Sophie and Flora bustled about, helping to organise her dress for the photographs.

Mel had never looked more beautiful or seemed so certain of what she was about to do. She and Harry had met as children, living on neighbouring farms, and all their lives since then seemed to have been leading to this special day. Walking down the aisle ahead of Mel and her nervous father, Flora knew that this was a marriage that was meant to be. It was the same certainty she had felt when she realised that she and David would never reach the same stage in their relationship. She caught Mac's eye as she passed him standing on Mel's side of the church and he gave her an encouraging grin.

Afterwards Flora could remember little about the actual service. She knew that Harry had stumbled over one of his lines, David was eyeing her curiously and the singing of a young soprano during the signing of the register was exquisite. Everything else tumbled into thoughts of Mac and why he was here, and she sensed his eyes watching her. When the wedding party was ready to leave the church, for an awkward moment Flora thought that she might have to walk back down the aisle with David, but Sophie's husband Eddie stepped in. Flora took his arm gratefully as they followed the newly married couple out into the spring sunlight, glad that she didn't have to deal with her ex just yet.

Outside, more photographs were required, as confetti was flung into the breeze, and Flora barely saw Mac. Other guests began to disappear, in a flurry of cars and shouted directions, as they set off for the reception in search of the first drink and, for a few, a sneaky cigarette. The photographer was relaxed and confident and had soon finished taking all the pictures he needed, to everyone's relief.

Harry helped his new wife into the carriage, waiting patiently whilst the bridesmaids reorganised her dress, and then he sprang in and merrily accepted a glass of champagne. Everyone waved and Flora helped Eva to fling the last of the confetti towards the carriage, and they laughed as it blew back over them and became tangled in their hair.

'Hello, Flora. How are you?'

Jolted out of her thoughts, she turned around to see David nearby, standing in the shadows cast onto the ground by the tall church tower. Her gaze softened as she looked at his familiar face, his eyes crinkling in the sunlight. 'Hello. I'm fine, thank you. How are you?'

'Yeah, really good, thanks.' A pause. 'Lovely service, wasn't it?' She knew they were making small talk as they didn't seem to know quite what else to say, their ease with one another already fading.

'Yes, it was beautiful. You look really well; did you manage to fit in that trip to Norway you were hoping for?'

'Yes, we did, thanks. You look well, too, Flora, that colour really suits you.'

'Thank you.' Flora was surprised by how quickly she had erased memories from her mind, and a few came sneaking back as she watched him. The way his dark hair curled if he left it too long and the gentle hazel eyes that were inquisitive and intelligent, capable of great compassion. They smiled at one another, an expression of understanding that spoke of how everything between them had changed. Suddenly, there was a warm hand on her back, and she jumped, whirling around to see Mac at her side.

'Sorry I was so long, Flora. Are you all right?' He removed his hand from her back as he smiled affectionately at her. 'Got chatting to Aunt Nora. She's quite a character, isn't she? Started telling me all about a guest house in Wales that she used to run with her husband about twenty years ago.'

'Did she?' Flora asked, surprised by the intimacy of his casual gesture and wishing he hadn't removed his hand. She composed her expression into one that wouldn't reveal what she was feeling, before continuing. 'Yes, I think she did. Near Lake Bala, somewhere out in the hills. I thought you'd left already.' She then noticed David eyeing Mac curiously and hurried out an introduction. 'Oh sorry! Of course, you two don't know each other.' She quickly explained that Mac was a work colleague, and watched as the two men shook hands, recognising a hint of reluctance from David.

'Good to meet you,' Mac said easily, managing to sound friendly and surprisingly sincere. 'I hear everyone's looking forward to your speech. Something about a wild weekend in Barcelona?'

Flora was astonished and still trying to work out how Mac had managed to learn so much already, whereas David's answering look was sharp and not particularly friendly.

'Majorca,' David replied brusquely, dropping Mac's hand as they stared at one another. 'It was a golfing weekend in Majorca.'

'So, no pressure then,' Flora jumped in, feigning brightness as she shot Mac a warning look. 'I'm sure the speech will be brilliant. Is Jayne with you? It is Jayne, isn't it?' Flora glanced around the churchyard for a glimpse of David's new girlfriend but had no idea what she actually looked like. 'I thought she was coming with you today?'

David shoved his hands into his pockets. 'Yes, she's here. She's probably waiting for me in the car; I should go and find her. I really ought to be heading to the reception anyway.'

'Of course. Probably see you later, then.'

'Are you ready to leave, too, Flora?' It was Mac who had spoken, and Flora hoped that he hadn't meant to sound quite so dismissive of David as he smilingly reached for her hand. 'I'll drive; Sophie asked me to tell you that she and Eddie have gone on ahead. They'll see us there.'

David turned away without another word and Flora was beside Mac as they set off. 'What was all that about?' she muttered, tugging her hand free. 'You don't have to try to make David believe there's more to our relationship than there really is. Just friends, if anybody asks. Or, better still, colleagues.'

Mac halted suddenly and Flora was surprised by the flash of disappointment that crossed his face as they stared at one another. 'Isn't that the point of all this?' he asked, lowering his voice as a family passed by, preoccupied with loading their protesting children into a nearby car. 'Inviting me here today just so you wouldn't be alone in front of your ex-boyfriend?'

Tension was beginning to make her head throb as she tried to deal with the flurry of emotions darting through her mind. 'Of course not,' she replied sharply, challenging his assumption. 'My relationship with David ended months ago. I knew he was bringing his girlfriend today, but I was perfectly happy to be here on my own. The invitation to you was just a silly dare that got out of hand and I never actually expected you to come. We were just playing games. And how do you know so much about David and me?'

'So, it really doesn't have anything at all to do with me? Anybody could've been your guest, is that what you're saying? I just happened to walk into the room at the right moment?'

'Yes.' It wasn't wholly a lie. In the beginning, all of this had been merely a game, and now Flora wasn't prepared to admit to him that she couldn't imagine wanting to share this day with anyone else. She was desperately trying to conceal the delight she felt in his company and the irresistible attraction she simply wasn't used to experiencing. She glanced at him again, aware of people passing by and eyeing the two of them curiously. 'This isn't really the right place for a discussion. Everybody's staring.'

Mac watched her for another moment and then he strode ahead, leaving her stranded on the path between the church and the lane, as he disappeared. Despite their heated exchange, Flora could hardly believe that he had simply marched away and left her. Kindness and honesty were surely things she had glimpsed in him, but she began to question her assessment of his character. Was she wrong? Was there really nothing more substantial than a boyish charm and the remarkable ability to look gorgeous in anything? A desire to play games, succeed at every challenge?

Slowly, she followed, aware of the inquisitive glances of the few remaining guests as she walked alone towards the car park. A rose slipped from its tie in her bouquet and slithered to the grass, and she kicked at it, realising grudgingly that she had been too dismissive of him and the effort he had made to be here today. Now he had gone, leaving her to explain away his even more sudden disappearance – and it was all her fault.

She reached the car park, hoping to find a lift to the reception from somebody. The wedding carriages had long since left and the last few people were climbing on board a minibus down the road. The sun had slipped behind a cloud and she shivered in her flimsy dress, as the warmth of the day faded. The trees around the churchyard rustled in a growing breeze and Flora was beginning to think that she really had been abandoned, and her dismay mounted. She turned around, squeezing back onto the lane through a gap in the hedge.

A silver Audi SUV pulled up sharply alongside her and she flattened herself against the hedge, out of the way, feeling the brush of leaves against her back. She saw the driver reach across to push open the passenger door. It was Mac. 'Get in,' he called to her.

'I'm fine.' Flora hadn't meant to sound so terse, as she tried to disguise her relief that he hadn't left. 'There's no need for you to stay if you don't want to.'

The door suddenly slammed shut, and she fully expected the car to spin away and shower her with gravel. But instead Mac's door opened, and he leapt out and strode around to face her. She noticed that he had loosened his tie and removed the suit jacket. Despite the more casual appearance, he still managed to look daunting and quite sure of himself.

'If you want me to go then I'll leave now,' he said shortly, ramming his hands into his pockets as he stared at her. 'But that might raise even more questions than my being here with you, now that most of the guests have seen us. What would you like me to do? It's your call, Flora.'

'Don't go, please.' The reply was soft, and heat coloured her cheeks when her eyes met his unwavering gaze. Her feet were aching in the high heels and she shifted from one to the other to relieve the discomfort. 'You're right. Of course everybody would wonder why you'd left. And you must have driven a long way. I'm sorry, I was just so unprepared to answer questions.' She dropped her head, aware that she had revealed more in her apology than she had intended. Happiness, anticipation, desire, doubt – all of these were making her afraid of feeling this way for someone she barely knew.

Mac reached out, gently lifting her chin with a finger. 'I know us meeting again was unexpected, Flora, given how far away we live,' he told her quietly. 'But every mile was worth it when I saw you getting out of that carriage.'

She could feel her resolve slipping away, his words hovering between them, suspended in the sharp spring air. She offered no answer as he opened the passenger door so she could get into the car and waited whilst she carefully tucked her dress around her. He moved quickly around to the driver's side, and jumped in, the atmosphere between them altered once again by his admission.

'Nice suit.' The teasing in her voice was clear and she allowed herself to go with it. His words and that light touch from moments ago lingered like a promise and she tried to trust him, not think of the distance. 'You scrub up well.'

'You think?' His voice was lower, matching hers and sounding just as playful. 'I was hoping to impress you.'

Chapter Six

Twenty minutes later Flora was still feeling warmed by Mac's comments when he pulled into the car park of the beautiful Georgian house where the wedding reception was being held. The front door was open, and a couple were climbing the steps beneath the portico. Most of the other guests seemed to have arrived, already spilling into the garden to enjoy the sun and accepting champagne from waiters slowly making their way through the growing crowd. Mac got out of the car and came around to open Flora's door, holding her arm as she stepped down onto the gravel below.

'Thank you.'

He was at her side as they crossed the drive towards a large terrace, filled with people clustered around tables and chairs, clutching glasses or the hands of small children. She glanced across to the French doors leading to the drawing room, hearing the exquisite sound of a harpist and the murmur of muffled voices. A Boston ivy clinging to the north wall of the house was just beginning to think about spreading and in her mind, Flora pictured it as it had been in the autumn, when she and Sophie had first visited the house with Mel, and the ivy had been gloriously burnished red, copper and amber. Despite the bright spring day, the air was cool, and she couldn't disguise a shiver now that they had left the car.

'Here, take this.'

Flora tried to refuse as Mac shrugged out of his suit jacket; somehow the simple gesture seemed incredibly intimate once she felt its weight and warmth across her bare shoulders. And yet once it was on, she didn't want to take it off and part with the comfort and the way it made her feel closer to him whenever she breathed in the sharply floral scent woven into the fabric.

A giant willow hung over the lake some distance from the house, offering shelter to those seeking privacy and the chance of a rest on the stone bench almost hidden amongst its branches. Flora saw Mel and Harry, standing slightly apart and encircled by guests at the edge of the terrace leading to the formal gardens. She and Mac made their way across to them, as the noise and laughter grew louder.

'Mac!' Mel saw them and broke away from the group, her delighted glance darting from Mac to Flora and then back again. 'How lovely that you came, isn't it, Flora?'

Flora's answering nod was deliberately vague, as she tried not to give away too much of what she was feeling with Mac at her side. She watched as he quickly leant forwards to kiss Mel on both cheeks, his hands briefly on her shoulders.

'Congratulations. It was a beautiful service and you both looked so relaxed. And thank you for the official invitation – it arrived just in time.'

'Thank you. We're so pleased you could come.' Mel turned to wave at Harry, and he excused himself from the growing huddle beside him to make his way to his wife's side. She grinned as Harry reached for her hand. 'Let me introduce you. Harry, this is Mac Jamieson, Flora's date. Mac, my husband, Harry.' She smiled up into Harry's eyes. 'I'm sure I'll get used to saying that very soon.'

'Not date,' Flora said hastily, inching away from Mac as she tried to appear indifferent to his presence amongst them. 'Mac's here as my guest, that's all. We've only met once or twice before.' She was aware he was staring at her, but then he turned his attention to Harry and congratulated him, too, as the two men shook hands.

Flora sensed curious eyes watching her as they tried to decipher what had really brought Mac here today. She grabbed a glass of champagne from a passing waiter and gulped at it, feeling the bubbles fizzing madly on her tongue.

'What a fantastic place.' Mac looked approving as he glanced from the house to the formal gardens, and then back to Mel and Harry again. 'I understand the hotel hasn't been open long?'

Mel laughed, waving at somebody emerging from a car. 'Casting a professional eye, are you?' She glanced at Harry. 'You remember I told you that Mac owns the fabulous hotel on Alana, where Flora and I stayed with Sophie last month?'

Flora saw Mac grin as he replied, 'No professional interest, it's not my field.'

'Mel tells me you're an architect,' Harry said to Mac. 'You don't work at the hotel?'

Mac shook his head. 'The hotel is part of a group that's run by my parents, who are based in Europe. Architecture was always my first choice.'

'Do you do private commissions or is it a commercial practice?'

'General practice. Our portfolio includes commercial as well as community; I specialise in modern residential projects, usually for clients looking to incorporate Arts and Crafts principles in their design.'

'Haven't you just won an award? For a commercial project?' Mel accepted champagne from a waiter, still looking at Mac.

Mac grinned as he reached for a glass of the sparkling elderflower cocktail for the non-drinkers. 'You've done your homework,' he said, amused, and she shrugged with a grin, perfectly unconcerned by Mac's realisation that she had googled him. 'Not me personally; the practice won with the design for a performing arts school in Newcastle.'

'Would you be interested in recommending someone to look at a barn conversion?' Harry got straight to the point. 'My parents are hoping to convert a small building about half a mile from our farmhouse and we're just beginning to kick around a few ideas.'

Mel laughed, as Harry slipped an arm across her shoulders. 'Mac probably has requests to view projects all the time, Harry, and we're too far away. You're based in Edinburgh, aren't you Mac?'

Mac nodded, seeming to consider the practicalities of Harry's request. 'I could have a look at it, if you like?' He reached into his pocket and drew a card from his wallet. 'I have a client who's moving to Harrogate and I'm meeting them in a few weeks. It's not that far away; give me a call when you're ready. I won't promise at this stage to produce drawings, but I'd be happy to give you some ideas. If I can't take it on, I should be able to recommend someone who could.'

'Are you serious?' Mel was elated and she reached out to touch his arm. 'That would be brilliant, Mac, thank you so much. Are you sure you aren't too busy?'

Mac grinned, and Flora sensed the quick dart of his eyes on her again. 'Not for friends of Flora's.'

The implication that he would put himself out to impress her was another surprise. When she had returned home after the weekend away, she had tried to dismiss the immediate and powerful attraction she had felt towards him on Alana. Back to an ordinary life, thoughts of work and a wedding occupied her, not foolish ideas of what might have been with a man who lived so far away and was as different from David as it was possible to be.

'Melissa Grainger, come here!' bellowed a sudden voice nearby, startling all of them. The crowd parted hurriedly to allow a little old woman, moving at some speed, to reach the bride and groom. Wearing a hat that would have been fashionable thirty years ago and fur-topped boots that were slightly different shades of blue, Flora smiled as great-aunt Nora scuttled forward to throw herself on Mel. Nobody in the family was very sure to whom Nora was actually related, she went so far back, but it was generally accepted that she descended from a batty old brother on Mel's father's side.

'Aunt Nora!' Mel shrieked delightedly, handing her bouquet to Flora as she bent down to give Nora a hug. 'It's so good that you could get away. Who's looking after the sheep? Not Gordon, surely! I thought he lost them last time? Are you staying over with Auntie Hazel?'

'Not likely,' Nora snorted, straightening her hat after Mel had dislodged it. She opened her bag and reached for the crackers in their plastic bag. 'She doesn't get up until nine o'clock and the day's half over by then. No, I'm better in one of those lodge places where they serve a proper breakfast nice and early, and you can leave when you like. When are we eating, Melissa? I haven't had any lunch and it doesn't do my digestion any good to go without.'

Mel smiled as she straightened up and collected her flowers from Flora. 'Soon, I hope,' she promised, pulling Harry's sleeve up to glance at his watch. 'I think the photographer wants us for a bit, but it shouldn't take too long. If you need anything, just order at the bar or find Dad and ask him to do it for you.'

Nora turned to Harry, giving him a fierce glare as she whacked him none too gently on the arm, her particular method of congratulation to those she considered to be outside the family. But the curious look she then gave Mac was remarkably warm and Flora turned to speak in his ear, surprised by Nora's uncharacteristically friendly interest.

'That's a step up for Harry,' she murmured to Mac. 'When they first told Nora they were engaged, she threw a bucket of water over him. But it was supposed to have been accidental: he just happened to be in the way when she set fire to a bale of hay. You've certainly made an impression; she doesn't normally smile at strange men.'

'I'm not at all strange,' Mac whispered back, bending closer so that Flora felt the soft tickle of his breath against her ear. 'You'll see.'

Helen appeared, drawing Mel and Harry away to greet more guests, and they all trooped dutifully back to the drawing room. The photographer was still busy, popping up seemingly everywhere and capturing the gathering of the guests, as they mingled with the bride and groom. Flora trailed slowly behind Mel and Harry, her mind wandering as she looked around the garden. The garden was divided into 'rooms' bordered by yew and beech hedges, and she loved how the use of different textures and forms emphasised the changing styles.

'Flora?'

She paused as she heard Mac, drawn back to the reality of his company, feeling the warm touch of his fingers on her arm underneath his suit jacket. She had forgotten that she was still wearing it and slowly they halted, drifting apart from everybody else.

'You seem a little distracted. Are you all right?'

Her look was steady, and she gave him a bright smile in reply. 'Of course.' Still, his hand was on her arm and she knew that she hadn't really convinced him.

'Are you sure? I know I've surprised you by turning up today, but I don't want to make you uncomfortable.' Mac had lowered his voice as a couple strolled past and Flora caught their curious glance, recognising old friends of Mel's parents.

'I should go,' she said quickly, pointing to the photographer arranging the guests into suitable poses. 'I think they'll be needing me any moment now. Why don't you go inside and have a drink? I'll catch up with you later.'

She shrugged out of the jacket and handed it back to him, admonishing herself for walking away and leaving him standing alone in the middle of the terrace. She really hadn't meant to sound quite so dismissive, but she needed space to think and drag her composure back under control.

As the photographer worked his way through each of the shots that Mel and Harry had requested, Flora was aware of Mac hovering on the fringe, chatting easily to the people around him and making himself unobtrusively at home. Finally, when there was just one picture left to take – the guests assembled on the lawn and the photographer hanging out of a bedroom window to capture the best view – Mac made his way to Flora's side, and their tiny little moment of togetherness was forever immortalised at her best friend's wedding.

–

There had been a little while to spare before the meal, and most people had brought drinks outside to enjoy the sun whilst catching up with friends or half-forgotten family, but now the wedding breakfast was about to be served and guests were nearly ready to take their seats.

'Flora, he's perfect,' Sophie exclaimed, as she followed her friend into the ladies, clutching Eva's tiny handbag and an iPhone. 'I'm going to chuck this thing in the lake if Eddie doesn't stop reading his emails. Oh Flora, he's lovely, don't you think so?'

'Mm…' Flora busied herself touching up her make-up, reapplying lipstick quickly. Sophie's comments were far too close to what she was already thinking, and she didn't want to hear any more about how lovely Mac was. She knew it for herself.

Flora saw Sophie's curious glance in the mirror and tried not to remember how Mac was often at her side, ready to chat with somebody or smooth over the details of how they had met. Since the conversation with David at the church, he hadn't tried to suggest that there was more to their being at the wedding together than simply friendship. And she was surprised by the easy way he took care of her, making sure that she had a drink, that her feet weren't hurting in her heels and even looking after her bouquet whilst she disappeared with Sophie.

'Don't you think so?' Sophie repeated incredulously as she shook out the contents of Eva's bag, sending paper and colouring crayons flying. 'Quick, grab them! I don't want the paper to get wet; we'll never survive the meal without it. He's so charming and friendly; quite different to the cool, reserved man we met back on the island. Surely you're going to see him again?'

'I doubt it.' Flora stuffed the lipstick into her bag and headed for the door. 'I'm sure he's only here to wind me up or make good on the dare. He's bound to be very competitive. And he lives miles away, Soph.'

'So?' Sophie switched the iPhone off and hid it in the depths of Eva's changing bag. 'That's better; Eddie will never find it in there. Mac likes you, Flora, it's quite obvious. And Edinburgh's hardly at the other end of the earth.'

Flora avoided Sophie's inquisitive glance, aware of her friend's hand reaching for hers. 'Flora? Just enjoy it. He came to see you, what other reason could there be?'

Flora nodded doubtfully, and then they left the room and made their way back to the reception. The children were sitting at their own table in the centre of the room, where parents could keep a vague eye and hopefully prevent them from hurling food at the groom, who'd promised them actual money if they could knock over a flower arrangement in the centre of the top table after the meal. Mac was waiting in the corridor when she emerged, still holding her roses.

'Thank you.' Flora reached out and reclaimed the bouquet, their fingers brushing together, touching, lingering. 'They suit you.'

He grinned as they set off towards the growing noise, now that the party had moved indoors. 'Yeah? Not sure that pale pink is my colour, though.'

'I think it is. It brings out the blue in your eyes and looks great against the grey.'

'Thanks.' They'd slowed down, and Flora sensed he was as reluctant as her to separate for the meal, as they were placed on different tables. 'Have you got any other compliments to offer?'

She felt the grin escape at his words, heard the layer of meaning in his casual question. 'I like that you're taller than me.'

'That's it? Oh, I get it now, you chose me for the dare because I'm taller than you?'

'Of course. I've never been a fan of dancing with men smaller than me. Too much hunching over.'

They halted at the seating plan and Flora didn't need to read it to know where she had been placed. She was completely aware of Mac at her side and he dipped his head to murmur quietly, 'I'm planning to dance the night away with you, Flora Stewart. Fair warning.'

She gasped and spun around, the seating plan forgotten. He was already making his way across the room, pausing to have a word with great-aunt Nora, who had flagged him down, and Flora heard the elderly woman's cackle of laughter. Flushed, she took her place at the top table, surreptitiously watching Mac as he introduced himself to his neighbours, who included Sophie's husband, Eddie. Flora settled down to wait for Mel and Harry, trying not to wish the evening had already begun. Sophie rolled her eyes and leant across to mutter to Flora that Eddie was probably boring Mac to bits with stories about sailing.

Once the meal was over and the master of ceremonies had called for the speeches, everybody quietened to listen to Mel's father. He had torn up all his carefully prepared notes, as he officially welcomed Harry to the family and expressed comical and yet emotional relief that the second of his daughters was safely off his hands. He didn't speak for long, clearly happy to retake his seat, and then the noise rose, as Harry clambered to his feet, ducking to avoid a bread roll lobbed from the back of the room. He stuck to his promise of keeping his speech short, and Flora was quite certain that she wasn't the only woman in the room about to cry as Harry bent down to kiss an uncharacteristically emotional Mel. Everybody broke into applause when Harry took his seat once more, just as relaxed as before he had begun.

Flora's ex, David, the best man, was well prepared and surprisingly natural, and coped easily with the remaining shreds of the children's patience and the rugby hecklers, who probably should have been relegated to the evening party. So the funny and witty speech went down well, as did the huge photograph projected onto a wall of Harry asleep on a beach in Majorca after a night out, smothered in chocolate ice cream and wearing a red bikini. This made Helen cover her eyes in horror, and great-aunt Nora was heard to mutter that she'd always known that Melissa was a very lucky girl.

Chapter Seven

Once the meal was over, there was still a little while to wait before the evening guests were due to arrive, and most people had gone to the bar or to freshen up in the bedrooms upstairs. Sophie and Flora had followed Mel to the bridal suite to help her out of her dress until the party began all over again. Once the dress was carefully hung and Mel had kicked off her shoes for a touch-up of make-up and hair, Flora headed to her room, quickly changed into jeans and escaped into the garden, hoping for a few minutes alone. She hadn't seen Mac for a while and she assumed that he was in the bar, probably chatting to Eddie.

She made her way through the garden rooms beyond the terrace until she reached a lawn, bordered by a belt of beech trees, and followed a leafy path between them. She found the lake and skirted around the edge until she came to the stone seat tucked underneath the willow tree. She sat down and gratefully eased her flat loafers from her feet, stretching them out luxuriously and wriggling her toes. Bluebells were fading now in the woodland, but the pungent smell of wild garlic still lingered, and she closed her eyes to enjoy it.

Her thoughts drifted back to the wedding service just a few hours ago, and a wave of sadness landed like a punch in her stomach. Both of her friends were married now, and she loved them so much and wished them well. She had watched Mel walk up the aisle beside her beaming father today, had fixed her smile in place and felt the quick grasp of Sophie's fingers reaching for hers.

Her own moment at her own wedding with her dad would never come. It had been lost not only to his sudden death but the revelation which had followed, leaving her family in pieces all over again. Her dad had been like a cuddly bear: big, lively and sometimes loud. She had been the little girl he spoiled, lifting her up to spin her around when he came home from his work trips away, making her squeal with excitement as he revealed yet more presents for her and her brother Charlie.

It had been her dad who had taught her what to do when a boy had pushed her over in the playground at school – the next time the boy had tried, Flora had sent him flying with a shove, her height always an advantage. Her dad had been the one who'd encouraged her to play the piano and stood on the side-lines to cheer Charlie on at rugby, their weekends as a family non-negotiable. Her dad, who was gone and had taken her cherished memories with him, leaving behind the pain of his loss and the realisation that she had never known him, not really.

The tears fell as she tried to picture her own wedding: someday hazy in the future and a space at her side, a chasm where her dad should be standing, her arm safely tucked through his as she stepped into her future. She pressed her hands to her face, trying not to let the tracks of her tears spoil the make-up so carefully applied.

'Flora? You're not very hard to find – I just had to look in the garden.'

She spun around so quickly she almost fell off the narrow seat, her hands flying down to grasp the stone. She knew feelings of surprise and then dismay were chasing one another across her face, revealing her distress to Mac. He was carrying a tray with two cups and he set it down on the ground, quickly moving to sit beside her. She saw him register her anguished expression and couldn't miss the new gentleness in his eyes.

'Hey, what's the matter?' He reached for her hand, smoothing his fingers across hers. 'Flora?'

She was still shivering and couldn't seem to stop now that he was here. Again, he shrugged out of his jacket to drape it across her shoulders, warming her at once. A moment passed and then she felt his arms going around her, too, pulling her against his chest, tightening his grip as she tried to gulp back a silent sob.

'What is it?'

'Nothing, really. I'm fine.' She mumbled the reply, hoping it would be enough but knowing it wasn't. He wouldn't settle for a lie; he would want to know all.

'You don't seem fine right now. Want to share?'

She no longer talked about her dad to anyone other than Sophie and Mel and her family; she and Charlie had gone over the events enough times when they had first happened. Now her brother had his wife, Sam, and a gorgeous baby daughter; her mum a demanding job which left her exhausted and with little time to think, just as she preferred it. Flora had found a way to live with the loss, too: she had flung herself into her work and appreciated the steadiness of a comfortable partnership with David. But then she had met Mac during the weekend she had spent on Alana and now he was holding her with a certainty and gentleness that threatened the barriers she'd erected around her heart.

'It's nothing you'd want to hear.'

'You can't know that,' Mac said reasonably, his hands stroking her back with a simplicity that only seemed to increase the amount of new tears gathering. 'If the prospect of dancing with me is making you cry, then you'd better say so now.'

Flora tried to laugh at the attempt at humour and sniffed instead, fumbling for a tissue that wasn't in her pocket.

'Here.' Mac reached for a handkerchief and instead of giving it to her, he ran it gently across her face, catching the last of the tears. 'Better than nothing.'

'Thanks.' She sniffed again, feeling herself surrendering to his touch and trying not to love the simple care he was offering.

'So? Are you going to tell me?'

The question hung between them, a moment to decide, and Flora knew she could still escape. She could stand and walk away, give his jacket back, promise to wash and return the handkerchief. She did none of those things. Her voice small, she began to speak. 'I was just thinking about my dad. He died two years ago and even though I don't think I'll get married, I still can't forget that he won't be there to walk me down the aisle.'

'I'm so sorry, Flora.'

'Thanks.' Her tone was flatter now. She had taught herself long ago to remove the emotion from her words, as though she were repeating someone else's history, because the facts still didn't seem to belong to her. 'It wasn't only that we lost him so suddenly. We found out in the middle of planning the funeral that he had had a second family, after us. Another partner and a child, who was fifteen.'

Mac instinctively pulled her closer to him, until it was impossible to know where he ended and she began. Her head was under his chin, his hands firm around her beneath his jacket. She was almost in his lap and her own fingers skimmed over the heat she felt through his shirt, unwilling to reject the tenderness he was offering.

'It was a terrible shock, especially for my mum; her hair turned white within a month and we were so, so angry. It felt like we'd lost him twice, because there was no possibility of discussing what he'd done. We'd lurch from really missing him to being totally furious and feeling so let down and deceived. He stole from us any possibility of grieving normally and being able to come to terms with losing him.'

'I'm so sorry,' Mac said again, his voice low, and Flora could feel the vibration against the top of her head. 'I wish I knew what to say.'

He moved his hands to clasp her face, tipping it back slightly. She saw his head bend toward her, until his lips had pressed a gentle kiss beneath one eye and then moved to do the same to the other. She drew in a gasp, caught between distress and sorrow, and the immediate flare of desire she tried to suppress.

'I hate that that happened to you,' he said simply. 'I haven't known you very long and already I can't stand to see you cry.'

'I can't stand that you've seen me cry, if that's any consolation.' Flora tried to make light of it, inching away from his strength and offering a wan smile as recognition of his gentleness towards her. 'It's not a good look.'

'On you, it actually is. You have the most extraordinarily beautiful eyes, Flora. Not even tears can diminish them.'

'Is that meant to be a line?' She tried to joke, to bat away his compliment. This shouldn't be happening; it was everything she sought to avoid. She knew this day was running away with her, but she could retreat no further without getting up from the seat. Mac's arms were no longer around her, but their hands were joined now, tightening the threads already beginning to bind them.

'I think you know it's not.'

There was nothing Flora wanted to add, unwilling to reveal how his words had awakened her desire, feeling the atmosphere settle into something different, something less casual. She knew Sophie would tell her to lighten up, not overthink it: enjoy the day with Mac and wave him off at the end with a kiss or maybe more – perhaps delay the parting until tomorrow. Maybe they'd each make a half-hearted promise to text, catch up if ever they happened to be in the same place again.

'It's been a fantastic day so far.' Mac broke the growing silence, shifting the conversation into something lighter. 'Sophie's trying to get Eva to have a nap and apparently Eddie's crashed out. I wanted to thank you for inviting me; I've really enjoyed meeting your friends properly.'

'You're welcome. Everyone seems glad that you came.' She bit her lip, surprised she had spoken the thought out loud.

'And you, Flora?' Mac's voice had dropped, and she noticed how it emphasised his Scottish accent, as he drew out the words; it was yet another thing about him that she liked. 'Are you glad that I came?'

'Well, it was better than leaving a gap on the seating plan after you'd accepted,' she quipped, dismissing his question with something that even to her sounded mean. 'Where are you staying this evening?' Flora hurried on, trying to explain herself. 'It's just that I think the hotel is fully booked and I'm not sure what else there is locally.'

'No need, I'm driving back later.' Mac reached out to swat idly at a bee floating around their heads and it droned away, settling onto a plant nearby.

'What, all the way to the island? Tonight?'

'My sister and a couple of her friends are coming to stay for a few days; I've promised to pick them up tomorrow morning. I'll crash out at a friend's place near the airport.'

'Oh.'

'Thank you for thinking of me but I won't need a room.'

'That's great,' Flora rushed on, desperate to make him understand that she hadn't been trying to issue a very different sort of invitation. She freed her fingers and saw him watching her gesture. 'I hope you won't be too tired; it's such a long way. Don't fall asleep at the wheel.'

'I won't fall asleep. Don't worry about me, I'll be fine.'

'Where does your sister live?'

'Paris. She's a painter; her partner is a sculptor. Every so often their artistic temperaments clash and she escapes to the island when she wants some time alone to work.'

'Are you alike?'

'I'm not sure. What am I like, Flora?'

'Tell me about your sister and then I can compare it with the little I know of you.'

'Cassie's very similar to our mother; they both have red hair and a wanderlust that keeps them on the move.

Since meeting her partner, she's stayed in Paris about three years – longer than anywhere else, I think. She's exuberant and sociable and has an ever-expanding group of friends around the world, and she loves adventures. She accuses me sometimes of being too predictable, but I know I'm always her voice of reason, and we speak often.' He paused, watching her. 'So how do you think that compares with me?'

It all sounded very lively and Flora felt embarrassed to reveal that her childhood home had been sold so her mum could move to a small new build in a larger town, and they could all try to move on without the glare of attention, offering sympathy and curiosity in equal measure.

'Well, I'd say that you're decisive, confident and creative, and those may be qualities you share with your sister. Will that do?'

'Impressive, Flora. My turn. I know about your passion for gardens. Tell me something – something that no one else would know about you.'

This was beginning to stray into proper date conversation, and Flora realised it had been a long time since she had bothered to try to be interesting on purpose. She scrambled about in her mind for something to tell him and blurted out the first wild thought that flared up. 'I missed getting my Gold award in Guides when I broke my wrist abseiling, trying to impress the instructor because I was madly in love with him.'

'Guides and abseiling. What else?'

Mac was laughing as he watched her. A tendril of brunette hair had escaped from its chignon in the breeze and drifted across her face. She stilled as he reached out and gently smoothed it behind her ear with a long finger, dislodging a wisp of confetti that floated to the ground.

'Stamp collecting? Crochet? Playing the recorder?'

'I was twelve,' Flora said indignantly, snatching her head away before she allowed herself to be distracted further. 'You're deliberately trying to make me sound boring.' She had learned to be very good at giving away little of herself and she preferred such anonymity to the alternative.

'I'm not, I promise.' Mac held up his hands in protest. 'I'm just trying to find out more about you, that's all.'

'Why?'

'Are you always this blunt?'

'Only when I know the other person is far more interesting than me. I'm sure you have much more to tell.' She crossed her hands firmly on her lap, gazing straight ahead to the lake in front of them.

'So what happened to the abseiling instructor?'

'It was an unrequited crush that lasted until I discovered he was already going out with somebody else.'

'Ah.'

'I have to get back,' she said, leaping to her feet. 'It's getting late, and I can't leave Mel and Sophie to manage alone, it's not fair. Sorry.' She slipped out of his jacket and handed it back to him. 'Thank you.'

Mac took it, and she turned and began to hurry back to the house, leaving him to follow.

Chapter Eight

Once Mel had been buttoned back into her dress and was looking suitably bridal – and Flora had also put on her bridesmaid outfit again – the evening party could begin. The noise was increasing, as more guests arrived and hurried over to congratulate the bride and groom, who were looking much more relaxed. The DJ was well into his stride, and a few young girls were already dancing to Ariana Grande songs and grumpily turning their backs on the boys sliding past on their knees and getting in the way.

Flora was busy greeting people, catching up with distant friends and marvelling at various children, either new or well grown. Throughout, she was aware of Mac hovering at the bar, his fingers idly resting around a glass of something she hoped wasn't whisky, seeing as he had a long drive ahead. Occasionally, she pointed him out with a casual wave to those who asked whether she had brought somebody to the wedding.

Mac wasn't alone; Eddie was keeping him company, and Sophie had expressed her amazement that somebody was managing to keep her husband away from his iPhone for more than five minutes. Flora glanced towards the DJ, as the music abruptly faded and he roared into the microphone, making himself heard above the noise.

'Okay, ladies and gentlemen – move over, kids! It's time for the brand-new Mr and Mrs Oliver to get the evening started with their first dance. Come on, everybody, give it up for your bride and groom!'

Most people stopped talking and turned to look, as the music was cranked up again, and Harry and Mel smilingly made their way onto the dance floor, holding hands. Flora stood in the shadows near the door onto the terrace, as a romantic track began to play. Harry drew Mel into his arms and slowly they danced, as their guests whooped and applauded, hastily pointing phones and cameras at them, and shooing children out of the way to capture this intimate moment in the special day. After a minute or so, the DJ invited the best man and bridesmaids to join in. Flora jumped, as she felt a hand on her back.

'Come on, Flora, you're not sitting this one out. Fair warning, remember?'

She was already smiling as Mac led her onto the dance floor. He placed a hand in the middle of her back and took hold of her right hand with the other. She gave him a casual glance, hoping it suggested that everything was fine. Really, it wasn't – every nerve ending was screaming in delight at his touch. Her smile was fixed as she looked away over his shoulder, watching everybody else so that she would not have to meet his gaze.

'You're tense again.' Mac lowered his head to speak into her ear, his breath light on her neck. She closed her eyes and pretended not to have heard. 'Relax, Flora.'

At first, he held her away from him, so that their bodies were not touching and a gap was maintained. But as the song progressed, Flora gradually softened in his arms, and the distance between them vanished, until she could feel the smoothness of his shirt and the contrasting hardness of his chest against her bare shoulders. His jaw, already shadowy with stubble, was against her temple and slowly his hand moved up her back until it reached her neck. Then his fingers trailed down her spine, sending her mind spinning as a searing heat lit up her skin.

As the people around them began to drift away, Flora realised that the song had ended, and very slowly they drew apart. But Mac kept a firm hold of her hand, unwilling as she was to let go. The DJ's sudden shout interrupted them, and a new track came booming through the speakers, blaring around the ballroom.

'You all know the groom's legendary taste in music, so once we've got this nonsense out of the way, we'll be onto the good stuff, starting with classic Stone Roses. Everybody – up on the dance floor and find a partner, preferably a stranger or at least somebody you've never danced with before.'

Carefully, Flora tried to prise her fingers from Mac's as she turned away, ready to go and sit down.

'Oh no, you don't.' Mac gently pulled her back, still holding her hand as the floor filled up around them. 'You're going to stay and dance with me again.'

Her voice was incredulous as she raised it above the din. 'You're not serious? Dance to this?' She recognised the implacable look on his face, and then they were jostled together as almost all the guests hurried up to get the party really started to The Nolans' 'I'm in the Mood for Dancing'.

He nodded, giving her a wicked grin as he started to dance, looking scarily like an extra from *Saturday Night Fever* but with better clothes, and Flora laughed. She tapped her feet, watching Mac in amazement as he danced wholly unselfconsciously, throwing himself into a disco routine. It would've looked desperate if he hadn't been so good: he was perfectly in time with the music and she couldn't have been more astonished if John Travolta had suddenly been parachuted in to take over. But then he reached for her hand and she was dancing with him, still enjoying every moment, as people crashed into them and spun away again.

Mac's performance was attracting attention and the crowd parted to form a circle around them. Before long Mel, Harry, Sophie and Eddie eagerly joined in. Sophie hadn't been a teenage dance champion for nothing, so when she cranked up the disco routine with expert moves, Mac copied her and everybody else could hardly stand, let alone dance, for laughing – it was so funny and brilliant. Once the track ended and another one began, Flora found she couldn't bear to leave the floor or look away when her eyes met Mac's. It was all such fun and Flora couldn't remember the last time she had felt so silly or enjoyed herself so much.

They managed another forty minutes or so, until Flora laughingly pleaded for a break and rushed to the bar, hurriedly finishing a glass of water. Mac was keeping his promise to dance with her all evening and she was loving every moment. She strolled back through the room, her eyes eagerly searching for him, impatient to dance again. Given his height, he shouldn't have been difficult to spot, but there was no sign of him, and she wandered onto the terrace, casually seeking him out.

He was standing on the far side, his back to her, phone clamped to his ear. She waited, safely out of earshot and therefore not feeling as though she was prying. A few smokers were nearby, and she nodded at them. Her gaze settled on Mac again, and she recognised the tension in his frame as the call continued, one arm gesturing to make a point to a person who couldn't see him, the other running through his hair. She was missing him, loath as she was to admit it, and she waited for another minute, still in the shadows.

She saw him turn and begin to walk across the terrace, and she heard his voice – resigned, fraught – as he ended the call and rammed the phone in a pocket. Flora slipped out of the shadows and moved inside, worried that he might think she had been trying to listen on purpose. She was chatting with another guest when Mac approached her, the tension she had recognised outdoors all but gone. He excused himself for interrupting, reached for her hand and they were back on the dance floor, the call seemingly forgotten.

As the party progressed, the evening flew away into the next morning all too quickly, and just after midnight, Mac took her hand and led her outside. They huddled in the light beneath the portico, facing one another without touching. She was horrified to realise that she might cry again, as she knew this moment would be a goodbye. She had long since kicked off her heels and had to lift her head to meet his eyes. She knew at once that he had withdrawn from her, had distanced himself to somewhere she could no longer reach him. The coolness was back, though she was surprised by the regret in his voice as he spoke.

'I have to go.' There was a suggestion of curtness in his tone, too, and Flora was very still.

'Of course.' She nodded coolly, clenching her hands into fists and determined not to give away her reluctance to say goodbye. 'Thank you for coming.'

Mac smiled then and she saw his face soften. 'So polite,' he said quietly. 'You make it sound like it was a business arrangement. Was it really nothing more?'

Flora didn't answer, in case she revealed the truth: how she'd loved every minute of the day with him and her regret that it was already over. She tried to slow down her racing pulse, wondering when – if – they might see one another again. *Better this way*, her mind tried to tell her heart. *Better this way. Say goodbye. Watch him leave.*

'Flora?'

He reached out and she felt the warmth of his hand on her bare arm, stroking her skin almost without thinking. He brushed his mouth against her cheek, and it was very different from the quick, impersonal kiss earlier in the day, when he had greeted her at the church. Flora was hardly aware that she had turned her head, but then his lips found her mouth and they were finally sharing the kiss she had been longing for.

She had known it would be like this. Her hands were already on his shoulders, urging him nearer, exploring the hard smoothness of the muscles beneath his shirt as he silenced every doubt with his mouth, offering a certainty and skill she had never before known. He pulled her closer still and she arched into him, until he was holding her tight against the hard length of his body. One hand was already exploring the curves outlined by the thin satin of her dress, while the other was on her neck and moved higher, until his fingers were in her hair, trying to loosen the pins that held it.

Somebody coughed behind him. She heard feet on the gravel and, abruptly, Mac let her go. His arms fell away, and Flora opened her eyes hurriedly, stunned by his absence. She was suddenly cold and trembling all over, and she stepped backwards sharply, grateful for the stone column of the portico steadying her.

'I have to go,' he muttered hoarsely, shoving his hands into his pockets as he turned away. Flora heard the uneven rasp of his voice and she was in no doubt that their kiss had affected him, too. She stared at him through the dim light from the house, hardly able to comprehend the words he tossed back over his shoulder.

'I'm sorry, Flora, I do have to leave now. Please will you say goodbye for me?'

She watched, astonished and hesitant, as he strode away into the shadows without looking back. She heard the sharp crunch of his feet on the gravel and a quick beep as the car was unlocked. The noise and laughter from the party seemed so incongruous, as she tried to process what had suddenly occurred between them. A kiss like that… surely it was a beginning, not a final farewell?

'Mac,' she called tentatively, her voice barely rising above a whisper as she took a step forward. He gave no sign of having heard her, and she saw the flash of lights as his car hurtled down the drive and then he was gone, leaving chaos and questions scattered in his wake.

Chapter Nine

The wedding was over. Mel and Harry had escaped to the Amalfi Coast on honeymoon, and life, for almost all the guests, had returned to normal. But as Flora wandered around her cottage, getting ready for work on a wet Monday morning two weeks later, she knew that something inside her had changed. She had been careful to try to conceal her feelings, especially from the eagle-eyed and intuitive Sophie. It hadn't been difficult to pretend with Mel; she was so wrapped up with her new husband and the two friends had barely spoken since the wedding. But Sophie was different. Flora knew from the way she had hugged her that she had guessed something had happened between her and Mac. She had also made her promise that she would pick up the phone or come and stay just as soon as she was ready.

Looking back, Flora remembered the wedding as a blur of excitement, filled with fun and the inescapable sensation of discovering that she was falling for somebody. But after Mac's abrupt departure, which had followed their kiss at the end of the evening, Flora had heard absolutely nothing from him, and she was hurt and surprised. With each day that passed in silence, the corner of her mind that told her he had liked her, too – had come all that way to be with her and had seemed to enjoy her company – was gradually being overtaken by the doubts pressing in. Was he too busy or not attracted to her after all? Maybe he simply had nothing better to do that day and decided to indulge her dare.

She threw herself back into her work in an effort not to think of him. After the way he had left, she was utterly determined not to contact him for fear of being turned down now that the wedding was over. But at night, alone in bed, she was tormented by the memory of their kiss and the feel of his arms around her – and sometimes she woke up believing that it had all been merely a dream, and almost wishing that it had.

But she couldn't think about that now. Soon she'd be leading a party of visitors around the garden at Middlebrook, and then the guests would have lunch, before exploring the grounds on their own. She took a quick shower, dressed in jeans and a Trust polo shirt, and headed upstairs to the kitchen, as she had something to do before heading out to work.

Flora loved her little cottage. Converted from farm buildings, it was a tiny upside-down house, with one bedroom and a shower room on the ground floor, and an open-plan living room and kitchen upstairs, with a small round table squashed between the two rooms. There was a compact deck outside, with views over woodland towards the town, two miles away. When she needed more space, she simply escaped into the estate and its gardens.

She plonked herself at the table, reached for her laptop and opened a file, absently chewing the top of a pen as she stared at a list of plants. She deleted a climbing rose and added two different varieties of clematis after a quick google to check availability, and then glanced through the window at the rain bouncing off the glass as she pictured, in her mind, the garden she was busy planning.

Her older brother and his wife, Sam, lived in nearby Thorndale in the Yorkshire Dales, where Charlie was the vicar of the village and three other parishes nearby. When they had moved into their large Victorian house, Sam had asked for help with the overgrown garden and Flora had come up with a simple yet effective plan, which improved the design and minimised the workload to accommodate their busy lives. Since the birth of their daughter, eight months ago, Sam had been on maternity leave from her job as a drama teacher, and Flora had made sure that the garden behind the house included a separate area for children to play, as well as comfortable seating to enjoy the south-facing views.

Sam had loved Flora's designs. She had been so enthusiastic that soon after Flora had received a call from Jon Beresford, owner of the Thorndale estate. Married only a few months ago, he was in the process of modernising a cottage that had recently been donated by his new wife, Annie, to an education trust they had set up together. The garden at the cottage had been created by Annie's godmother many years ago and had fallen into disrepair.

Flora had met with Jon and he had asked her to restore it to how it used to be, as a surprise for Annie. Flora was thrilled with the commission and was now finalising the planting scheme before work began. She knew that time would be tight, but everything was in place and the contractors ready to begin. Jon was taking Annie away and he wanted the garden to be finished by the time they returned. Sam was going to project-manage in Flora's absence and she intended to visit in a couple of weeks to complete the planting.

Flora enjoyed designing, but her heart absolutely lay in restoration and she was passionate about the ability of a garden to change lives for the better. Taking a blank space and creating something new and beautiful was exciting, but for her that didn't compare to stepping around history and discovering the past. Her grandmother had largely been responsible for Flora's love of gardening: during long periods spent at her grandparents' home, she had been given her own little plot to plant as she liked, and they had enjoyed visiting historic properties together. Even now, whenever she first entered an abandoned garden, her mind always took her back to that first glimpse of the Lost Gardens of Heligan, when she was fifteen, and she had understood then what could be achieved with love, time and careful thought. It was this same sensation she had experienced when she had stumbled upon the forgotten garden on Alana – the excitement of discovery, what it had once been and could be again.

Her mobile rang, startling Flora, and she looked at it, tempted not to bother answering. But the call was from Sophie, so she picked up the phone warily.

'How are you, love?'

Sophie sounded unusually hesitant and the realisation made Flora immediately suspicious. 'I'm fine.' Her pen dropped to the table, as she tried to imagine what might be coming next. 'What's up? You don't usually ring in the middle of the morning for a casual chat. Is everyone okay?'

'Yes, all good, but you're right: I haven't rung for a natter about the family. Have you seen any of today's posts from *Belle* magazine?' Sophie got straight to the point.

Flora's heart sank and she jumped up impatiently, taking two steps into the kitchen. 'No, of course I haven't.' She switched the kettle back on to make a second cup of coffee, more to distract herself than because she wanted another drink. 'Why would I? You know I don't read that stuff.'

Social media was a stranger to Flora, despite Sophie's best efforts down the years. She flatly refused to join any of the usual platforms, certain that she would never suffer from fear of missing out. She understood only too well how a simple comment could sometimes be translated into a whisper that became more hurtful and less truthful as it travelled.

'Okay… Here goes. I just wondered if you knew – about Mac?'

Flora dropped the spoon she was clutching and tried to keep an alarmed yelp from escaping, as she bent down to retrieve it. 'What about him?' She heard Sophie sigh and her dread spiked again, shooting adrenalin through her limbs.

'He's in a post of theirs with someone who looks very much like a girlfriend; there are pictures of them on holiday in Ibiza. I'm so sorry, but it's Chloe Berkeley, Flora. There's no official confirmation that they're actually together again, but the images look right.'

'Again?' Flora whispered the word, winded by the sudden and terrible news she had not seen coming. Together. Again. Tears gathered in her eyes as she remembered her and Mac at the wedding, the evening they had danced into another day and his kindness over her dad. 'What does that mean?'

'That they were a couple for nearly two years and apparently split up in February. Usual story: separate careers, travel, too far apart. No one else, blah blah.'

'So they weren't a couple when we were at Mel's wedding?' Still a shocked whisper, a moment of hope.

'Doesn't look like it. I've done some digging and I can't find anything else on social media that's linking them beyond this. No comments from mutual friends, no official statement or relationship status from her publicist. I just thought you would want to know, and I didn't think you would've seen it. I'm so sorry to give you such bad news.' Sophie paused. 'Have you heard from him?'

'No.' Flora was astonished that her voice sounded fairly normal, even though her heart was still crushed in despair and her hand had balled into a tight fist. Of course he wasn't single. She was almost more upset that she had allowed herself to be deceived, when usually she was so careful, and she slammed her still empty cup onto the counter, muttering angrily under her breath, before she continued. 'There's no reason why I should. Thanks, Soph, but it doesn't matter. The wedding's over and I won't see him again. This just confirms it.'

'Flora?' Sophie's voice had lowered in sympathy. 'I know you like him. And it was perfectly obvious that he liked you, too. Why don't you call him, ask him if it's true?'

'Absolutely not,' Flora answered furiously, her mind still restless, as memories, both good and bad, kept darting back in. She was definitely *not* going to call him; that much she was sure of. 'I've already made a fool of myself once, I'm not about to do it again. Thank you for telling me; I don't suppose it was fun for you either.'

Sophie sighed again, her sorrow for Flora clear. 'Sure, babe. Let's speak again tonight, when you've had time to process it.'

They said goodbye and Flora hung up, shoving the phone away, as though it was responsible for her sudden black mood instead of the news about Mac. All thoughts of planting schemes and coffee were forgotten, and she ran down the stairs, desperate to be outside in the fresh air. She grabbed a coat and shoved her hair up into a baseball cap, as she closed the door behind her. Flora marched across the yard and followed a track from the farm into the estate, skirting around the edge of a wood as she crossed the deer park towards the main house.

She reached for the keys in her pocket and let herself into the garden through a narrow gate in the elaborate wrought-iron fence. Normally, she couldn't look at the house without appreciating its beauty and enormous, solemn façade. But today she barely noticed it, furious with herself for allowing Mac to intrude even here. Yet, she found it impossible to forget him, and her mind churned over the few details she knew about his girlfriend.

Chloe Berkeley was the latest in a line of former models turned actress and television presenter. Popular and friendly, she was part tomboy, part style icon, as she raced around the world on wildlife adventures and threw herself into the latest extreme sports in between acting roles. Slight, with sharply styled short dark hair, she managed to pull off a look that was wholly unique and yet copied by teenagers everywhere. She was always denying rumours that she was planning to pose for men's magazines, and her signature look was definitely girl-next-door with an edge, which seemed to appeal to dads as well as their daughters. Flora walked faster and faster, as she tried to drive the image of Mac with such a beautiful and sophisticated girl from her mind.

Flora headed around the west side of the house, past a huge eighteenth-century orangery, her eye quickly taking in details of things in the garden that she would have to attend to later. A check of her watch confirmed that she still had twenty minutes before assembling her group, so she crossed the walled garden and emerged in a cobbled courtyard, dodging visitors and a group of volunteers selling plants from the garden. She smiled at them as she passed by, but didn't pause until she reached the shop and stepped inside.

It was busier than a normal Monday morning, presumably because the house wasn't open yet and few visitors wanted to brave the garden in the rain. Flora squeezed past a couple of people and disappeared into the stock-room behind the till. Grumpily, she flung herself down onto a chair. As usual, the small room was cluttered with DVDs of the latest production to be filmed in the grounds and spring catalogues crammed with last year's woodland pictures.

'What's the matter?'

The voice belonged to Sheila, the shop manager. Small and round, with curling grey hair, Sheila was highly competent, and in her twelve years at Middlebrook she had come to know every inch of the house and its gardens. 'It's not like you to be miserable, Flora. I thought you liked taking groups out.'

Flora stifled a sigh. 'Sorry, Sheila, of course I do. Do you know how many? I haven't seen the list yet.'

'I heard sixteen, one or two last-minute additions this morning. Come on, tell Auntie Sheila, I've got big ears and a little mouth.'

Flora laughed. She knew that Sheila was entirely trustworthy and whatever she learned would not be repeated. 'Another time,' Flora said, feigning brightness as she leapt to her feet. 'I'd better go and round them up.'

The rain was heavier when Flora returned to the courtyard and she tugged her cap down, trying to divert the water from her face. The volunteers were still toughing it out with their plants and she went over to have a word.

'If it doesn't stop,' she told them sympathetically, admiring their commitment to the cause, 'you can move the stall underneath the gatehouse and catch people on the way out. I'll send somebody over to help.'

They thanked her as she moved away and she switched on the radio attached to her belt, so that she would be in contact with the rest of the team whilst working. She noticed a few bedraggled people hovering on the lawn in the centre of the courtyard and headed towards them quickly.

'Hi,' she called, turning up the collar on her coat, trying to prevent the rain from trickling down her neck. 'Are you waiting for the garden tour? Okay, come with me. I'm Flora; I'm going to be taking you round today. We can wait underneath the gatehouse – might as well stay dry for as long as we can. Have you come far?'

Flora listened to the chatter as they headed for shelter, but by the time she had found everyone and brought them together, she was soaked, even though the rain had ceased and a patch of blue sky was looking promising. She frowned as she did a quick head count again and checked her watch impatiently. Fifteen – one missing.

'Two minutes,' she called to the group over the noise of polite chatting. 'We're just waiting for one more, but if they're not here shortly then we'll go. The weather's probably put them off.'

Flora peered over heads and checked the courtyard once more, but nobody seemed lost and she decided to begin the tour. 'Okay, everyone,' she called loudly, pausing for a moment as people turned towards her. 'Thank you for coming today; welcome to the Middlebrook Estate. I'm Flora Stewart, one of two assistant head gardeners, and I'm going to show you around the garden, parts of which are still undergoing restoration. If you'd like to follow me?'

Flora led the group across the courtyard towards the entrance to the garden and then, out of the corner of her eye, she spotted a man running towards them. She turned her head to look at him properly, guessing that this was her missing guest. He slowed down as he neared the group, and the blood rapidly drained from her face. It was Mac Jamieson.

He had obviously just arrived; he was still dry, and carrying a messenger bag slung across one hip and wasn't wearing a coat. Her mind went completely blank as she stared at him, terrified that her expression would betray her feelings. Flora knew that she looked decidedly different from the glamorous bridesmaid of two weeks ago, with no make-up, soaking hair, and wet and muddy jeans clinging to her legs.

'Sorry I'm late,' he said in a low voice. She saw him taking in the details of her bedraggled appearance. 'I was held up in traffic.' He smiled at the group and one or two older ladies softened at the gesture, but Flora was determined not to be quite so forgiving. She noticed his tanned face and the realisation of where he'd very recently been on holiday didn't improve her mood.

'We were just leaving,' she said shortly, desperately trying to regain her composure, as she turned towards the garden. 'You can follow at the back.'

She didn't care if anyone else thought she was being rude, as every memory she had stored away came rushing back into her mind. She remembered his voice and the lilt of his accent; she knew his eyes and how they could soften when he smiled, and most of all she recalled the feel of his mouth on hers and what it was like to be held in his arms. Absolutely livid with him for turning up at her work after two weeks of silence, she tried frantically to drag her mind back to the garden and focus on the rest of her group. She saw that Mac had obediently positioned himself at the back, as she had requested.

'Once we're in the garden, I'll explain a little bit of its history, what we're currently doing to restore it and the Trust's plans for its future. I'm very happy to answer questions as we go along and there will be time at the end if you would like to know anything else. The garden today covers approximately forty acres and the tour will last about an hour and a half. Lunch will be provided for you in the restaurant, and then this afternoon you're free to explore the house and grounds on your own. Thank you, I hope you enjoy your day.'

Flora was amazed that her words made sense and people were following her, as they were supposed to do. For all she knew she could have been speaking utter gobbledegook, and she was still finding it hard to remember what she had planned to talk about this morning. She sensed Mac watching her as she held open the entrance door, but she didn't wait for him; she scurried through and left him to fend for himself. She waited as the group huddled around her and then she began, concentrating carefully on what she knew.

After a few minutes they moved on and as Flora continued with the tour, she was still feeling uncomfortable, despite her attempts to relax and enjoy it. Bad enough that she had allowed herself to think of Mac, to become attracted to him, but much worse was having to deal with him in person, here of all places, where she had always felt at home. She struggled to keep anger at bay, as she wondered why he had kissed her and then simply walked away. And now he was suddenly back, and she would have to begin the process of forgetting him all over again.

She had led the group to the rose garden, and as she completed her talk and answered questions to bring the tour to a close, she was already eyeing an escape route so that she would not have to deal with Mac. The group murmured their thanks as they drifted away, and Flora saw her opportunity. Whilst Mac's back was turned, she bounded up a short flight of steps that skirted the edge of a deep pond and disappeared through a small summer house into the folly garden behind. Surrounded by tall yew topiary and dominated by a square tower, this corner was secluded and filled with shade-loving plants.

'Flora, wait!'

She heard his voice and ignored him, her pace increasing as she crossed the lawn. She intended to sneak away into the expanse of the huge parkland beyond the boundary of the formal gardens.

'Please, Flora. May I just speak with you for a minute?'

Mac's voice was louder and she heard his footsteps right behind her; he had easily found her route and quickly caught up. Hating the realisation that she was reduced to skulking around her own garden in order to avoid him, she whirled around to face him.

'What?' Her baseball cap had skewed to one side and she grabbed at it impatiently, loosening her damp ponytail. Her wet hair cascaded over her shoulders and she tried to ram the cap back into place to tame it. She noticed his eyes narrowing as they followed her movement. 'What could you possibly want with me, Mac? Why are you here?'

Her voice had dropped to a muffled hiss, as a family strolled past, the mother wheeling a pushchair and eyeing Flora curiously. She smiled blankly, hoping to project that all was well but knowing that she hadn't convinced them, as they turned to stare at her again before wandering slowly out of sight.

'I have two things I'd like to say to you.' Mac spoke quickly, nervously. Flora realised, with a jolt of surprise, that she had never seen him like this. 'I'd like you to come and look at the garden properly, on the island. I haven't done anything with it yet and I'd be really grateful if you would advise me.'

An unexpected thrill of elation raced through Flora, as she listened to his request. To be the first to document such a garden as the one on Alana – to search for plans, uncover its history and reveal its secrets little by little – was everything she sought to do, and she could hardly believe he was offering her such an opportunity. But then those thoughts abruptly disappeared, as she remembered their time together at the wedding. How they had talked, the way he had offered comfort when sorrow for her dad had found her again. And, at the end of the evening, the incredible kiss she had been utterly unable to forget. She had no idea if she could return to the island, feeling the way she did about him. Confused, hurt and afraid, she feared being overwhelmed once again. And yet, the garden: undiscovered, asleep, untouched.

'And the second?'

Flora saw his eyes narrow again as he watched her. His expression had become serious; he had reverted to the cool and distant man she had met on her first evening on Alana.

'There's something you need to know, and I'd prefer if you heard it from me.'

She was ahead of him and keen to appear unconcerned by anything he might say. 'Oh, you're not going to tell me about you and Chloe, are you?' Flora laughed lightly, her eyes glittering with something she hoped he recognised as dismissal, still feeling the unwelcome flare of colour in her cheeks. 'That's old news, surely? How great that the two of you are back together again.'

She'd stunned him, that much was clear. He stilled, his arms hanging loosely at his sides. He took a step forward, his hand reaching out and then falling straight back. 'You knew?'

'Doesn't everyone? Isn't that the point of social media?'

'I guess. Well, right. So you know.' Mac was mumbling and it gave Flora a strange satisfaction to see him rattled for once. 'Have you seen the pictures? What do you think?'

'I'm sure you both look fabulous together.' She was incredulous at this question and choked back an even more sarcastic retort. 'And why the hell would it matter to you what I think? She's your girlfriend, Mac, not mine. It's your life. We barely know one another – surely you didn't expect us to see each other again?'

'So, the dare, the wedding... our kiss. Are you saying it's all over and forgotten?'

'It was a silly dare, a day out. Just a kiss, Mac, nothing more.' Flora willed herself to relax, to remove the tension from her shoulders, and she deliberately allowed her attention to wander. 'People do it all the time. We've both moved on since then, haven't we?'

The pointed question seemed to take him by surprise and his nod was uncertain as he swallowed. Another thought struck her, and she voiced it quickly, before she could change her mind.

'Is that why you really came to the wedding? To ask me about the garden?'

'It wasn't the only reason. But then you knew that,' he told her quietly, his composure almost recovered. 'I had a really great day and there didn't seem to be a moment when it was right to ask you about the garden.'

'That was quite an act you put on,' she retorted, struggling to keep bitterness from her voice. 'Some people actually thought we were a proper couple. Anyway, thanks – you certainly managed to convince everyone that I'm over David. And I already have a job. Goodbye, Mac. I'm sure you can find your way out.'

Rain was beginning to fall heavily again as Flora brushed past him, intending to return through the rose garden and disappear into some secret corner where he couldn't follow. But Mac was quicker, and he took her arm, heading across a patch of lawn to the shelter of a small wooden hut out of the worst of the weather. She furiously shook her arm free, as he dragged a hand across his face to wipe the raindrops away. She noticed that his shirt was already damp and beginning to cling to his skin, outlining the shape of a chest that her hands had already explored, and looked up sharply.

'Please, will you think about it – the garden?' he asked, gentle and serious all over again. 'I saw the way it made you feel, and how you immediately understood its history and what it could be in the future. I have no expectations, Flora. I only want to say that I'd very much like you to come.' He paused, a frown creasing his brow. 'If you agree, then of course I'll make sure that everything between us is purely professional this time.'

The radio on Flora's belt began to squawk and she picked it up, listening to the voice speaking through it. 'I have to go; I'm needed back at the house.'

'May I call you in a couple of days? If you say no, then of course I won't bother you again. I'll accept whatever decision you make.'

She nodded and hurried away to the house without saying goodbye, all too sure that she had allowed her imagination to take flight and soar to somewhere she obviously now had no right to be.

She tossed and turned for the next two nights, as she considered every possibility. The most sensible decision, on a personal level, would be to refuse his offer and have nothing more to do with him. Professionally, she knew that the garden was a marvellous opportunity for her. But, as she kept reminding herself, she had her cottage and had recently been promoted; she loved her job and the role she was playing in the estate, and she really didn't want to give it up just yet.

On the third evening, she was at home, heating pasta in the microwave, when Mac called. Briskly, she told him her decision and all too soon the conversation was over. She had accepted his invitation, trying to convince herself that the only reason for going back to Alana was the work opportunity. But it wasn't only that. She so wanted to be the one who would reveal the garden's secrets, to share with him how every story the garden would tell fastened its history so firmly to its future.

Chapter Ten

'I think you're mad,' Mel said incredulously when she heard what Flora was planning to do. She almost tilted a full wine glass at Flora to emphasise her point but hastily tipped it upright again, just in time. 'He's totally messed you around, and you're going to go back and poke around in that grotty old garden for him? Why? What about your job?'

Sophie and Mel had arrived to spend the weekend with Flora – their first together since the wedding – and they were crammed into her cottage, eating a Thai takeaway and already on a second bottle of red wine. Flora had planned to cook something nice for supper, but the idea had to be shelved once she had been delayed at work, so she had texted her friends to ask them apologetically to pick up something en route from the station.

'I'm not giving up my job,' Flora said patiently, reaching for the last shrimp spring roll as she glanced at Mel. 'I know you're angry with him, Mel. I'm only taking a couple of weeks' holiday and I'll spend it on the island, doing preliminary work on the garden, until I have to be back in Thorndale for Annie's cottage. Mac has at least one of the original designs and I'm just going to see what's left and try to gauge what's needed, if he decides to restore it, and point him in the right direction for professional help.'

'I still think you're mad. What about him? How are you going to manage, seeing him every day, feeling the way you do? I can't believe he turned up at my wedding, cool as you like and pretending to be your date, when he already had a girlfriend. She's away, so he's coming out to play. The lousy little—'

Flora shot Sophie a cross look and interrupted Mel before she could vent any more of her temper. 'Soph, I thought that conversation was just between us. And, anyway, apparently they weren't together when he was at the wedding with me.'

Sophie shrugged, unconcerned, as Mel continued to glare, refusing to allow her opinion to be swayed. Sophie then informed them that Chloe Berkeley was currently filming a television drama series in South Africa, and her Instagram was full of stunning locations and cute animals, as well as the odd bikini shot, which endeared her to the thousands who followed her. 'Sorry, babe. But it's only the three of us; you know we've always shared everything. And I don't think you're mad, by the way. I think it's a great idea, spending all that time with him.'

'He almost certainly won't be around.' Flora hoped she had successfully concealed the little pang of disappointment that she hadn't quite come to terms with yet. 'He's made it quite clear he'll be working or seeing clients, probably in Edinburgh, so there won't be any misunderstandings between us this time. And when this silly crush passes – and it will – I know I'll never regret the chance to work on that garden.'

'Hmm...' Sophie sounded suspicious as she tipped the last of the bottle into their glasses and crossed to the fridge for another, throwing her friends a glance over her shoulder. 'I'm not so sure, Flora. You can pretend it's business as much as you like, but I saw the way you were looking at each other at the wedding.'

'Don't, Sophie, please,' Flora pleaded, replacing her cutlery on her plate with a sigh as she pushed it away, her appetite gone. 'The whole thing at the wedding was just a game, I can see that now. And I really am only going back because the garden is such a marvellous opportunity.'

'Huh,' Mel snorted, refusing more wine and jumping up to switch the coffee machine on instead. 'Anyone else want a cup whilst I'm making it? You're so much prettier than Chloe is, Flora. At least you would be if you didn't live permanently in jeans and muddy boots. And look at your nails! How do they get in that state so quickly?'

Flora laughed ruefully. 'I know, but I don't seem to ever have a minute to go into town. And thanks for your loyalty, Mel, but I'll never be prettier than Chloe Berkeley, no matter how good my nails look.'

Casually mentioning Chloe's name still didn't make her relationship with Mac seem any more tangible to Flora, but she was all too aware that she would have to deal with the reality of it sometime during the coming days. It still felt like something that lived in the pages of a magazine and through the whirl of constantly updating social media accounts – not someone she had kissed and whose face was imprinted in her memory. After learning about Chloe, Flora had become even more set in her belief that, as far as she was concerned, romance was overrated.

'Are you staying in the hotel?' Sophie looked envious as she scooped the remains of the food into a bag, and Flora nodded. 'You are! You lucky, lucky girl. Let me come with you; I'll be your labourer or assistant, or whatever it is that you all do. I can bring my own trowel and gloves. You're bound to need someone who can take notes or something.'

Flora was still smiling as she opened the fridge and pulled out the remains of a chocolate cake she had scrounged from the restaurant at closing time. 'Haven't got much choice, really, other than the hotel. I know, what a shame. At least I should be able to have a manicure. And you'd hate it, Sophie, it's bound to rain.'

They laughed and Sophie accepted the truth of Flora's comment with a wry nod. They shuffled up on the sofa to settle down for what remained of the evening with their dessert and Flora was thankful that her rapidly approaching return to Alana wasn't mentioned again.

Three days later, shortly after a snatched lunch on a sunny Monday afternoon, Flora loaded everything she needed into her trusty car and headed north. Everybody had laughed when she had swapped her nippy little hatchback for the old estate, but Flora was fond of it. It was practical for her job; it didn't matter how dirty it got and it never let her down. So she took the jokes, mainly from Eddie, in good humour and carried on enjoying driving it.

The decision she had finally reached had seemed reasonably rational at a safe distance from Alana, but as she neared the island, her misgivings grew with every mile. No matter how many times she had told herself that Mac was unavailable, not interested in her and unlikely to be around, she knew she was going to find it very difficult to pretend complete indifference to him if he did turn up.

After the initial conversation with Sophie about his girlfriend, of course Flora had looked up the photos of Mac and Chloe online. There were only three: one showing Chloe as she emerged from the sea in a bikini, looking fabulous and in another Mac was sitting on the side of her lounger, massaging oil across her shoulders. In the third, they were walking down a busy street; Chloe was laughing up at him, as Mac faced the camera, and both of them were holding shopping bags. Flora had been informed by Sophie, who had naturally checked, that the images Chloe had posted of the holiday on Instagram had not included Mac. What did that all mean?

After almost five hours on the road and a ferry crossing from the mainland, Flora did her best to push him from her mind as she caught her first glimpse of the island. Since she had last been here, spring had abandoned its first cautious peek and the landscape had flung itself wholeheartedly into the new season. She noticed so many differences as she drove off the ferry that she had to stop the car as soon as she had let the other vehicles pass by, and jump out to look properly.

Only a few mountaintops in the far distance still clung onto their snow topping; the hills below boasted patchwork patterns of green shoots and clumps of slowly unfurling bracken, interspersed with the tiny white dots of grazing sheep and long-haired ginger Highland cattle. The early evening sunlight was still warm, and Flora shrugged out of her jacket as she turned full circle to absorb the views from every direction. The sea seemed still and smooth; yachts moored off the jetty swayed gently, the light bouncing off the water back to the hills. It was silently, astoundingly beautiful, and a sharp thrill of excitement stole through her as she thought of the days ahead exploring the garden. But this was Mac's place. Whether he was here or not, she knew she would be unable to escape him. He had been everywhere she would be and no matter how hard she tried, she knew she could not completely push him from her thoughts.

When she arrived at the hotel a short time later, guests were milling about: strolling through the gardens, drinking on the terrace, playing a late round of golf and enjoying their leisure time in a way that Flora knew she would not whilst she was here. The porter came out to meet her and collected her bag, and she dutifully followed him inside, feeling strangely lonely without Mel and Sophie to share this with her. The hotel looked as beautiful as ever – in fact, more so now that it wasn't smothered in rain and mist disguising its ancient charm.

Flora had no idea in which room she would be staying but was really hoping it wouldn't be the same as last time. That room, Islay, held memories she didn't want to have to deal with just now. That whole weekend had been filled with glimpses of Mac and snatched conversations she had tried so hard to forget.

So when Flora was shown into Arran, she was thrilled and surprised. Huge windows on the south and west walls gave her views of both the garden and the coast, and she wondered if Mac had chosen this room for that reason. But then she realised that he almost certainly wouldn't have been the one to pick it.

Cranberry and chocolate colours were lightened by cream panelled walls and subtle lighting, and a pair of checked armchairs sat either side of an oak writing table in front of the south window. Curtains were full length and heavy, and a queen-size bed was hardly able to dominate the ample space. The room was beautiful, and she loved it.

Aware that she'd be late for dinner if she didn't get a move on, she hurried towards the bathroom to freshen up but on the way she noticed an envelope on the table beside the bed, addressed to her. She picked up the typed note and opened it.

> Flora,
>
> Sorry I can't be there to welcome you. Please make yourself at home – all the facilities of the hotel and spa are available to you whenever you like. I've left a key to the garden for you with reception.
>
> Mac

It couldn't have sounded more impersonal and businesslike, and Flora read it once more, before crumpling the paper and dropping it in the bin. The brief lines he had written confirmed that their relationship really was purely professional and a wave of sadness swept over her. She turned away from the bed and headed into the bathroom.

-

She didn't need an alarm to wake her early the next morning from a restless sleep. She showered quickly, grabbed some breakfast and collected the key that Mac had left for her on her way out of the hotel. It was a warm, bright morning already and she decided to walk to the house; she would come back for the car later, if she needed it. For now she only needed her camera, sketchbook and laptop.

She saw a few early golfers already out, dragging their trolleys and seemingly oblivious to the emerging beauty of the day. She could smell the change of season in the air since her last visit and she breathed deeply, enjoying the fresh spring scents. She found her way back to Róisín House quite easily, and the familiar sense of excitement grew as she approached it. The curved and tree-lined drive had been cleared since she was last here, and that somehow extended the perspective of the house to meet her.

The house was different, too. The outline of the building had disappeared behind layers of scaffolding, and plastic sheeting covered some of the worst of the wooden window frames. Although there were not yet signs of builders on site or work in progress, Flora knew it couldn't be long until they arrived. The drive widened as it met the house, and she crossed to the scruffy green door, slipped her key in the lock and pushed it open, bashing down the nettles that had only grown bigger since she was here last.

She stood silently for a few minutes, just listening. The sea slithered over the rocks below, and gulls swooped and called, but no footsteps came to seek her out, no warm voice announced a welcoming smile as she took her camera from its case. Carefully, she made her way down the uneven steps to the bottom of the terrace, glancing back towards the house when the abrupt sound of cars roaring up the drive startled her. Their noisy din and the shouting, as builders slammed doors and set to work, seemed quite wrong in this peaceful place.

Several hours later, she realised it was almost four o'clock already and she was starving. She had made sketches of different areas, following the sun through the day as she thought about what might have been planted and where. She had also taken photographs, beginning at the very top and working her way down. Tomorrow she intended to sketch the walled garden and photograph it, before returning to capture the site of the formal south-facing garden beyond the terrace. She was in the sunken garden, lost in thoughts of roses that might have been planted a hundred years ago, when a sudden voice nearby made her shriek in surprise, and her camera and sketch-book fell to the ground with a clatter.

'I'm sorry, I didn't mean to make you jump.'

Hearing Mac's voice had surprised her very much, and their heads almost bumped together as they both bent down to retrieve her things. Flora was thankful for a hurried moment to take a deep breath, as the thudding in her heart slowed only the merest fraction. The day was lengthening into a warm, late spring evening and there was a glow on her skin that hadn't come from the sun. She hadn't really been expecting him to turn up and her sadness had grown throughout the day, with the realisation that she might not see him at all.

'Thank you.' Flora wiped a bit of soil from her hands on her rather grubby shirt as she straightened up and reached out to take the camera from him. She was uncomfortably aware of the faded jeans and wild hairstyle that her colleagues had nicknamed 'Flora's nest'. Self-consciously, she tucked a strand of hair behind her ear, as the warmth on her skin began to settle down.

'How are you getting on?' Mac was leaning against a low wall, watching her. He was wearing a suit without a tie, and black Oxford shoes set him even further apart from their wild surroundings. Yet she knew that he had never looked sexier and more at home, as he pushed sunglasses onto his head.

'Really well, thanks.' Flora's response was confident; she was at home in such a place as this. 'I've photographed some of the garden now and sketched basic designs; I can let you have a copy of these, along with notes on possible planting schemes, once I've done each area and scanned them. Most of the sketches are my impressions based on Lassiter's style and the setting of the house, as well as climate and any evidence of the little original planting which remains. But if I could see any plans you have, then I should be able to be more specific about what restoration would involve, depending on what you envisage for the future of the garden and how authentic you want it to be.'

'I'm impressed. You have been busy, thank you.' He paused, as though he were unsure what should come next, how it should be between them. His hands were restless on the wall and she felt his eyes on her.

Flora, surprised by his hesitation, raised one shoulder in a brief shrug. 'It's why I'm here,' she reminded him, as she switched her camera off, relieved that it was still working. 'I'm leaving in a few days; it isn't much time for a garden of this size.'

'Of course.'

His reply was short, to the point, and she sensed the return of efficiency in his tone. There was a moment of silence while she waited for him to say something else, and when he didn't elaborate, she stepped past him with a smile she knew was forced. 'Well, I think I'll head back. It's been a busy day.'

She had reached the top of the steps leading from the sunken garden before she heard the quiet sound of his voice behind her. It was gentler, its richness absorbed by the overgrown garden all around them, as though his professionalism had already disappeared to the secret depths of their surroundings.

'Flora?'

She paused, aware she was only too happy to linger. 'Yes?'

'Complete restoration? Or should I just tidy it up a bit, shove in a few conifers and let nature take its course?'

She turned to face him, only partly feigning horror as she threw up a hand in protest and saw his grin. 'Not conifers,' she pleaded, feeling a softening of the tension that his arrival had produced. 'You already know what I think, so you're probably asking the wrong person if you want a different reply.'

'I'd like your opinion.' The smile in his voice faded as they stared at one another. 'I can ask any number of people for advice, Flora, but I'd like yours.'

'Of course, restoration,' she replied quietly. Her gaze finally left his and searched out the neglected remains all around them. The builders had left for the day; they were alone now, and the thought secretly thrilled her. The only sounds she could hear were the breeze drifting through the trees and waves rolling onto the beach below them.

She knew the garden much better now. Her short time here had already taught her what the architect had been trying to achieve when he had designed it to be an extension of the family home. Flora understood the design had become less formal as the garden stretched away from the building behind it, so that the plants gradually blended into the naturalness of the land beyond its boundaries, and walls were built for terracing and to shelter tender plants, not to keep people away.

'My opinion is that it would be desperately sad to lose a garden such as this. So few of Lassiter's original properties remain, and I'm sure you know there are organisations who would be prepared to help you with restoration. But of course, it also depends on what you want to do with the house. Are you planning to convert it into another hotel?'

Mac shook his head, suddenly leaping up the unsafe steps towards her and reaching for her hand, as he had on that very first day here.

'What are you doing?' Startled by his gesture, her protestations fell silent, unable to snatch her hand from his and break the sudden intimacy of the contact. Mac gently pulled her alongside him onto the terrace, until they were in the centre, and then he let go, placing his hands on her shoulders. He turned her around until she was facing the sea and then his arms fell away.

'What do you see?'

She stared at the water, already understanding its ebb and flow well enough to know that it was slipping away from the shoreline as the tide turned. She sensed the presence of the house behind them, perched above the sea, the tangled garden somehow joining the two together.

'What Lassiter saw,' she replied eventually, understanding exactly what it was that Mac was trying to show her. They shared an ability to design, to take something blank and make it beautiful. 'How he created the house to be part of the landscape and allowed the garden to belong to both the land and the building.'

'It won't be for sale again, Flora, nor is it going to be a hotel. I'm going to make it my home.'

She heard the note of excitement in his voice and whirled around to face him, the enthusiasm in her eyes matching his. 'That's brilliant! But what will you do about your job? I thought you were based in Edinburgh?'

'I'm committed to projects at the practice until the end of the year but by then I hope to be living in the house; I'll work from here and travel as necessary.'

'How lovely.' Flora dropped her gaze. 'I should be going.' She began to retrace her steps and collect her belongings. 'It'll take me a little while to walk back to the hotel.'

'Would you like me to drop you off?'

'No, thanks. I enjoy the exercise and it's probably out of your way.'

Mac followed her until they were at the green door and he pushed it aside so she could exit first, stepping over the weeds still trying to trap them. He pulled the door shut and they hovered on the drive, both turning in surprise when the sound of an approaching vehicle caught their attention. A little red car rattled to a stop as it neared them, and Flora watched as a middle-aged woman emerged and grabbed ineffectively at a terrier that managed to leap out before she could slam the door.

'Stop him! Quick,' she shrieked, as the dog shot off towards the house, barking gleefully. 'Rex! Come here, you little monster.'

Flora made a grab for the dog with her free hand, but Mac was quicker: he lunged and caught him by the collar, bringing the terrier to a halt, even though he continued to wriggle in protest as Mac lifted him easily and tightened his grip. The woman hurried over and Flora read the relief in her face. She clipped a lead onto the dog's collar and took him from Mac, who was still grinning as he released the terrier to her.

'Thanks so much! Sorry about that, we're still working on recall. I didn't want him getting into the house – heaven knows where he might have gone or what he'd have peed on.'

Mac was laughing now and as the woman swung her jolly gaze to Flora, he began the introductions.

'Flora, this is Maggie Connors and you've already met her delinquent dog; Maggie's the headteacher at the primary school on the island. You remember, Maggie, I told you about having a professional historian to look over the garden? Well, this is Flora, Flora Stewart.'

'Hi, Flora,' Maggie said eagerly, still trying to hang onto the wriggling dog in her arms. 'How lovely to meet you. Mac did tell me about your coming to the island, but I must confess I was expecting a fifty-something in tweed or dungarees.'

Flora laughed, liking Maggie immediately. She had dark hair, caught in a wayward bun that emphasised an attractive face and brown eyes, and she was smaller than Flora. 'Left the dungarees at the hotel,' Flora said. 'But I don't have a tweed jacket. Your dog is very lively.'

'He's a swine!' Maggie gave the terrier a loving look which belied her words. 'But he's the apple of my eye and very young, so I can still make excuses for him.' She glanced at her watch and looked at Mac apologetically. 'I can't stay, I've got a PTA meeting in half an hour.

Actually, Mac, Flora's the reason why I'm here. Look, I hope neither of you will mind, but I was wondering if I might borrow Flora for a couple of hours one afternoon, if it won't interfere with her work here?'

Astonished, Flora listened to Maggie's explanation. 'We've been trying to set up a proper garden at school, but it's ground to a halt and turned into a bit of a tip just now. Seeing as we don't get many visitors to the island with your level of expertise, Flora, I wanted to ask if you would consider popping down to the school and having a look at what we've done? And perhaps letting us know how we might improve and make some progress?'

Flora was already nodding, delighted by the invitation and the opportunity to offer her skills to help engage children in the joys of gardening. 'Of course,' she told the headteacher, whose smile became even brighter at Flora's words. 'I'd love to, if you think I can help at all.' She glanced sideways at Mac, who was looking at her. 'I'm sure I'll still have enough time here. It's light until late so I can use the evenings, if necessary.'

'I think you having a look over the school garden is a great idea. I'm not worried about how much time you spend here; you know you're free to come and go as you please.'

'Perfect.' Maggie was beaming, still clinging onto the squirming dog. 'Thank you both so much. I really had better dash; we can sort out the details later. Oh, Mac, before I go, you haven't forgotten about the ceilidh tomorrow evening, have you?'

The smile Mac gave Maggie was apologetic. 'I haven't, but a client has requested a last-minute meeting on site, and I might end up taking them out for dinner. I'll try to be back in time, but no guarantees.'

Maggie nodded, accepting his explanation as she lifted the dog down, seemingly tired of the battle to keep him still. 'Why don't you come, too, Flora? It's just a fundraiser for the school at the community hall. There'll be music and dancing and great food. Whoever is on the island, even if they're just visiting, is always invited. We like to keep an open door for any events.'

'Oh, I'm not sure,' Flora said awkwardly. 'It's very kind of you to invite me but I won't know anyone, and I don't want to intrude on a private event.'

'Och, don't be daft! It's not private at all, you'd be very welcome,' Maggie pointed out. 'And you'll know me – and Mac, if he turns up – and I'll introduce you to lots more people. And Scottish dancing is great fun.'

'I won't promise,' Flora warned her. 'I'll see what time it is when I've finished here.'

'Lovely, see you tomorrow,' Maggie called as she headed back to her car. 'I'll pick you up about seven from the hotel, if you like – save you bringing a car or having to walk, and then you can have a glass of wine or a beer? Bye, Mac, hope the meeting goes well and you're free in time. Thanks for lending Flora to us.'

'But I haven't said—'

Maggie was in the car and speeding away, with the dog bouncing on the back seat, before Flora had even finished her sentence. She looked at Mac, bemused, and saw him grinning.

'You may as well just go,' he said. 'She'll only send someone to find you, if you don't turn up.'

Judging by what she had seen of Maggie already, Flora didn't doubt his words. They said goodnight and she began the walk back to the hotel, leaving him standing alone in the driveway, sensing the weight of his stare following her steps.

Chapter Eleven

The community hall wasn't quite what Flora had been expecting. Maggie had turned up, as promised, at the hotel to pick her up and Flora enjoyed listening to her chat about the island, even though she was glad the journey in the bouncy little Ford lasted no more than ten minutes. They soon arrived and, once out of the car, Flora looked at the modern and bright building with appreciation.

'Oh, how lovely.'

The hall sat just below a small hill overlooking the sea, perched behind the hamlet where most of the islanders lived. Clad in dark sheeting, no doubt robust enough to withstand the island's weather, huge skylights made the most of the natural light and three sets of bifold doors opened onto a deck running the width of the building. Surrounded by a stone wall with a belt of pine trees behind, the playing field was scattered with tables and chairs, full-sized goals for football and a couple of barbeques.

'It really is. We're so lucky to have the hall, it's a real gathering place for the islanders and we've all used it for some reason or another over the last couple of years. The previous one blew down in a storm, but it wasn't up to much anyway. Mac designed this one to last for an awfully long time, and we're certainly benefitting from his expertise.'

The music was already spilling outside as they made their way to the entrance. A light drizzle didn't seem reason enough to keep the doors closed and they were pulled wide, as more people headed inside. A folk band, complete with fiddles and accordions, was set up at the furthest end, away from the makeshift bar, and Flora followed Maggie as she searched for a free table. She made a mental note to thank Sophie, as the simple grey dress she'd packed on her insistence fitted the occasion well. Cheerful, handmade bunting was strung across the light-coloured walls, and she noticed a sports court marked out with white lines on the floor and a basketball hoop at either end. Small groups of people were clustered together, holding drinks and chatting over the noise as a few excited children raced around, the smell of hot dogs filling the room.

'Not many tables left,' Maggie called across her shoulder to Flora. 'Quick, there's an empty one – let's grab it.'

They settled down at the table and Flora was happy to sit on her own for a few minutes whilst Maggie headed off to find glasses. Mac had warned her in a text this morning that there would not be a proper bar so she had brought a couple of bottles of wine and some beers from the hotel, as her contribution to the evening's refreshments. She watched the room, her eyes falling on people laughing together and clutching drinks whilst children played together. She thought about Mac and wondered if he would turn up or whether dinner with his client would keep him from the island all evening. She told herself firmly that she didn't mind either way.

Maggie returned with glasses and Flora poured drinks for them, distracted by the constant flow of islanders who came over to say hello and welcome her. Maggie introduced her to everyone as 'Mac's gorgeous gardener', and eventually Flora gave up trying to insist that she wasn't. Finally, making the most of a lull in visitors to their table, she and Maggie joined the queue for the buffet.

'Don't eat too much,' she warned Flora, waving at someone she recognised across the room and trying not to drop the slice of quiche slithering around on her plate. 'Save yourself for the set dances; it's not much fun if you feel sick.'

'Oh no, I won't dance,' Flora told her with a firm shake of her head. 'I don't know the steps, and I'd only be in the way and trip somebody up.'

'Och, don't worry about that! The simpler ones are easy enough, if you keep an eye on someone nearby. We'll find you a good leader and then you'll be flying.'

'Not literally, I hope!' Flora's silent resolve was still to sit them all out and enjoy watching everybody else instead. Maggie was side-tracked by a couple of governors from her school and apologised as she turned away to speak with them. Flora was content to slide a little food onto her plate, before returning to the table and topping up her glass of red wine. The band had settled down to eat, too, and the room was quieter, as only the noise of chat and laughter filtered through the crowd.

Her gaze constantly flicking to the wide-open doors, Flora saw Mac before he spotted her, and her heart hitched in surprised pleasure as he strolled in, greeting people with ease. He was still in a shirt and tie, the formality of his clothes at odds with the casual nature and fun of the gathering. She watched as he removed the tie, ramming it into a pocket and undoing the top buttons on his shirt, as though distancing himself from the city he had just left behind. He looked tired as he pushed a hand through his damp hair while he spoke to an older man who had come to stand beside him.

She shrank back in her seat until she felt the wall behind her and could retreat no further. The man left, and she saw Mac's eyes scanning the room quickly. When they eventually found hers, she gave him a brief smile and he nodded in return with a lift of his brows, acknowledging her presence but no more. She dropped her gaze and sipped the wine slowly, pushing aside the disappointment of his greeting. Still, she felt the pull of his presence in the room, as though the space had contracted to contain only them, and it was an effort to refuse her eyes permission to follow him, to wonder and watch where he went.

Soon the band was in place once again, tuning up as tables and chairs were pushed to the walls, and couples began to line up together down the length of the hall, experience telling them where to go. Some of the men were in kilts, which Flora found very appealing, whilst others were in jeans, and quite a few of the ladies were wearing dresses or tartan. Flora watched, shrinking back in her chair at the far end, hoping that Maggie had forgotten about her. But it was not to be. Maggie dashed over and grabbed Flora's hand, pulling her to her feet with a cheery grin.

'Come on, Flora, I've found you a partner.'

Hesitantly, Flora found herself being towed into the middle. As soon as she saw Mac staring at her with some reluctance, she tried to protest and back away to the safety of the chairs along the wall.

'Oh no, really, I'll just watch. I'm not a very good dancer.'

'Don't be daft,' Maggie scoffed, only letting go of Flora after she had handed her over to Mac with a smile. 'You'll be fine. Mac's an excellent partner; he's had plenty of practice. Just try to follow him.'

Slowly, she approached him. Flora felt herself stiffen when he placed his right hand on her back and took hold of her free hand with his left, joining them. She couldn't look at him, couldn't let him see that every touch reminded her of the wedding, when she had danced in his arms for the first time and they had spent most of the evening together. She sensed that he was equally uncomfortable and avoided touching her any more than was essential.

'You don't have to do this,' she muttered, every part of her responding to his closeness with a delight she tried to disguise. 'I'm more than happy to sit it out.'

'Let's just get through it, shall we? Maggie will think it strange if we don't dance now.'

His curt reply was more than enough to dash away any pleasure their proximity had brought and she remembered how, in the garden at Middlebrook, he had tried to tell her about his relationship with Chloe. The sharp reminder made her realise that his unwillingness to dance with her again was their reality and the way things were going to be between them now. Tension lent her frame a stiffness that made her awkward in his arms, but when the dance began, the intricacy of the steps and the sheer pace demanded all her attention. Suddenly, she was half-dancing, half-skipping across the floor, as she tried to keep up with Mac and realised it was much more fun than she had been expecting.

Somehow they stumbled through the opening barn dances, thanks to Mac's obvious skill, and when they had completed the faster 'Eightsome Reel' and the 'Dashing White Sergeant', Flora was laughing, despite her initial reticence. She didn't need to see Mac's face to know that he was beginning to enjoy himself, too, as she felt the rigidity in his muscles softening. She was still getting hopelessly lost at times and felt dizzy after being twirled from partner to partner and back again. During a short pause in the music, she broke away for a quick drink.

'Where did you learn to dance like that?' She had to gasp out the words in between breaths as she leant against a table, still smiling at what had just taken place. 'I'm impressed.'

'Misspent youth,' Mac told her drily.

They had both downed half a bottle of water when Maggie called them loudly back to the floor. '"Strip the Willow", you two, come on!'

Flora dashed back to line up opposite Mac once again and he gave her a brief, impersonal smile as he bowed slightly, copying the other men. They were third in line when the music started up and Flora was glad, as it gave her a few moments to watch the other dancers before it was their turn to take part. They joined hands and Flora was entirely aware of the taut strength of his arms, crossed with hers; as he spun her around, their eyes never connecting as he led her through the steps. The dance seemed to last for an age, and when she and Mac finally reached the end of their row and the music stopped, she was hot and breathless all over again, her hair escaping from her high ponytail and framing her face with long tendrils that curled into soft waves.

'I'm done,' she told him with thankful relief, tucking her hair behind her ears as they drifted away from the centre of the floor, their arms no longer linked. 'I'm going outside for some air. Thanks for obliging Maggie and showing me what to do.' She could have told him she had loved every minute because she had danced it with him, but that would be going too far.

'You did great, for a first time.' His gaze was settled somewhere in the distance, but she heard more warmth in his voice this time, as they slowly drew to a halt.

Flora laughed at that as she searched for Maggie amongst the people milling around the hall, topping up drinks in the break between dances and finishing the last of the food. 'I think you're being generous. It's exhausting and I'm sure I stood on your feet a few times. Night.'

She was tired, probably as a result of the long drive on Monday and the constant battle to conceal her emotions around Mac, and decided to make her way back to the hotel. She found Maggie, refused her offer of a lift and thanked her for the invitation. It had been much more fun than Flora had imagined and, despite the awkwardness with Mac, she was glad she had come – everyone had made her feel very welcome, as Maggie had promised. She and Maggie made plans to meet at the little village school the following afternoon and Flora headed out of the hall, waving to the people who wished her good night.

It was cool outside, and she appreciated the breeze drifting from the sea as she slid her jacket loosely over her shoulders. It was only nine thirty and the evening was still light, despite the clouds tumbling overhead. Setting off towards the hotel, Flora looked forward to the prospect of a brisk walk to free her mind. She was getting used to seeing sheep scattered across the rough fields, penned in here and there by cattle grids crossing the few roads, and she saw a couple of lambs spilling onto the lane in search of excitement, jumping out of her way into the fresh, emerald green fronds of bracken. She had only been gone for ten minutes or so, when a car drew up alongside her and she recognised the purr of the engine without having to check who was driving.

'Flora? Let me drive you back; it's probably going to rain again.'

She carried on walking but glanced into the vehicle. Mac had slowed to a crawl and was leaning across towards the passenger seat, the window down, one hand on the wheel to keep the car under control.

'I'm fine, thanks. I think you've done your duty for one evening.'

The car lurched towards the grassy bank on the other side of the road and then Mac cut the engine and leapt out, striding around to face her. She stopped, too, and tried to disguise the dismay she felt as she read the tension in his face.

'I'm sorry, about before. I didn't mean to seem offhand. I just wouldn't want to give anybody the wrong impression about you and me.'

'*Again*, you mean. Like we did at the wedding? I suppose it was different then, since you weren't officially back with Chloe and it didn't matter who saw us.' Flora crossed her arms, eyeing him suspiciously. 'Unless you *were* together even then? You did leave in rather a hurry.'

'What? Of course I wasn't with Chloe.' His answer was sharp. 'Is that what you think of me? That I'd fall for someone else and cheat on my girlfriend at the same time?'

Shock plunged through her stomach, and Flora's voice was shaky when she found it. 'Fall for someone else? What do you mean?'

His face was suddenly expressionless as he rubbed one hand across his neck in agitation and ignored her question. 'Flora, look, things have got a bit complicated since the wedding. It's not what you think.'

'It really doesn't matter at all what I think, Mac. Only what's happening between you and Chloe.'

'If I asked you to trust me, to give me time, would you?'

'*Trust* you?' Flora's laugh was bitter, and she heard the sneer in her voice. 'You hurt me! I told you things I hardly ever share, and you kissed me like it really mattered, and then left me with barely a word. Then I see you strolling down the street with your girlfriend like nothing ever happened between us! What am I supposed to think?' It was impossible now to disguise the despair she was feeling, and her voice fell. 'Just leave me alone and let me do my job. That's all I need.'

Mac's shoulders slumped and he stared at her for a long moment, his hands balled at his sides, before he retreated to the car without another word. Flora continued to walk, the pounding in her temples increasing, despite the even pace she soon re-established. She was a good distance from the car before she heard the engine re-start and then fade into the night as he drove away. She reached the hotel and hurried through reception, desperate for a shower to wash away the entire evening. However simply they tried to behave around one another, somehow complications seemed to arise with every encounter, and Flora was beginning to look forward to leaving the island and returning home to the steadiness of her ordinary life.

The next day she was excited about seeing the school garden, so she finished at Róisín in good time and drove straight there. Maggie had wanted her to come before the children left for the day and Flora arrived promptly at two, giving them around an hour before the grown-ups arrived to take pupils home. Nestled in the hamlet just behind the houses closer to the bay, it was a long, low stone building, surrounded by a wall, with a playground at the front. Flora worked out that it faced east, and she automatically looked to her right, searching for signs of the garden and spotting the high dome of a polytunnel sitting behind a hedge. Maggie met her at the office and, once Flora was signed in and issued with a visitor pass, they headed straight through the school to the garden.

Maggie began to explain its origins. 'We had a family on the island who were as self-sufficient as possible, and they helped us with ideas and practical upkeep. We registered the school with a gardening charity, which gave us access to lots of support, and put up the polytunnel with the help of a grant. But then the family had to leave the island for work elsewhere and the project stumbled to a halt. I'd love to get it up and running properly – it would be such an opportunity to engage the children in nature and to develop scientific, as well as practical, knowledge and skills. Quite a bit of our learning is done outdoors, weather permitting, as we have a fantastic environment and community around us.'

'Absolutely.' Flora was pleased by Maggie's enthusiasm for restarting the garden and what that could mean for the pupils. 'You won't hear any argument from me! I think it's a wonderful idea and I'd love to help if I can, whilst I'm here.'

She saw at once that it was a tip. The polytunnel was still in good order but the rest of the plot was a mess, with flourishing weeds and abandoned pots dumped in heaps, some still with plants inside. The plastic compost bins had blown over and spilled their contents, adding to the chaos. Four raised beds looked to have contained fruit at one time, but they were long since past their best and the strawberry patch was full of mare's tail, which would be almost impossible to eradicate. Nevertheless, Flora felt her excitement grow, as she pictured the plot as a productive and working garden – and the results which could, given plenty of hard work, be achieved in the coming months.

'It really is a disaster,' Maggie said sheepishly, bending to pick up a watering can and tossing it into a nearby wheelbarrow. 'I'm sorry, Flora, I haven't looked at it for a while and I feel embarrassed to have dragged you here, now I've seen the state of it again.'

'Oh no, don't be,' Flora assured her, already making her way over to the polytunnel to explore. 'I've seen far worse. It will need some work for sure, but it can definitely be sorted out.'

Just then there was a roar behind them and they both turned to see children erupting from the building and running over to discover what was going on. They were followed more slowly by two adults, who Maggie explained were a teacher and classroom assistant. The children skittered to a halt as they spilled into the garden and Maggie asked them all to stand quietly so she could introduce Flora.

'This is Miss Stewart, who is a professional gardener, and we're very lucky that she's visiting the island for work just now and has agreed to look at our garden to see how we can improve it.'

Flora smiled at the little group, noticing the glum stares of two older boys and the wide-eyed wonder of three tiny children, almost certainly reception age. She hoped she could engage everyone's interest, eventually. The nine remaining kids looked the most interested and a couple of them were already scrabbling about in the soil.

'Hi,' Flora said, dropping down so she was roughly on the same level as them. She picked up a handful of the soil, and was pleased with the quality and texture. 'Who knows what this is?'

It was a question with an obvious answer and almost every hand went up, so Flora picked one of the older boys to reply. She thanked him for his answer and gave them a very quick and simple explanation of why the soil was so important to everything in the garden. Maggie asked her to tell the children how she became a gardener, and Flora took a breath as she began.

'Well, I was planning to be a musician at first.' She was standing with her back against one of the compost bins and she smiled at the little group, pleased by their attention. 'I went to a very good school to learn about music but then, when I was fifteen, I was really poorly and had to miss quite a lot of lessons.'

'What was wrong with you?'

Flora smiled at the direct question from an older girl. 'I had glandular fever, which is a type of infection, and it caused a swelling in my tummy and then another illness called pneumonia, which made me very poorly. Even though the symptoms went away eventually, I was very tired for a long time and couldn't go to school. My parents were working every day, so I went to stay with my grandma to get better.'

Flora had never forgotten those weeks and months. She remembered the endless sore throat, the constant sense of being unwell, and the shivers and aches that left her feeling cold on even the warmest days. Nausea that nibbled away at her appetite until it was gone, and the weight and strength that slipped away with it. And then the days when she was too tired to do barely more than lift her head from the pillow, before finally she was able to emerge outside, blinking in the sunlight in her grandma's garden, her symptoms eventually improving.

Flora dragged her mind back to now, aware that everyone was listening, and endlessly grateful that she had recovered. Her gaze fell on a little girl with a neat blonde bob, topped with a fringe, and big blue eyes. She was standing further back, next to a slightly bigger girl – perhaps a year or so older – and they were holding hands tightly. Flora smiled at them, surprised when the younger girl just stared back without responding. The older girl looked down and gave the little one a nudge, which resulted in the merest stretching of her lips.

Flora couldn't fathom why, but she felt that her story had been worth sharing just for the sake of this little blonde girl alone. So she continued. 'My gran has a beautiful garden, even though it's small, and when I started to get better, I was able to spend time outside and help her. It wasn't long before I had completely fallen in love with nurturing plants and watching them flourish, and I honestly believe that the garden made me better. Not because it could heal me physically, but I was feeling quite sad about missing school and home. Growing things in the garden helped me to feel excited again, and then I minded less about school and not seeing so much of my friends.' She paused, smiling at each group in turn. 'The garden I'm visiting here on the island is big, definitely special and important because of its history, but it doesn't matter about the size of the space you have. What really matters is what you do with it and how it makes you feel. When I was still at my grandma's, I decided I wanted to become a horticulturist, which is just a big word for a gardener. I went to university to study and worked hard, and here I am.'

'Thank you, Miss Stewart, what a lovely, happy ending. We're awfully glad to hear you got better, aren't we?'

There was a chorus of agreement and Flora stood up with a grin. 'Well, who wants to explore in the polytunnel and see what we can find? But please be careful – it's important not to touch anything and then put your hands near your mouth, okay? You must always wash them when you've finished outside.'

It was a bit of a scramble to get in and the teachers had to organise the children in an orderly queue to make sure no one was pushed aside. Flora glanced around for the little blonde girl and saw her standing with her friend, just inside the door. She gave her another encouraging smile, but knew not to expect a response this time. She made her way over to a section of shelving, where there were some seed trays and pots, and picked up a couple to examine them. She felt a movement at her side and when she looked down, the little blonde girl and her friend were standing next to her, watching with wide eyes. Flora picked up another small pot and bent down, still taller than either of the girls.

'Look,' she told them, holding the pot out in front of her. 'These are sweet pea seedlings. Someone must have planted the seeds a while ago and they've germinated. Do you know what they look like?'

A shake of the head from the older girl, but still no reply from the smaller one.

'Well, they're plants of course, but they have the most beautiful and delicate flowers, which smell amazing and come in all sorts of pretty colours. I love them; we grow lots in the garden where I usually work. If you look after these plants by giving them room to grow in the sun and some water, you'll have flowers in the summer, too. These little plants are like a promise of happiness to come.'

Flora smiled at them and then she paused, the pot in her hands, as the little girl's lips parted, and she tried to speak. It was a few moments before any sound followed and Flora had to stoop low, her ear close to the little girl's face.

'Will they be pink?' It was a tiny noise, a whisper that Flora heard through the clamour around them. The simplicity of the question from this little girl, who had somehow captured Flora's attention, brought a rush of emotion she hadn't expected.

'They might be,' Flora told her quietly, unwilling to say yes and then risk disappointment if they turned out to be anything but. Flora felt that trust from this little one could be lost in a heartbeat if she didn't offer the truth. 'They're usually a mix of colours so they probably won't all be pink. Is pink your favourite colour?'

A nod, while those still, blue eyes watched her steadily. 'What's your name?' Flora asked.

The older girl looked down quizzically as the blonde girl opened her mouth and, again, it was a minute before any sound followed. Flora was ready this time, close enough to hear the tiny murmur she made.

'Tamsin.'

'That's a really pretty name,' Flora told her, looking at the other girl and repeating the question, quickly learning that she was called Bonnie. There was a call then, from the teacher, and the children were bustled away, some protesting, to return indoors. Flora watched them go and it was only as they lined up that she saw Tamsin was still holding the pot of sweet pea seedlings in her little hands. Her eyes softened as she looked at the small girl, and then they were gone.

'Oh, Flora, you were fabulous!' Maggie was enthusiastic as ever and Flora laughed, her thoughts still with the little girl. 'I wouldn't be surprised to hear you've got a couple of budding horticulturists after that. They loved you.'

'They're very sweet, especially the little blonde one – Tamsin, is it? She asked me if the sweet peas we found would be pink.' Flora was busy straightening pots that had fallen over but she heard Maggie's gasp and looked around curiously. Maggie was staring at her in astonishment and Flora wondered what on earth she had done.

'Did you say that Tamsin spoke to you? Did Bonnie tell you her name?'

Flora was worried now, a frown creasing her brow. 'No, I asked Tamsin and she told me. That was it, I think. She didn't say anything else, apart from asking if the sweet peas would be pink. What's the matter?'

Maggie shook her head in wonder. 'Absolutely nothing. Tamsin has barely said ten words together to anyone other than Bonnie at school and none at all since her parents died nine months ago.'

Chapter Twelve

At Róisín, Flora had managed to unearth a wheelbarrow and some not completely useless tools which she carted back to the formal garden, dumping them in the long grass beside the hidden herbaceous border. After a couple of hours of good hard labour, hacking at brambles and nettles, she had cleared a space about two metres squared down to perennial weeds and the stumps of a couple of shrubs. Experience had taught her not to rush into removing anything that could prove important, so she took photographs and made notes of what she had discovered.

Since the visit to the school garden yesterday, she hadn't been able to stop thinking about Tamsin and the appalling bereavement she had suffered. Flora felt a closeness and connection to Tamsin that she couldn't explain, given the very little she knew about her.

When she had returned to the hotel after visiting the school, she'd called a colleague at Middlebrook and requested some help. She knew they had hundreds of sweet pea seedlings growing in cold frames and she had asked for around a dozen of a particular variety to be carefully wrapped and sent up to the island by courier as quickly as possible. There was a part of her that knew the gesture to be fanciful, but if it meant that Tamsin would have her pink flowers come the summer, then Flora was prepared to do whatever it took to get them to Alana, even if she had to drive back and fetch them herself. The only shop on the island, a mix of post office-cum-general store, sold compost and basic pots, which she planned to buy once her package had arrived and before delivering the plants to Tamsin, so she could show her how to care for them. She was still thinking about the little girl as she carried on clearing the patch of ground, digging out the remains of a dead shrub.

'Hey, Flora, are you about?'

She heard Mac's call and stood up, spade in hand, to see him pacing impatiently on the terrace outside the house, an urgency in his body that she was beginning to recognise. He spotted her and quickly ran down the steps. They hadn't spoken since the night of the ceilidh, although she had seen his car on the drive and knew that meant he was somewhere on site. It wasn't hard to imagine he was avoiding her on purpose after the way they had parted, and Flora squirmed whenever she remembered her agitated admission that he had hurt her.

'Hi.' There was a look of apology in his eyes, slightly at odds with the suggestion of exuberance on his face. 'Are you really busy? I've found some more old papers boxed up in the attic and I think they could be significant. I haven't read very much yet but there's stuff about the garden and the family who built the house. I thought maybe we could go through it together, if you'd like to and can spare the time? Two heads and all that, and I know you like doing research.'

Flora immediately grasped his excitement, under-standing only too well his desire to know more about the people who had created this special place. 'You mean am I busy apart from trying to clear this lot?' She waved her hand over the remains of the plants at her feet and saw his grin. 'But I'd love to see it.' Her passion for research was another thing she had forgotten she shared with him and yet he had remembered, and the knowledge pleased her.

'Flora, look… about the other night.' He hesitated, the exuberance fading as concern flashed across his face. 'I'm truly sorry if I've hurt you. That was never my intention – it's the last thing I want, after everything you've already been through.'

'Mac, don't, it's really not necessary.' Flora bit her lip, trying to hide her frustration that yet again she had revealed more than she had intended. 'I'm not going to be here for too much longer. Can we just put the wedding and everything behind us, and focus on the garden? Please? I really don't have anything else to say.'

'If that's what you want?'

What else was there? She didn't voice her question; a shrug sufficed as her reply. She pulled off her gloves and dropped them to the ground as Mac hovered, waiting for her to join him so they could go and explore.

She dusted off the worst of the soil clinging to her jeans and boots, and they ducked underneath the scaffolding stretching across the back of the house. They reached a French door set beside a wide, curved bay window and Mac pushed it open, standing back so that Flora could enter first. They were in a large, mostly empty drawing room, except for a couple of old armchairs, a desk with an office chair in front of it, a laptop sitting on the surface and a messy pile of boxes propped nearby.

The high ceilings and painted panel walls were still bright, despite the discolouration they had suffered over time. The oak floorboards were scuffed and worn but the room still retained its spacious and innate beauty – from the chipped, ornamental plasterwork to the marble fireplace and huge sash windows overlooking the garden. Dust clung to everything and the remains of a broken chandelier lay abandoned in a corner, and Flora began to realise the extent of the restoration project that lay ahead. She spoke, her voice loud in the vacant space around them.

'Shall I take my boots off? I don't want to make more of a mess.'

'No, they're fine, leave them on. It's better not to be wandering around without anything protecting your feet whilst the house is like this.'

She glanced outside, her view of the garden partially obscured by the scaffolding poles poking up from the ground. It was the first opportunity she had had to view the garden from inside the house and she studied the perspective of the design for a minute, noting tiny details that she had missed outside. She sensed Mac watching her as she rearranged her long hair back into a ponytail that drew it away from her face.

'This is a stunning room, so beautiful. I haven't seen any of Lassiter's houses before and I was expecting something more formal, more masculine, I suppose. The light in here is amazing; it must be exceptional on clear days.'

Mac smiled and she saw that he was pleased by her approval. 'The design is quite unusual in that all of the principal rooms are on the ground floor and open directly onto the garden. There's a library next to this room and a dining room at the far end of the house.'

'What will you do with the house? Are you planning to alter it?'

He leant back against the desk as he watched her. 'No, just modernise it, keeping to the original principles of using local craftspeople, wherever possible, to take it from the last century into this one. I love all the personal, private details that turn it from a building into a home and I'm still exploring, still finding stuff that was left behind.'

Flora looked away first and Mac moved towards the armchairs positioned to capture the view from the windows. 'Shall we sit here? It's probably more comfortable than the desk and I haven't got two chairs to fit around it.'

'That's fine.' Flora watched Mac as he lifted a couple of the boxes across to the bay window and dumped them between the chairs.

'There's no Wi-Fi here yet and the 4G's pretty rubbish. Sorry, I know it's not ideal for doing research.' Mac pulled the lid from the box nearest his feet. 'Hopefully, we'll find some information in this lot that I can follow up later in the office or when I finally get Wi-Fi in a couple of weeks. Or you could at the hotel.'

Flora knelt to remove the lid from the second box and a thrill stole through her when she saw the packets of letters – some loose, others tied together – and books that she hoped might be diaries or journals, as well as ledgers.

'You ought to know something more of the history.' Mac was close as he dropped down beside her. 'The island belonged to Fraser Campbell, who had inherited it from his uncle; it had been in their family for generations and they'd always farmed. Campbell also had a manufacturing business in Glasgow, where he lived most of the time. This house was designed to be a modern home where he brought his family on holiday. He'd travelled quite extensively as a young man and the differing styles he incorporated were inspired by what he had seen. There was a manor house on the site before, most of which was pulled down, although the old kitchen on the north side still remains.'

Flora nodded, keen to hear more about the story of the house. The gardens she had worked in were always intimately attached to the buildings, and she loved learning their history and immersing herself in the details of other people's lives.

'Campbell was married, and had a son and daughter. The son left for university in London and didn't return often; he wasn't interested in the island or the manufacturing business. Eventually, the business was sold, and the Campbells moved here full time with their daughter. Campbell had included a clause in his will, allowing her to remain in the house for her lifetime but when his son died and the nephew inherited, the son's will had made no such provision. The nephew probably saw an opportunity to get her out – he clearly didn't want any dependants making life difficult and preventing him from doing what he liked with the house. Doesn't sound like he was a nice guy, since he had no qualms evicting his own aunt from the home she was promised.' Mac pointed to the boxes. 'I'd love to think we might actually have stumbled on some more information about their lives in these. If you find anything you think is useful, let's pile it on the desk and take photos, and then we can research it properly later.'

They settled down in the chairs to begin work. Before long, she wriggled to the floor to make herself more comfortable, and it was only a few moments until Mac copied her. They sat near to each another, long legs stretched out, as gradually the contents of the boxes were emptied around them. They read through and photographed what they had found, enjoying a naturalness in the quiet that enveloped them. Flora separated everything she thought might be informative and after an hour or so, when the only sounds were the builders crashing about somewhere in the house behind them and the scrape of their feet as they repositioned sluggish limbs, she stretched her neck, placing a record book onto the growing pile of documents beside her.

'Anything good?' Mac asked, giving her a quick glance, before returning his attention to the ledger in his hands.

'Possibly. Most of what I've seen so far is invoices and orders for the build – some of it includes materials for the garden, but nothing too personal yet. How about yours?'

'Not really.' He sounded frustrated as he put the ledger down. 'It's nearly all stuff relating to the management of the island and the crofts. I'm sure there'll be more information somewhere in the house... I just have to find out where they hid it. Campbell's study had been cleared long before I came here and I'm hoping the most important items were saved.'

She rummaged around in her box and found several journals at the bottom; she picked one up carefully, lifting it past the business papers and a yellowed folder that surrounded it. Made from a red and now cracked leather, it was bound with a loose ribbon. Mac stood up as she untied it and she sensed his attention on her new find.

'That might be interesting,' he said idly and she agreed. They were both still for a moment and he looked away first. 'I'll make us some coffee.' He sounded awkward as he turned away and she heard the door close behind him.

Flora opened the journal and gasped as she saw the intricate and beautifully detailed watercolour painting of a faded pink rose on the first page. She couldn't be certain, but it looked to her experienced eye like an Old Garden Rose and the image was exquisite. Even though she was itching to rush on, Flora quickly took a photo on her phone and slowly turned the page. It was only moments before she understood that she had stumbled on a very personal journal and realised she was holding her breath. The name inside read *Rose Campbell* in elegant handwriting and Flora carefully turned the yellowed pages one by one, her anticipation intensifying with every glimpse.

It was the diary of a young girl who was very much in love for the first time. Begun in 1908, when Rose was twelve, she described her excitement about the new house on the island and especially the garden, which she was longing to make her own. Scattered into hurried passages with some gaps in between, Rose had written of long summers on the island with friends, mostly left to their own devices and allowed a freedom that would probably have been unthinkable anywhere else. Flora was wholly captivated as she tracked Rose through the seasons and the development of the garden, and she didn't hear Mac return until he nudged her leg with his foot. Startled from the world set out in the pages on her lap, she tried to drag her mind away from the lives and escapades in this place over a hundred years ago. She watched as he set their mugs down on the floor and settled next to her once again.

'Sorry it took so long.' He pointed to the mugs. 'The builders needed me for a decision and then it took ages to make drinks for them, too, with only one working kettle between us.' His eyes searched hers with a keenness that she was becoming used to, as though he saw her more thoroughly than anyone ever had before. 'What have you found? I can see from your face that you've got something useful.'

'They're Rose Campbell's journals,' she told him jubilantly, unable to disguise the exhilaration she felt at her discovery. 'Written over several years but there's so much detail about her life here. I've only managed to read one from beginning to end so far, but I've glanced at the others. Exploring the old manor house and its grounds before this one was built, helping to choose plants for the garden, sailing around the coast, picnics and playing out until the light had gone every day and sleeping in tents... It's extraordinary, and in places she's sketched pictures or painted tiny watercolours of things that caught her eye.'

'But I don't know who Rose is,' Mac told her, his brow furrowing. 'The daughter was called Caroline and, as far as I know, she lived here with her parents until the nephew turfed her out.'

'She must be Campbell's daughter – there's too much in here for her to be just a friend or more distant family member. There's even a sketch of the house, look.'

Mac leant closer as Flora passed the journal across and she felt the weight of his arm against her side. His thigh was close to hers as they peered at the book together and, effortlessly, she remembered their unforgettable kiss and the sensation of being held in his arms. The thought was distracting and she blushed as she tried to wrench her concentration back to the journal.

'Maybe there was another child, another girl?'

'Possibly, but I would expect we'd have come across her name by now. There were three boys who visited the island regularly and the eldest was the same age as Rose; he was called Archie and they more or less grew up together. I'm guessing they were friends of the family or perhaps distant cousins. I skipped ahead to one of the other journals and it starts with her turning eighteen. She and Archie fell in love as they became older and got engaged on Rose's eighteenth birthday; she wrote about the party and who was there, and she talks about a guest called Rupert. I wondered if he might be Lassiter. It was in the summer before the start of the First World War, and then there are a few lines about Archie joining up and being sent away for training. There are fewer entries after that, mostly to do with the garden and their letters to each other, and then it stops, in May 1915.'

Flora's voice had dropped in sadness as she imagined Rose and Archie tearing around the island as teenagers, and exploring the beautiful new house and garden, only dreaming of the future as an extension of childhood fun and endless games. In those days, Flora imagined, summer must have seemed endless and everything possible, until calamitous events in the world reached even here and brought disaster long before they were ready to understand it.

Mac whistled as he scanned through what Flora had already read, propping the book so it fell across their legs. He grinned then, something carefree lighting up his face – a look which would have her follow him anywhere. She shoved away the thought, feeling his fingertips skimming her thigh as he turned the pages.

'She must have been a very talented artist, judging by these little sketches and drawings.'

Flora hummed in agreement, happy to share in Mac's progress through the journals as she tried to glimpse details she might have missed the first time. He seemed oblivious to his fingers brushing her leg and gradually she relaxed, unwilling to draw away from the intimacy they had unthinkingly created. They read on and it was almost another thirty minutes before they reached the end. Flora laughed when she saw their coffee, forgotten and cold, still on the floor, and Mac's chuckle was wry.

'Sorry. I'll make some more.'

Gradually, they moved apart and Mac climbed to his feet. He raised his arms above his head to stretch, the gesture casually lifting his polo shirt above the waistband of his jeans and revealing the hard stomach muscles beneath.

Flora reluctantly wrenched her eyes away. She glanced at her watch as she stood up, too, realising that most of the afternoon had passed and she hadn't achieved what she had planned to get done in the garden. 'I'd better get going; I'd like to finish up outside before it gets late. Thanks anyway.'

'Flora? Before you go, I wanted to thank you for going to look at the school garden. Maggie was thrilled with your visit; I've heard she's arranging a volunteers' day tomorrow to start clearing up and that you've agreed to run it.'

'Well, I'll just be helping with work on the day so we can get as much done as possible in a short time. Maggie's hopefully going to get enough people along to help; it's not much notice but she said that word gets around and some will come, as it's a Saturday. I can sort out which areas to focus on first and what can be recycled or stored for later.' Flora retied the ribbon around the first journal and placed it carefully on top of one of the armchairs – a precious find indeed from their afternoon together.

'I just wanted to say thank you, too, for what you did with Tamsin.' Mac's voice had dropped, and Flora was astonished by his words. 'I heard that she spoke to you.'

'Wow, news certainly travels fast on this island!' The thought of the little girl brought a sad smile to Flora's lips. 'She was adorable, and I really didn't do anything.'

'Well, it wasn't nothing.' Mac was staring at Flora, as though trying to decipher exactly what had occurred between her and the small, blonde girl. 'Whatever you did, you managed to capture her interest enough to enable her to speak to you and that's quite an achievement.'

'How do you know about Tamsin?'

'She's my god-daughter. Her father, Angus, was my best friend before he died.'

Chapter Thirteen

The sweet pea seedlings for Tamsin had arrived when Flora reached the hotel in the early evening. She usually felt a bit self-conscious, marching through reception in her working clothes, but the staff were used to her now and greeted her cheerfully each time she returned. One or two liked to enquire about the garden and ask how she was getting on.

The island shop was closed until tomorrow so all she could do was stand the small plastic cases of seedlings in a little water in her luxurious bathtub. She hoped the plants would survive their journey, and was pleased to see that they looked healthy and strong, with the growing tips to encourage more flowers already pinched out. She emailed her colleagues at Middlebrook to thank them and received a cheery reply in return. When she thought of the garden at work back in England, she realised she hadn't really missed it yet, caught up as she was with Róisín and its history, thoughts of Mac and Tamsin, and now the school garden to try to untangle before she had to leave the island next week.

-

The shop was open early on Saturday so Flora popped in and collected some supplies to repot Tamsin's little plants.

It took her longer than she expected to get away, as the chap behind the counter, as well as a couple of customers, remembered her from the ceilidh and wanted to know how the garden at Róisín was progressing. She was happy to answer all their questions, before saying goodbye and dashing back to her car. She was thrilled when she arrived at the school to discover around a dozen helpers and some extra tools, plus children and a particularly useful-looking flatbed truck. There was a mist hovering below the hills and Flora was hopeful, as she got out of her car, that it would soon clear to reveal a lovely, sunny day.

Sheep were bleating in the field beyond the school and a couple of curious Highland cattle had stuck their heads over the wall to see what was going on, making Flora smile when she spotted their hairy, ginger heads. Maggie had done wonders in gathering help in such a short space of time and Flora went to search her out, saying hello to everyone she passed. She found Maggie in the polytunnel, which in the cool of the morning was usefully doubling up as a canteen.

'Hi, Maggie,' Flora called cheerfully, moving a couple of pots holding small trees to one side, ready for inspection later. They looked almost dead, but she would make sure before they were scrapped for good. Her hair was still loose, and she quickly wound it into a plait that ought to keep it from getting in her way whilst they worked. She noticed Maggie's terrier securely tied up out of harm's way and looking miserable about it, whining when he spotted Flora. 'This all looks brilliant; you've managed to find so many people to come along at such short notice.'

Maggie grinned, adding a lid to the large teapot balanced on a section of wooden staging. She was wearing a pair of green overalls and practical shoes, and her long dark hair was swept off her face by a scarf; the style suiting her perfectly.

'Yes, they've all been marvellous, especially as it's the start of a bank holiday weekend. I asked everyone to bring as many tools as they could, too, as some of ours seem to have got broken or disappeared altogether, I've no idea why. Thanks so much, Flora, for doing this; I know you must be busy at Mac's new place.'

'It's my pleasure. Any excuse to work in a garden, especially when it will make a difference to the lives of children and encourage them to learn about horticulture.'

'How do you want to organise everything?'

'Let's get everyone together and then we can chat over a cup of tea in here.'

Maggie set off to round people up and gradually they made their way inside, where Flora was pouring drinks into mismatched mugs and handing them out. Her eyes searched the group, who were chatting excitedly, hoping to find Tamsin. She was not surprised, but simply disappointed when she couldn't find her amongst the others. Maggie was distributing biscuits and just when Flora thought everyone was settled, she saw Mac walking through the garden towards them.

To her delight, Tamsin was at his side, their hands tightly linked, and Flora's heart tilted with a feeling of such tenderness that she almost gasped. Mac was wearing jeans, a dark hoodie that emphasised his wide shoulders, and boots, and Flora knew her face was flaming at his unexpected appearance. She smiled brightly at Tamsin, not anticipating a response, but her spirits lifted again when the little girl's lips twitched shyly. It was enough for

Flora and she was so looking forward to telling Tamsin all about her new pink-flowering plants whenever the opportunity arose. Mac was greeting people cheerfully as they made their way over, while still keeping an eye on Tamsin, and then he pointed at the tray in Flora's hands.

'Morning. Hope we're not too late for one of those.'

'Of course not, there's plenty. Maggie has biscuits and there's hot chocolate for anyone who wants it. Hello, Tamsin, how lovely that you came today.'

'Thanks.' Mac lifted a mug from the tray and Flora watched surreptitiously as he smiled at Tamsin again, his voice gentle. 'Glass of milk?' Tamsin nodded, her blue eyes looking up at him. 'Come on then, let's go find you one.'

Flora busied herself with emptying the teapot. She had barely been able to stop thinking about Tamsin or the fact that Mac was her godfather. She hoped that by the end of the day she would have shown the little girl just how special creating and nurturing a garden could be. She had made rough plans for the work they would be carrying out and, as Maggie shushed everyone, Flora stood ready to explain her strategy, enjoying the sense of excitement building. She had quickly assessed people as she had been moving amongst them, recognising some faces from the ceilidh.

They all listened as she offered an enthusiastic welcome and divided them efficiently into three teams: one to begin clearing the rubbish outside and sorting it into piles for removal, a second team to carefully turn over the soil and remove weeds, and a third to repair the sorry-looking raised beds. She asked the children to join her in the polytunnel and set them to sorting out pots into sizes, throwing away those which could not be salvaged, with Maggie to supervise.

When everyone had dispersed into the relevant groups and begun to work, Flora headed into the garden. She wanted to look over the ground and see what sort of perennial weeds were lurking beneath the soil, ready to erupt, and her eyes automatically sought out Mac amongst the others. She had set him to work with a small group, and she noticed that Tamsin had not joined the other children but was outside with Mac. He was still holding her hand but talking to another man, their arms resting idly on their spades. The others in the group were already hard at it, their backs to Mac, and Flora made her way over, lips twitching at the scene before her.

'Looks like you two are doing more leaning than digging,' she told the two men, shifting her head to include Tamsin in the gesture. 'The spades won't work unless you actually push them into the soil. Would you like me to show you how to do it?'

Mac laughed and she saw the other man smile at her playful tone.

'Come and meet Lewis,' Mac said, holding out his arm. 'Then we'll do some work, I promise. Lewis is a cousin of Tamsin's somewhere down the line, don't ask me where.' He hesitated for a moment before continuing, casting a quick glance down at the little girl at his side, who was listening to every word. 'He and I spent quite a lot of the school holidays mucking about together on the island.'

'Hi,' Flora greeted him warmly, shaking his hand. 'I'm Flora. It's lovely to meet you.'

'I know who you are,' Lewis told her, his eyes twinkling as they met Flora's. He was a couple of inches smaller than

Mac and a bit younger but of a much broader build, with brown eyes and untidy hair, chopped into uneven lengths that didn't show much preoccupation with styling. Lewis crunched her fingers between his and Flora tried not to wince at what passed for his handshake. 'I've heard a lot about you, and I saw you at the ceilidh the other night, dancing with this fella.'

'Oh!' Flora was startled, wondering exactly what Lewis knew about her and who was responsible for telling him. Mac looked uncomfortable for a moment, as Lewis carried on in the same cheerful tone, his local accent very different to Mac's more urban one.

'All good, I swear. Mac's been going on about your brilliance to anyone who'll listen and then Tamsin came over after school the other day and told me about your visit. I think she's pretty excited to be working with you today.'

Now Flora was completely astonished, and she crouched down to speak to Tamsin, who was watching her silently but with interest. 'I've got something for you,' she told Tamsin, unable to subdue her excitement. 'Do you remember those sweet peas we found here the other day?' A nod. 'I've got some pink ones for you. They're still very small and you'll have to look after them to make them flower. Do you think you can do that, if I show you how?' Another nod and then Tamsin smiled for a second, her eyes huge.

'Thank you.'

A faint whisper but precious words nevertheless, and Flora had to gulp down the lump that formed in her throat and she stood up slowly, still looking at Tamsin. 'Shall we leave your cousin and Mac to do some work out here, and we'll go and explore with the others in the polytunnel?'

She held out her hand, uncertain whether Tamsin would accept it or not, and felt another rush of emotion when the little girl slipped her fingers between hers, and Flora squeezed them gently. She spoke to the two men, her tone brisk to disguise the tears threatening to betray her. 'We'll be back later to see how you're doing, okay?'

Mac grinned, already turning away, as Lewis shoved his large boot down onto the spade and it slid effortlessly into the ground. Flora led the little girl back to the polytunnel and they joined the others, carefully working their way through the mess, storing everything they could save and making piles of rubbish to be taken away. Throughout, Flora was aware that Tamsin barely left her side and she made sure to include her in everything she did, without demanding too much of her. Flora was careful to divide her attention between the others, too, and offer explanations that she shared amongst her group.

Bonnie was there with her mum and she stuck close to Tamsin, too, and Flora appreciated how the older girl took care of the younger one. Before long it was time to stop for lunch and Flora was really pleased by the progress they were making. It was clearly going to take more than one day to turn the space into a proper garden, but it was certainly looking more promising. She had been called away a few times to go and identify a weed or a plant, or decide whether something should be dumped or saved, and each time Tamsin had followed her solemnly, until Flora was automatically checking to make sure she was beside her. She had a little shadow and she loved spending time with her. Tamsin had spoken to her a couple of times

– quiet little words that fell from her lips – and each time Flora had paused her work to listen, appreciating the effort that the little girl had made to communicate.

Outside, the ground was gradually being turned over and weeds removed, and Flora planned to swap people around, so they wouldn't get too tired or stuck with the same job all day. The mist had cleared to reveal a lovely sunny day and she was distracted by the view down to the sea for a moment, loving how the light played on the water and the expanse of clear, white sand. Maggie had arranged for lunch to be delivered and at twelve thirty a car turned up, loaded with plenty of sandwiches, fruit and salad that everyone devoured with relish, settling into a big circle on the ground in the sunlight. More tea was brewed, cold drinks handed around, and a couple of huge, home-made cakes were sliced up and gone in moments. Flora sat down with her sandwich and, as Tamsin was still with her, she was soon joined by Mac and Lewis. Flora tried not to let her imagination run away as her eyes flickered over Mac, who was eating his lunch hungrily and chatting easily with the people around him.

They relaxed for a while, letting their lunch settle, before Flora stood up and reorganised the teams for the next shift. Mac and Lewis were happy to load the truck with rubbish, and Flora watched them go. Her breath caught in her throat when she saw Mac pull off his hoodie, revealing a plain grey T-shirt that clung to the width of his shoulders and stretched over his chest. She looked away hastily, glancing down to see Tamsin's eyes on her, and she smiled blandly.

'Shall we go and repot your plants?'

Tamsin nodded eagerly and they made their way back to the polytunnel. Soon, Tamsin had gloves on, her hands wriggling through compost as she filled new pots and carefully lifted the seedlings into them. When they were done, Flora showed her how to water them and they left them safely on a bench, ready for Tamsin to take home later.

Flora called a halt at four o'clock, aware that everyone had worked hard and was beginning to tire after a very physical day and the remaining children were becoming bored. Most of the soil had been turned over and weeded, the raised beds mended, and the polytunnel made ready to be cleaned. She called everyone together to thank them and say good night, standing by the gate to offer individual praise, as people left for home. Finally, it was just her and Maggie, Mac, Lewis and Tamsin, and she dropped onto one of the benches with a yawn. Tamsin settled down beside her, the tray of seedlings nearby, and Flora smiled at her. Maggie had disappeared into the school to replace the tea things and lock up, as Mac threw a final bag of rubbish into the truck.

Lewis crouched down next to Tamsin and tapped a gentle finger on her knee. 'Tamsin? I think it's time for me to take you home now, don't you? Your nanna will wonder where we've got to. I bet you're tired and I'm ready for a shower.'

Tamsin shot a glance at Mac as he joined them, the hoodie in his hands. She hopped off the bench and trotted briskly over to him, tugging his arm. Flora watched as he bent down to listen to what she was whispering to him.

'I'm sure it will be fine,' Mac was saying, looking at Tamsin lovingly. 'Shall we ask her?'

The little girl nodded and then pulled Mac back to Flora, who was still enjoying the sun on her bench. She was looking at Maggie in the distance, who had gone down to the beach now with her terrier.

'Flora, I hope you don't mind,' Mac said, squeezing Tamsin's hand. 'Tamsin was hoping you would show her the garden at Róisín, sometime before you have to leave? She'd really love to see it with you.'

Flora laughed, cross with herself for not suggesting it before now. She knew that whatever Tamsin wanted, she would do her very best to make it happen. 'Absolutely,' she replied. 'Do you like exploring? There's lots of secret places I can show you. We could do it on Monday, if you're not already busy, as Maggie's told me there's no school then.'

Tamsin's smile was widening into something very close to a giggle and Flora looked up to Mac as he spoke. 'If that's okay with you? I'll need to check with Tamsin's grandparents but I'm sure it will be fine. How about the morning?'

They finalised the plans to meet and then Lewis left with Tamsin, holding her hand as they began the walk back home. At the last moment, the little girl turned around to wave and Flora waved back merrily. She walked to her car with Mac beside her, unlocking the boot to throw her dirty gloves inside and change her boots. Mac was still hovering and she glanced around the car park for his Audi, seeing no sign of it.

'Would you like a lift?' she asked him casually, opening her door and waiting for his reply.

He hesitated, apparently undecided, then stretched and the tension in his expression quickly disappeared. 'Thanks.

It's been a rough day, all that digging and shifting for a terrible taskmaster, and I'm exhausted now.'

'You lightweight,' she retorted as they climbed in the car together and she started the engine. 'If that's all it takes to wear you out then you're not half the man I thought you were.'

He laughed at her teasing and Flora blushed as she turned out of the car park, hoping he would read no more into her comment than she had intended. She drove slowly along the road beside the coast. A few other people were out enjoying the late afternoon sun, strolling along the beach, and she noticed a couple of riders cantering through the surf. It all seemed so relaxed and carefree, a long way from her real life back on the mainland.

Mac tried to disguise a yawn, one hand covering his mouth. 'See, I told you I was tired!' He stretched his long legs as far as he could in the small footwell of her car. 'I did a bit of research last night.'

Flora reached for her sunglasses as they left the small hamlet behind and headed out into the country. 'So did I. You go first.'

'I started looking at Rupert Lassiter. Would you be surprised if I told you he had three sons and the eldest was called Archie?'

'Oh, that's amazing,' Flora exclaimed, her head swivelling round and seeing the pleasure on Mac's face. 'Of course! Rupert Lassiter was a guest at Rose's engagement party! He must have been there as her future father-in-law.'

'That's what I thought, too. Lassiter and Fraser Campbell had apparently been friends since they were at school, so it makes sense that their families spent time together here and knew each other well, if she was Campbell's daughter. You remember how Rose's journal ended suddenly, in 1915?'

'Absolutely.'

'I found out that Archie Lassiter was killed at the Second Battle of Ypres, in May 1915, when he was nineteen. It looks like Rose stopped writing the journal after he died, unless we come across another one that she wrote later.'

Flora's face fell, clouding with sorrow as she thought of the joy and love, hope and promise that she and Mac had discovered in the pages of Rose's book. 'That's utterly tragic,' she said wretchedly, feeling as though they had lost the young couple almost at the same moment they had discovered them. 'How awful. She must have been bereft.'

He nodded; his sympathy reflected in his gentler tone as he continued the story. 'Rose was mentioned briefly with Archie on the page I found online, presumably because she was his fiancé and connected to the Lassiters. There was no mention of her own family or official announcement of their engagement. It said she had been a talented and promising young artist but that's all, and it fits with what we saw of her sketches in the journal. I'm wondering if she stopped painting after Archie died?'

'Oh, I hope not. She was so gifted.' Flora was still thinking about the young couple, so exuberantly and passionately in love, and yet destined never to spend a long life together. She heard the softness in Mac's voice when he spoke again.

'What did you find out?'

Flora sighed, thinking over what she had learned after spending the evening alone in her room, hunting for information online, thoughts of Rose, her extraordinary garden and Archie tumbling through her mind. 'That there definitely wasn't a third child or second daughter. Caroline was the only girl, and her middle name was Rose. Did you know that Róisín means "little rose", in Gaelic?'

Flora noticed Mac's astonished expression. 'No, I had no idea! I only know a few words in Gaelic, and nobody's ever suggested that the name was personal. Do you think then that the house was named after Rose?'

'I do, absolutely, it makes perfect sense. She adored the garden; we saw for ourselves that her love for it shone through every line she wrote and then later for Archie, too. I think she might always have been known as Rose, never Caroline.'

'Wouldn't it be great to see if we can find out what happened to her paintings?'

Flora heard the suggestion of exuberance again in Mac's voice, and her smile was still sad as he continued. 'I've no idea how many there were, and I couldn't find her name linked to any sale or gallery, so they could still be hidden away in the house. Unless they were dumped by the nasty nephew.'

'Maybe she took them with her when she left the island?'

'Yes, that's more likely. So we might never know what became of them.'

'She must have been distraught all over again when she had to leave the island and spend the rest of her life mourning Archie from somewhere she couldn't truly call home.' Flora paused, thinking back over Rose's life and what she had lost. 'There could be lots more about them for us to find, in the house.'

Us. Flora heard how easily she had used the term, and knew that her excitement and delight in their discoveries were binding her to a place she would find hard to forget. Already she was beginning to dread leaving Alana and everything she was coming to feel so much for here and returning to Middlebrook. They were both silent for a minute, until she finished the story. 'The photograph you showed me – do you remember, back at the hotel? – of the family and children in the garden?'

'Of course.'

'I'm guessing then that the boys were most likely Lassiter's three, with Rose; her brother would've been grown-up and gone. The timing's right and we know now that they were often together. There might be more photos somewhere in the house.'

'How sad,' Mac murmured, and he shook his head. 'What an incredible story. It makes the house even more special, more personal, now that we know a bit more about their lives.'

'Yes, I thought that too. Thank goodness it hasn't been lost.'

'Or the garden,' Mac said thoughtfully. They were at Róisín already and Flora slowly halted the car near the house, unwilling to end their time together. He seemed in no hurry to leave either and Flora felt the space between them narrowing, as a swift look of longing crossed his face, before he quickly disguised it. 'Once I met you, there was no decision to be made about that, really.' He winked as he reached for the door handle and pushed it open. 'What else could I do but restore it, put back the garden they made as best as I can?'

Flora was thrilled, not just because the garden would be rescued before it was too late but also because she knew that it was becoming important to him, tightening its hold on the house as the Campbell family history bound both to the future. Mac still wasn't out of the car, the door half open, and she had no time to tell him of her joy before he spoke again.

'I don't suppose you'd like to come in, see what else we can find about the family? I could make us something to eat. You must be as hungry as me after all that work?'

Flora would have liked nothing more than to spend the evening with him and explore, searching for more information about Rose's life and the garden she had loved, over supper with Mac. But she slowly shook her head, her glance steady on the old house before them. 'I think we're both tired.' She hoped she had disguised the regret she was feeling, as her mind went back over the day. How their eyes had connected with ease whenever they were near, searching one another out and finding a waiting smile of encouragement each time. 'I'm just going to crash at the hotel, if you don't mind.'

Her final comment wasn't a question, and Mac got out and swung the door shut with a simple good night. He headed towards the house, and Flora turned the car and drove away, glancing in her rear-view mirror until he was lost to her sight.

[illegible]

[illegible]

"I don't suppose you'd [illegible] to come [illegible]"

"[illegible] about the family? [illegible] to one you must [illegible]"

[illegible]

[illegible]

[illegible]

Chapter Fourteen

After spending the rest of the weekend alone in the hotel, Flora was back at Róisín by eight on Monday morning. She knew that Mac had arranged to meet Tamsin and her grandparents at ten, so she busied herself taking photographs in the walled garden and making notes. She was climbing through the mess in the glasshouses attached to the south wall when Mac found her, sticking his head inside and indicating the two mugs in his hands.

'Morning. Thought you might like one of these – it's chilly just now. Hope it's not gone cold; it took me a while to find you.'

'You're a mind reader,' Flora told him gratefully, clambering over the gnarled remains of a vine just waiting to trip her up, as she made her way back to the door. 'I've forgotten my flask and it's a bit warmer in here out of the wind.'

'You shouldn't need to bring a flask with you.' He handed over one of the coffees and she thanked him, wrapping her hands around the mug. 'I'll show you the basic kitchen facilities that the builders are using in the house, and then you can go and help yourself whenever you want. Sorry, I should have done that for you sooner.'

'Thanks.' Flora knew she probably wouldn't take him up on his offer; she liked not having to stop work to wander off and make a drink. Her trusty little flask usually went everywhere with her, and if she hadn't been awake half the night thinking of Mac and then slept late, she wouldn't have forgotten it. 'Are you going back to Edinburgh tomorrow?'

'No. I'm working here, sort of.' He made room for them to sit on a couple of crates, and his smile and the low timbre of his voice, as he shoved some pots out of the way, was enough to increase her pleasure in the morning. 'I can speak with clients from here and it's useful to be around if the builders need me. I've arranged not to go into the office this week unless it's essential. I can use the hotel's Wi-Fi, if I need to.'

Flora felt a thrill steal through her at his words; this meant he would almost certainly be at Róisín whenever she was, and she knew she would be happy to snatch more time in his company before she had to leave at the end of the week. They drank their coffee in a comfortable silence, enjoying the warmth of the sun through the glass, as it slowly climbed higher. Flora thought of Tamsin arriving here this morning, and the little girl's family, as she quietly voiced the question which had been in her mind for the last couple of days.

'I hope you don't mind my asking, but I wondered what happened to Tamsin's parents? Maggie said very little, other than that they died several months ago.' Flora hesitated. 'I quite understand if you'd rather not say.' She knew well that not everybody wanted to reveal their grief.

Mac was silent for a minute and Flora thought she might have overstepped the mark and that he would not wish to share something so personal and upsetting with her. He dipped his head and then turned it towards her, the loss evident now in his eyes and the sorrow stilling his smile.

'It was an accident. They'd gone to a restaurant on the mainland to celebrate ten years since they had first met. There was heavy rain and a lorry skidded into their car on the way home. The awful irony is that they were driving back instead of staying over because they didn't want to leave Tamsin overnight. It wasn't even dark.'

'I'm so sorry.' Flora's voice was barely more than a whisper and he acknowledged her words with a twist of his lips.

'Angus, her dad, was my best friend on the island; he grew up here but, like everyone else, he had to go away to board for high school, and so we'd both be here for the holidays and spent most of our time together. He moved away after university and met Rachael, and when they knew they were expecting Tamsin, they decided to come back and settle on the island so they could all benefit from the way of life here. Angus's parents ran a B&B, so they already had family here; Rachael had lost her mum years ago.'

'Oh, Mac,' Flora whispered, tears filling her eyes as she thought about such a tragic loss. 'You must all have been devastated. I'm so very sorry. Poor, poor Tamsin.' Her free hand reached for his, and she covered his fingers with hers, caressing them lightly. His look moved to their joined hands and he squeezed, trapping her fingers between his.

'Thank you.' His voice was very quiet in the broken building and Flora leant towards him until their shoulders were touching, wanting to give him every scrap of empathy she could offer. 'It affected the whole island in different ways, but everyone has been so supportive and helped however they could. Rachael's dad was distraught, but he has MS and can't offer the practical help he would like. Angus's brother farms in New Zealand, so he's out of the picture and, in place of a legally appointed guardian – as Angus and Rachael died without naming one – Tamsin lives with her grandparents here, as they are in a better position to take care of her. If it hadn't been for Tamsin and the overwhelming need to look after her, I don't know what Angus's mum would have done. It nearly broke her, losing him and Rachael.'

'What about you?' Flora couldn't have disguised the softness in her voice even if she had wanted to.

Mac shrugged and when he tilted his head sideways to look at her again, she saw the tears in his eyes, glistening against the grey. 'I lost my best mate and sometimes now the island only feels like half a home, like it's missing a piece of its heart somehow. He was such a madcap when we were kids and I keep expecting him to burst in to tell me about some crazy stunt he's planning. But it's worse for their families, whatever I feel. One of the reasons for moving here permanently will be the opportunity to be a proper godfather to Tamsin and help take care of her however I can.' He blinked, the tears retreating as his tone became more reflective.

'I don't know whether Maggie has already told you, but Tamsin has a form of anxiety called selective mutism. She's perfectly fine at home and with people she's comfortable with, but when she started school and didn't really speak, it was assumed at first that she was just shy. Eventually, it became apparent that there was more to it and then it took about a year to get a proper diagnosis, and it's another thing for her grandparents to worry about.

She's having treatment and there were signs of improvement, but of course after what's happened, she's not doing quite as well.'

Mac raised his head to look at her, and Flora wanted to cup his face, to smooth away the sorrow lining his skin – and the realisation hurt. It was not her place. 'Until she met you, Flora. She's really taken to you.'

Surprise raced through her at his comment; Flora understood only too well how they were all having to adapt to a life no one had ever imagined or wanted. 'I'm so glad if I'm helping her in any way, Mac.' Shoulders still touching, she glanced at her watch. 'Do you think we should go? They'll be here very soon.'

They chatted about the garden as they walked back and Flora pointed out anything she thought would interest him, pleased by his curiosity in what she was uncovering. She opened the garden door after they had crossed the terrace and saw that there was already an additional car on the drive. An older man got out of the vehicle, immediately followed by Tamsin from the back seat. They called a greeting to her and Flora was thrilled when Tamsin came shyly towards her, a cautious smile beginning to reveal a little of the excitement that was bubbling in her eyes.

She was wearing pink flowery wellies with a purple coat, her love of pretty colours evident. Flora's arm naturally extended towards Tamsin and she felt the warmth of her small hand slipping into hers. She squeezed it gently with a smile, feeling that bump in her chest again, as Mac made the introductions.

'Flora, this is Doug Hardie, Tamsin's grandad. Doug, Flora is the horticulturist I told you about.'

Doug reached out to shake Flora's free hand, his bemused glance landing on his granddaughter as he observed how she had already snuggled up to Flora. He must only have been in his early sixties, but thick lines were carved through his face and his cheeks looked thin. Blue eyes were faded and his grey hair blown about by the breeze circling from the sea beneath them, and Flora guessed that this was a more shrunken version of the man he used to be. Not that she was surprised; she knew first-hand what sudden grief could do to a person.

'I'm really pleased to meet you at last,' he said warmly, his accent sounding very much like Lewis's. 'We've heard a lot about you around the island and Tamsin is thrilled with those little plants you gave her. It was very kind of you.'

'Not at all,' Flora brushed away his thanks, swallowing down the lump forming in her throat. 'I just hope Tamsin enjoys them and they flower well for her.' She looked at Tamsin, her sapphire eyes meeting the little girl's softer blue ones. 'Shall we take your grandad and Mac with us or would you like just us girls to explore on our own? I don't mind which.' Flora tilted her head towards the two men as she bent down and caught Tamsin's faint reply.

'Just girls.'

'Perfect,' Flora whispered for Tamsin's ears only, before turning to Mac and Doug. 'This is a girls-only expedition for now, so we'll see you in an hour or so, okay?'

The two men nodded, although Doug looked a bit doubtful. Then Mac pointed to something high up on the house, distracting him, and Flora turned away, her hand still in Tamsin's as she grinned at the little girl beside her.

'Let's go. I'll show you some things I think you might enjoy but if there's anywhere you see or want to explore, providing it's not dangerous, let me know and we'll go and look together. You can just squeeze my hand. Okay?'

Tamsin nodded as they set off back through the door and onto the broken terrace, and Flora warned her to be very careful as they descended the steps together. She began to explain a bit about the garden, unwilling to put her off by speaking too much and bombarding her with information that Tamsin would find hard to remember. She took her down to show her the rose garden and explained why they believed the house was called Róisín, but left out anything to do with Archie or his death. Every so often, Tamsin would tug her hand and whisper a few words, questions which Flora was more than happy to answer. She talked briefly of the architect and how it related to Mac's job, and why the garden might be important for teaching people in the future.

'Are you sure I'm not boring you?' Flora was watching Tamsin, who shook her head fiercely. 'I promise to stop when you've had enough, okay? My friends say I talk too much about gardens sometimes.'

They had made their way up to the north garden above the house, and Flora led the way carefully through the tangled mess of lawn next to an overgrown border, until they reached an old summerhouse. A tiled roof was still mostly in place, despite the ivy climbing the walls and threatening to choke the stone. Flora checked to make sure it was safe, before she settled on a seat and invited Tamsin to sit beside her. She lifted an arm, indicating the view before them.

'This summerhouse was built exactly here because it's completely hidden from the house, but if you look down there, towards the old hedge, can you see the small gap in the hedge, a bit like a circle? When the garden was built, the gap would have been bigger so that people could sit here, look at the garden and catch a glimpse of the sea. It's a clever idea and Rose, the girl who used to live here with her family, loved to come to this spot and write a diary about some of the things that happened to her. Mac found some boxes in the house with journals she had written and they're helping us to find out more about her and the garden.'

Flora recognised that Tamsin was content to sit for a few minutes and rest her tired little legs. 'We can stay here for a bit and then we'll go and see where your grandad and Mac have got to. Do you think they might be lost, without us to show them the way?'

A smile, a nod, blue eyes resting on Flora's face, questioning. Suddenly, Tamsin reached up and touched Flora's hair, which was already trying to escape from its unruly ponytail, and Flora stilled, unsure what to do next as Tamsin's hand fell away again.

'My mummy had long hair.'

Quiet, heart-breaking words that made Flora pause to blink away tears, before she could offer a reply. She could barely breathe, and she swallowed anxiously, uncertain of how to reply without upsetting Tamsin, her voice tremulous. 'Was it blonde and straight, like yours?'

Tamsin shook her head matter-of-factly. One pink welly was dangling off her small foot and she bent down to pull it firmly back into place. 'Darker but not as dark as yours.'

'I see,' Flora murmured slowly, giving Tamsin time to continue if she wanted and aware of her looking straight down into the garden as she spoke again, just a few more whispered words.

'I like your hair. I think Uncle Mac does, too. He's always looking for you.'

Astonishment rendered Flora speechless after Tamsin's confession. Sliding an arm across her narrow shoulders, she pulled her closer, holding her as tightly and as fiercely as she dared. Flora had no idea what to say or how best to respond, other than to show Tamsin that everything she had been brave enough to say mattered very much. They sat huddled together for what seemed like only moments, as Flora gently stroked her arm. Whatever else she might have to leave behind on the island, Flora was already dreading having to break the connection that she and Tamsin were developing through the garden.

'Are you ready to head back to the house before we get too cold? The sun doesn't reach here until later.' Flora's voice was low, her arm still tightly holding Tamsin. 'I think Mac said there might be hot chocolate.'

Tamsin nodded and hopped down from her seat. As they set off on the walk back to the house, her little hand found Flora's again and they returned to see Mac and Doug waiting for them on the terrace, sitting on green plastic chairs that looked incongruous in the historic and decades-old garden. There was a wrought-iron table, too, on which Mac had got a camping stove going, with a kettle and frying pan. He waved when he saw them climbing the steps carefully, hand in hand.

'Who's for sausages?' he called, his eyes going to Tamsin before coming to rest on Flora. 'They're ready – you timed it well.'

'They smell amazing.' Flora squeezed Tamsin's hand gently. 'We're starving after all that exploring. Hope you've got the hot chocolate you promised.'

'Of course I have. Sit down and I'll sort it out.'

Doug climbed to his feet when Flora and Tamsin reached him, scooping Tamsin up and spinning her into a hug that made her giggle. 'Have you two had fun?' Tamsin seemed serious as she looked at her grandad, who was staring at her with such love that it made Flora want to gasp at the unfairness of what they had lost. 'What did you find out?'

Doug put her down and pulled out a chair beside his for Tamsin, but she didn't sit on it; instead, she dragged it the few yards across the terrace until she was next to Flora and looked at her anxiously. Flora reached for her hand reassuringly and Tamsin began to speak tentatively, the noise of the sausages spitting behind her.

'We saw an old stream that hasn't got any water in it. It's called a…' Tamsin hesitated, looking at Flora again for confirmation.

Flora leant close to Tamsin, hoping to encourage her. 'Do you remember? It rhymes with pill. It doesn't matter at all if you've forgotten; you've listened so brilliantly to me chattering on for ages.'

'A rill! It's called a rill. But there's no water in it.'

'One day there will be.' Mac had joined them, bringing plates with sausages stuffed into rolls, and Flora couldn't miss the love in his expression as he looked at Tamsin. He pushed a plate onto the table in front of Flora and another one in front of the little girl.

'Can I come and see?'

'Absolutely! I'll probably need your help, too, Tamsin, if you're going to be a gardener like Flora. There's so much to do.' Mac reached down and stroked her hair, and she looked up at him, hanging onto his words as though they were a promise. 'Not for a while yet, though, little one. There's lots to do first.'

Flora watched as he slid another plate in front of Doug, and she couldn't allow herself to think about the progress that this magical place was going to make in the future without her. All too soon she would be leaving, and these people would continue their lives as though she had never been amongst them. A thoughtful silence fell over them as they ate hungrily, broken only when Tamsin asked for another hot chocolate.

Mac joined them again after he had made more drinks, pulling out a seat beside Flora. His eyes sought hers for a moment and she was startled afresh by Tamsin's observation. Doug pushed his empty plate aside and spoke, easing the sombre mood that had fallen over them.

'I almost forgot and then I'd have been in trouble! Moira asked me to invite you both to an early supper with us at the B&B, tomorrow night. Will you come? She's very keen to meet you, Flora, and say thank you for everything you've done for Tamsin. She's even getting the baking tray out and Mac can tell you how famous her lemon meringue pie is, can't you, Mac?'

Flora was certain that Mac would want her to refuse, as he would surely be unwilling to share an evening in her company with such close friends, especially given the distance he had tried to keep at the ceilidh. But she caught a glimpse of Tamsin's face, beseeching and excited all at once.

'Please, Flora?'

Flora knew she couldn't say no, whatever Mac's wishes might be, and she quickly plastered a bright expression on her face, careful not to reveal any reluctance to come for supper and risk hurting the small girl. 'That's really kind, if you're sure it's not too much trouble?'

'Of course not. We'd love to have you, wouldn't we, Tamsin? Mac?'

Flora couldn't see Mac's face but sensed his shrug beside her, his shoulders rising in a gesture that suggested he wouldn't mind either way. 'Thanks, Doug. Sounds great.'

'Perfect. See you both about five thirty tomorrow then. That'll give us some time together before Tamsin goes to bed.'

The impromptu meal over, Doug thanked them and said goodbye, and Flora watched as he and Tamsin crossed the terrace to the drive. Tamsin glanced back to wave at Flora, as she had done on Saturday at the school, and Flora couldn't help but smile as she waved in return. She stood up, piling the plates together to help Mac clear away, and thanked him for the food. Then she turned around to leave, intending to carry on working for as long as possible in the walled garden.

'Flora? I may as well pick you up tomorrow night, if you like. There's probably not much point in both of us driving and the B&B isn't that near the hotel. Relatively speaking, given the size of the island.'

It seemed churlish to refuse his offer and Flora's reply was casual. 'Thanks. That'd be nice.'

When Flora arrived back at the hotel the following day, later than she had intended, she showered hurriedly and searched for something to wear – something that wouldn't suggest she was trying to dress for a date. She pulled on skinny jeans and low-heeled ankle boots with a lemon-yellow shirt, tugging a jacket from her wardrobe that suited the casual style she was aiming for. There wasn't time to dry her hair properly so she swept it into a messy bun above the nape of her neck that left tendrils drifting loose. She stroked her lashes with mascara, added lip gloss and her favourite perfume, and she was ready.

Excitement blended with nerves at the thought of spending the evening with Mac and she made her way through the hotel reception, holding the bottle of wine she had quickly collected from the bar. She saw immediately that he was waiting outside, probably keen not to draw unnecessary attention, given his relationship with Chloe. The passenger door to the Audi opened as she neared it, and she thanked him politely as she climbed inside. She glanced across, noticing that he was in jeans, too, with a slim-fitting indigo shirt, the top two buttons undone.

They barely spoke during the journey, and soon Mac pulled off a narrow lane and bumped up a track that was fenced on one side by sheep netting and an open meadow on the other, sloping down to a beach below the headland. He drew the car to a halt outside a two-storey stone house surrounded by fields; the nearest building glimpsed perhaps half a mile away, further along the coast.

'Thanks for coming this evening, Flora. I'm sure Tamsin will love seeing you again, even though it's maybe not for the best, given how she is around you. You've been amazing with her but you're leaving in three days and I don't suppose you want to spend any more time with her than absolutely necessary, just in case.'

'In case of what?' Flora was astonished by Mac's comments. Her only reluctance was in battling the constant desire not to miss a moment of his company and spend another evening with him – something she could not reveal. The realisation that he didn't want her to be around Tamsin any more was a shock. 'And don't forget that none of this was my idea!'

'She's formed a bond with you already, whether you know it or not, Flora, and I don't want her to be hurt again. I only realised yesterday in the garden just how much she's taken to you.' He sighed, a frustrated sound that made her search his face in an attempt to understand.

'Of course I don't want to hurt her. I only ever wanted to help!' Flora couldn't restrain the incredulous note still rising in her voice. 'I've only known her a few days and already I can't bear to think of what she's lost. Do you really believe that I'll just drive away without a backward glance and not mind leaving everything behind?'

'Everything?'

Flora shrugged, swallowing down the truth. 'The garden. Tamsin. The island.'

'And is that everything, here, for you?'

'What difference would it make if it wasn't?' She knew there was a sharp bitterness in her tone, and she refused to look at him and reveal any more of what she was feeling. 'We'd better go inside before they start to wonder why we're still out here.'

Chapter Fifteen

Flora was still rattled by Mac's warning and what she'd almost confessed, but there was no time to dwell on it, as the front door was flung open and Tamsin stood there, ready to receive them. Mac bent down to fold her into a hug with gentle tickles that had Tamsin giggling, and Flora resisted the temptation to copy him, her heart softening as she watched the two of them. Tamsin looked up timidly and then her hand reached for Flora, who found herself being pulled into the living room. She laughed as she clutched the bottle of wine precariously under her arm. Tamsin stopped in the centre of the room and Flora paused in surprise, her eyes widening at the view.

Flora hadn't realised that the house was perched so close to the headland, making it seem as though they were virtually on the water. A large extension, reaching across the back of the building and made almost entirely of glass, allowed light to flood in, highlighting the Scandinavian feel of the open-plan living room and ultra-modern comfortable kitchen.

'How beautiful, I wasn't expecting such a view!'

'It never fails to take people by surprise. We must have been lucky with our architect, when we decided to extend.' Doug grinned wryly at Mac, as he crossed the room to greet them, reaching out to grasp Flora's hand between both of his and shaking firmly. 'Hello, Flora. Very glad you could make it tonight. Ah, here's Moira.'

A woman – like Doug, probably in her early sixties and much the same height – had appeared from the corridor behind, glanced at Mac with a loving look and directed her attention to Flora. She hurried over, a smile lighting her face, as Doug stepped back to hug Mac, the obvious ease between the two men speaking of years of familiarity. Slim and elegant, Moira had short, grey hair tucked behind her ears and stylish black glasses framing hazel eyes that, like Doug's, looked sad.

'Flora, I'm so pleased to meet you! How lovely of you to come and join us.'

Flora wasn't sure that Mac would agree. Moira's accent wasn't so obviously local as her husband's, and Flora wondered if she had moved to Alana from the mainland.

'You're most welcome in our home. Tamsin has told us all about you, including how beautiful you are, and I can see she was right.'

Flora's face flamed at the unexpected compliment. 'That's very sweet of you,' she murmured to Tamsin, giving her a grateful smile, which was cautiously returned. Then she remembered the bottle of wine. 'Oh, this is for you. A small thank you for inviting me tonight.' Flora retrieved the bottle and proffered it to Doug, standing nearby. 'I can't claim any glory for choosing it, but I was assured it would make a suitable aperitif, as I wasn't sure what we would be eating.'

Doug thanked her, pleased, as he examined the bottle and Moira crossed the room to greet Mac properly. He pulled her into an embrace that had her sniffing as she wriggled away. She joined Doug in the kitchen, taking a salad from the fridge and searching for something to dress it with, as he busied himself collecting plates.

'Something smells delicious,' Flora said hungrily, trying to stop her mouth from watering in anticipation of what smelled like a marvellous meal.

'Well, it's just a vegetarian lasagne; I hope that's all right with everyone. I'd already decided to err on the side of caution, and Doug only remembered to tell me you'd had sausages yesterday once the lasagne was in the oven.'

'I eat anything,' Flora told her gratefully. 'I don't cook very often for myself so a home-made meal like this is an absolute treat.'

'Shall we open your wine?' Doug directed the question at Flora, his voice carrying easily across the room. 'I understand Mac's driving, so can I pour you a glass?'

'That sounds perfect, I'd love to try it. Thank you.'

Doug reached for glasses and Mac indicated to Flora the bar stools on the sitting room side of the kitchen. She pulled one out and sat down, checking what Tamsin was doing and wondering if she would join them. She was staring up at Flora, her eyes flicking to the door. Flora tried to guess what the little girl wanted and hopped back down from the stool, as an idea came to her.

'Shall we go and have a look at your plants? They might need watering.'

Tamsin nodded excitedly and Flora was happy to follow her outside. She had barely looked at Mac since she had almost blurted out the truth to him in the car and she was glad of some time to gather her scrambled emotions.

There wasn't much of a garden outside, beyond a practical patio stretching around three sides of the house, enclosed by a hedge on two sides and a few scattered pots of evergreens. Tamsin's precious plants had been carefully positioned in the sunniest spot, attached to bamboo canes and in larger pots. Flora knew that Tamsin was watching as she examined the plants to check if the little girl had done everything right, so she quickly reassured her that they were doing fine. She reminded Tamsin to keep them watered and the canes secure as the plants grew taller. Tamsin visibly relaxed at Flora's assessment, and she felt her heart melt at the girl's concern and determination to take care of her plants as best as she could. They returned to the house; Moira was still in the kitchen and Mac had settled on a stool, his fingers wrapped around a bottle of non-alcoholic beer, whilst Doug laid the table.

Flora sat down next to Mac, sipping her wine, and listened to Doug chatting and perhaps trying to make up for Moira's silence as she put the finishing touches on the meal. Tamsin was on a stool, too, on Flora's other side, colouring a picture of *The Tiger Who Came to Tea*. Every so often she paused, waiting for Flora to choose the colour that she should use next. It wasn't long before Moira declared the lasagne ready and they all moved to the dining table nearby. Doug brought the salad across and Moira asked them to help themselves, lifting a small portion onto a plate for Tamsin.

Flora was surprised to notice that her glass was already empty, and Doug refilled their drinks before he joined them at the table and they began to eat. Tamsin was sitting between Flora and Moira, with Mac and Doug opposite. The lasagne was fabulous and Flora was already beginning to feel the effects of the wine; it usually made her sleepy, but tonight her senses seemed sharper, more aware of her surroundings, and she was finding it difficult to control how her body responded to Mac's attentiveness whenever their eyes met.

To distract herself, she asked Moira, 'Mac mentioned that you run a B&B here? It's an amazing location, I can see why people would want to visit.' She noticed the look that passed between Moira and Doug, and he replied first, a small sigh escaping as his gaze quickly went to Tamsin.

'Aye, Flora, we do – or did, anyway, and it kept us busy during the summer months when it's easier to travel to the island. But since the, er, well you know… what happened,' he lowered his voice, a flash of grief skittering through his eyes, 'we decided not to take in guests for the time being. It was just too much to think about. We have a small croft, too, you see, that belonged to Moira's family. The cottage is rented out, but we farm the land and look after the livestock, and that keeps us occupied enough.'

'Sorry, Flora, I didn't make that clear before.' Mac had softened his voice and Flora sensed him gazing at her. Moira sniffed sharply, and Doug reached across the table to touch her arm.

Flora opened her mouth, not quite sure what she was going to say, but desperate to make amends for inadvertently making the conversation awkward.

'I like seeing the lambs.' Tamsin's voice was a whisper but it carried through the open space around them. Her steady blue gaze was flickering between Flora and Mac, and it was to her she directed her words. 'Can you come with me and see them?'

Flora's hand stilled somewhere between the table and her glass as she thought hurriedly of an appropriate response. She saw Mac's frown opposite her as Doug jumped in.

'Och, Tamsin, Flora won't have time for that,' he told her, softening his words with a kind smile. 'She has to go home soon, remember? We talked about this.'

Flora wished she didn't have to refuse Tamsin, but understood it was probably for the best, as Mac had said. 'Your grandad's right,' she told Tamsin gently, seeing the little girl's eyes fall to her plate and disappointment outlined in the slump of her shoulders. 'I still have some work to finish in the garden before I leave. I'm so sorry, I wish I could. Maybe if I leave my email address with your nanna and grandad, you could send me some photographs?'

The idea of staying in touch with Tamsin had been taking shape in her mind over the past couple of days. Irrespective of Mac and what their relationship was – or wasn't – she was dreading never seeing Tamsin again or being able to find out how she was getting on. Doug was already nodding, although she noticed Moira looking more doubtful. 'And I'll need to see pictures of the sweet peas, too, when they flower.'

'Won't you be coming back?'

Another whisper, a collection of letters brought together and forming words that Flora did not want to consider. She blinked back the sudden tears scratching at her eyes, desperate for Tamsin and Mac not to see. 'I don't think so, I'm sorry. I live a long way from here.'

Flora saw the look then which passed between the older couple, a shared glance of concern. Mac had been right after all: this evening was a mistake. She wondered how soon she could escape this dinner, before her inability to remain on the island unsettled Tamsin any further. The talk turned to more general matters, and Flora was relieved to move on and learn more of the island's history and stories, which she encouraged Tamsin to share. When the lasagne was finished, Tamsin suddenly hopped down from her chair, looking up at Flora earnestly.

'Please will you come and see my new bedroom, Flora?'

This Flora could do, and she returned her glass to the table with a smile for her hosts, as she excused herself. She followed Tamsin along the hallway past three doors, before they reached her bedroom. Flora saw at once that it was a picture-perfect little girl's room, with pink walls and a low, white bunk bed, with bookshelves and space to play underneath. Fairies and a unicorn were stencilled onto a wall, and there was a photograph of Tamsin's parents on a dressing table. Flora tried not to stare but her eyes fell on it anyway, and she immediately saw the kindness and energy that seemed to shine from Rachael's eyes, so like Tamsin's. Angus had his arms around Rachael, holding her from behind, and his look above her head was very like Doug's, their faces so similar. Flora was almost winded by the laughing casualness of the picture, barely able to believe that two such young people could have been lost so suddenly. Tamsin took Flora's hand again and tugged her over to a squashy lilac beanbag, big enough for two, and pulled her down.

'Please will you read me a story?'

Flora settled into the beanbag with a smile. 'Of course. Shall we do this one?' She reached for a book close by. It was a story of unicorns, magical horses and a princess who rescued them from a cruel master, and she began to read, with Tamsin snuggled into her side. Before long, she noticed that Tamsin's breathing had changed, and Flora saw that she had fallen asleep. Long, fair lashes swept down onto pale skin, her fringe falling to one side, and Flora's heart clenched with a sudden sweep of love mingled with sorrow for all that the little girl had lost.

She read on, her voice growing quieter, until she reached the end of the book and placed it on the floor. Unwilling to disturb Tamsin, she sat cuddling her for a few more minutes, until the door opened and Mac appeared. At once his eyes darkened with an unfathomable expression at the sight of Flora snuggling the sleeping child, and she fumbled for an apology as her pulse rocketed.

'I'm sorry, I didn't mean for this to happen,' she whispered, trying very carefully to disentangle herself. 'Tamsin wanted a story and then she fell asleep. I didn't want to disturb her.'

Mac shook his head, stepping quietly into the little pink room. Immediately, he completely filled her view and it seemed as though the walls were contracting around her. He was too big, too masculine, to be contained in such feminine surroundings, and she swallowed nervously, moving her gaze to Tamsin.

'She looks so peaceful,' he muttered. 'Doug's on the phone, there's a crisis with a neighbour and a tricky calving, so Moira asked me to see if you were both okay, whilst she shuts up the chickens. Should we lift her onto the bed?'

'Probably best. Hopefully, she won't wake up.' Flora wriggled slowly away from Tamsin, who seemed deeply asleep already. Mac bent down, his head very close to Flora's, and she felt his breath on her neck as he gently slid his arms beneath Tamsin, carefully lifted her up and settled her onto the bed. He turned to Flora with a light smile and whispered, 'Think we got away with it.'

Flora was all too aware of Mac watching as she untangled her legs from the beanbag and tried to stand up quietly. She had been leaning with her back against the wall and the pins that were holding her messy bun in place had fallen out. Her long hair, which had dried into uneven waves, spilled down her back and she automatically brought her hands to her neck to gather it back up. Mac spoke, his voice low and hoarse in the quiet of the room, and her heart began to race.

'Don't.'

Flora froze, her hands stilled above her shoulders, before letting them slowly fall away. Her eyes flew up to meet his, and she saw the intensity blazing in them, before his gaze dropped to linger on her mouth, and her lips parted in stunned reply. Her body responded immediately: held in check for so long whenever she was around him, and desire raced across her skin, leaving her quivering in anticipation of his touch. He lifted a hand, reaching for her face, and then Tamsin murmured in her sleep, and Mac quickly stepped away. Shock registered in his expression, before he tore his eyes away from Flora's and they both whirled around to stare at the sleeping girl.

Horrified by the realisation that she had allowed Mac to see how effortlessly he could arouse her, Flora carefully pulled the duvet over Tamsin with trembling fingers, tucking her in as the racing of her pulse began to slow. Mac was hovering behind her and she stepped past him to return to the living room, thankful that her hosts weren't there. She reached for the glass of wine that Doug had refilled again and gulped it quickly. She was pulling her hair into place, facing the extraordinary view from the huge windows, when Mac soon followed.

'Flora, I—'

'Just leave it,' she said bluntly, refusing to give him her eyes and let him witness any more of her heart revealed in them. 'Nothing happened.'

Doug reappeared a moment later and he sounded cheerful, unaware of the tension between Flora and Mac. 'Crisis over! The heifer's delivered a healthy calf, just in time.' He looked around the room, only just seeming to notice that Moira and Tamsin weren't there. 'Moira must still be outside. Where's Tamsin?'

'She's asleep,' Flora told him quickly, her hair more or less back in place, and she gave him a bright smile that couldn't quite ease the strain she still felt. 'She dozed off whilst I was reading to her so Mac helped me tuck her into bed.'

'Ah, bless her, it's been an exciting and tiring day. Thanks, both of you. We'll pop in and check on her later; she'll probably need the loo at some point. Well, who's for the famous lemon meringue pie? I'll get some coffee going while you decide if you'd like cream or ice cream with it.'

Flora groaned inwardly, torn between being a polite guest to her lovely and generous hosts and her desire to escape Mac's company as soon as she reasonably could. The highs and lows of this evening had already depleted her, and all she wanted was the impersonal space of her hotel room. 'Not for me, thanks, Doug. It was so kind of you to invite me, but I ought to head off now. I don't want to keep you both up.'

'Och, Flora, don't be daft, there's no need to rush off. Moira will think there's something amiss with her baking!'

There was disappointment in his teasing tone and Flora felt torn. She glanced over at Mac, who was standing beside the bar stools, watching her with a questioning expression she didn't attempt to decipher.

'Please stay, if you can. We'd love to get to know you better and hear about your work.'

Flora knew she was trapped by Doug's almost pleading words. 'If Mac doesn't mind?' There was a pointed tone in her voice she knew he would recognise, as she left it up to him to decide.

'Of course not,' he answered blithely, crossing the room to join her near the window overlooking the sea. 'We can stay for lemon meringue pie and coffee at least, Flora. I'm sure you told me once that it was your favourite dessert.'

Flora could have screamed, as she backed up and sat down on the large, L-shaped sofa and shot Mac a furious look. She reached for her glass again and sipped at the wine to distract her from his gaze. Her body was still buzzing after what had just occurred between them in the bedroom, and the cushions sank when Mac joined her on the sofa, causing another unwelcome spike in her pulse.

Moira had emerged into the kitchen after shutting up the chickens, and Flora and Mac were silent until the older couple joined them, bringing coffee and bowls filled with soft meringue and a creamy yellow filling. Flora was persuaded to copy Mac in having ice cream with her pudding, and it was so good that she laughingly threatened to steal the rest away. Moira looked pleased, and Doug reached across to squeeze her hand encouragingly, before his gaze returned to Flora.

'So how long are you staying on the island, Flora?'

'Just until Friday. I have another commitment over the weekend, before I go back to work next week.'

'Do you think you'll be coming back to help Mac with the restoration?'

Flora felt her breath catch in her throat at the question from Moira. The air between her and Mac seemed to stretch and bend, its tautness humming in the pause before she answered.

'No, I don't think so. There's a great deal of work to do and I'll be able to put Mac in touch with organisations that will advise him once I'm finished. I'm sorry, of course, that I won't be around to see it or help with the school garden but it's not a practical option, with my own job being so far away.'

Moira nodded, surprising Flora as she reached across the sofa to take her hand, her hazel eyes sincere and kind. 'Doug and I, well, we just wanted to say thank you for everything you've done for Tamsin since she met you.'

Flora began to protest but Moira shook her head firmly, speaking across her insistence that she hadn't done very much at all.

'No, Flora, you really have made a difference already, even though you probably can't tell, as you've known her for such a short time. I don't know how much of it is to do with gardens or just you, or both of those things, but these past few days she has come out of her shell a little and it's marvellous for us to see. She loves those plants you gave her and if we didn't stop her, I think she'd watch over them night and day.'

Flora was silent, absorbing the joy that Moira's words had given her, despite Mac's bleak warning earlier.

'Tamsin was always chatty enough at home but since the accident she seems to flee sometimes to a place we can't always reach, and I do worry that we'll never properly find her again. I don't know that you ever get over a thing like losing your parents the way she did. Bad enough to lose a son and the woman who loved him.' She paused; her eyes laden with grief, and sadness was etched into every line as she gripped Flora's hand even tighter. 'She wants us to make a proper garden here. As you can see, it's hardly been a priority; we've always been busy with the B&B and the farming, but she seems to think a garden could make all of us feel better. She told me about you being poorly, Flora, and how gardening helped you. I want to ask you; do you really think it will help her? Truthfully? Because sometimes I just have no idea what will, and we're prepared to try anything.'

Moira seemed to notice then that she was still clutching Flora's hand and she let go, leaning back into the sofa and wiping her eyes with a tissue she fished from her sleeve. Flora knew that everyone's attention was on her now; she could only speak the truth from her own experience and that of others she saw at work every day.

'I absolutely believe that being in a garden can help to heal people, so my genuine answer to your question is undoubtedly yes. There are lots of studies showing it to be hugely beneficial in many ways, and I would be more than happy to send you links to the information and relevant organisations. I have to tell you, though, that it doesn't necessarily work for everyone, but from what I've seen with Tamsin, I do think that it could be helpful for her.'

'Well then, we'll have to try to make a garden here.' Doug's tone was light and hopeful. 'Top tips, please, Flora?'

She was thrilled with their willingness to try, and the offer to help them in any way she could was on the tip of her tongue, until she remembered Mac's words about her imminent departure from the island. 'Get to know your soil,' she told Doug eventually. 'So that you can learn how to improve it and what plants will do best in a location like this.' She waved a hand casually towards the view with a wry smile. The landscape was stunning but wind and salt-laden air would not make their task any easier.

'What does the counsellor say now?'

Doug looked across as Mac spoke, removing their attention from the sea. 'That she's making a little progress and to continue not applying any pressure to encourage her to talk when she isn't able to. It'll likely come in time; we have to be patient and use the methods we've been taught to help her. We all know grief is a terrible thing and we react to it in different ways. Maggie's great with her at school, and everyone on the island is, too – the community here is a huge source of strength, but then you know that, Mac. It's one of the reasons why Angus settled back here with Rachael. And we still go across to the mainland every month to meet with the child bereavement group—'

'It's so unfair!' Moira burst out, sorrow easily turning into anger as her eyes darkened in despair. 'Why should a seven-year-old girl have to meet with a counsellor every month to show them all the ways she misses her mum and dad, and how we are all trying to go on without them? It's just not right.' She slumped back on the sofa and

Doug reached across to slide his arm around her, trying to replace anguish with love, as the tears slid down Moira's face and she covered it with her hands.

Doug offered Mac and Flora an apologetic glance. 'We haven't really had people over for supper since we stopped having guests to stay, but Moira was adamant she wanted to invite you both before Flora has to leave.' They clung together and Flora felt her sadness and empathy growing as she looked away, trying not to intrude on their sorrow. Her eyes easily found Mac's, and the compassion and understanding she read in his expression almost undid her. Slowly, she dragged her gaze back to the sea crashing onto the headland below them.

'I'm all right,' Moira sniffed from the depths of the sofa and she smiled weakly at her guests. 'It always gets us just when you think that every day is getting a bit easier than the last.' She nodded at Doug, who stood up and headed to the kitchen. Flora heard him gathering glasses and retrieving something from a cupboard. 'It really worries me, what sort of life we can give her, being the age we are. She should be running around with brothers and sisters, and having a normal life. Nothing about this is normal anymore.'

'That's perfectly understandable,' Flora told her quietly, and she hesitated before carrying on. 'I lost my dad two years ago in difficult circumstances, and all any of us wanted was to have him back and cling to everyone we loved. I know it's not the same, as my brother and I were older, but it was still a big shock.'

Moira's expression changed, as she understood that Flora, too, knew the measure of loss. Flora could feel the solidity of Mac's stare and she looked down, noticing his hands clasped loosely between his legs. The merest movement would erase the tiny space between them, but she drove the image from her mind, knowing it was pointless to think such things about him.

'Well, I think it's time to break open the last of the damson gin, don't you? Seeing as Flora isn't going to be with us for very long.' Everyone looked at Doug as he spoke from the kitchen. He waved a bottle of ruby-coloured liquid and the atmosphere shifted into something easier with his casual gesture. 'I'll fill the glasses. Mac, you can have a taste but that's all, as you're driving. This has put you on your back before now, laddie, as you well know.'

Flora laughed, as Mac's hands rose in defeat. The smile died on his lips as their eyes locked and she looked away first, her skin igniting once again at the unguarded ache in his expression. Moira stood up and excused herself to go and check on Tamsin.

Short of sticking her fingers over the glass Doug proffered, Flora was unable to prevent him from pouring her a shot of the home-made gin, served neat with ice, which smelled gorgeous and tasted utterly delicious, sure that it would quickly render her incapable of even standing up should she have too much. The evening was beginning to lengthen into dusk as Moira re-joined them, satisfied that Tamsin was comfortable and still asleep.

They chatted together of simpler things and, as it grew later, Flora relaxed sufficiently to laugh with Mac again. By the time they left, close to midnight, Tamsin still hadn't woken, and Flora realised that she had drunk much more than she'd intended, as the bottle of damson gin had gradually dwindled to nothing. Doug and Moira hugged them both as they said good night and she walked unsteadily back to the car, shaking off Mac's hand when he tried to prevent her from stumbling on the grassy path.

'I'm fine,' she told him, taking her time as she climbed into his car, sitting down heavily and letting her bag slide to the floor. 'Perfectly all right.'

'Sure? You look a bit wobbly to me.'

She heard the grin in his voice as he joined her and started the engine, and she could only laugh huffily at his comment.

'It's that blasted hooch of Moira's! It's probably illegal to even make that stuff and certainly lethal if you're mad enough to drink it. Just drive me back, please, to somewhere that serves tea, chocolate and water, not necessarily in that order.'

Flora was relieved that it was only a ten-minute journey before the hotel came into view, and Mac was pulling up on the gravel drive close to the front door. It was quiet at this hour and she knew she would have to knock to gain entry from the night porter before she could reach her room.

'Are you enjoying the hotel, Flora? Is there anything else you need?'

She hesitated before replying, one hand on the door, ready to escape. 'Of course. It's very generous of you to let me stay here.' She knew she hadn't disguised the pause quickly enough to prevent his noticing.

'But?'

She shook her head as she started to laugh and stopped abruptly, the additional movement not helping with her ability to look straight ahead. 'I don't want you to think badly of me if I tell you.'

'Go on,' Mac said, waiting in the darkness for her answer.

'The hotel is fabulous but then you know that. It seems so formal and I still haven't got used to eating such amazing food and not making my own bed. The hotel is perfect for holidays, but this is work and I feel a bit out of place. I'm sorry, I know I'm being very ungrateful, and you can blame it entirely on Doug and the damson gin – it's like he's given me some kind of truth serum.'

'I see. In that case, is there anything else you'd like to tell me?'

'Nope.'

She glanced at him and saw that he was smiling, his profile outlined by the light above the front door. Eventually, she managed to push open the car door and heard him laugh again as she tried to position both her legs onto the drive to stand up.

'Stop it,' she told him crossly, finally managing to extricate herself from the Audi and bending down cautiously to glare at him, her handbag sliding to the gravel. 'This is all your fault, anyway. Everything's your fault.'

Slamming the door shut, Flora scooped her handbag up from the ground and strutted away from the car, proud of her suitably dramatic exit, even though she was struggling to identify which of the front doors was actually real through her double vision.

Chapter Sixteen

Flora was dreaming of thunderstorms crashing above her head, when she struggled from sleep a few hours later. She realised that the din was not merely a dream, but a very real banging on her bedroom door. Relieved that the pounding wasn't all in her temples, she climbed gingerly out of her huge, cosy bed and unthinkingly opened the door, trying to blink away the gritty sensation in her eyes, as she peered at Mac in surprise.

'Morning. I know it's early but there's something I want to show you.'

'What?' Flora mumbled as she stared at him, uncertainty quickly replacing surprise. He looked bright, full of energy, and she felt a scarlet heat racing across her face as his gaze took in the details of her short turquoise pyjamas. 'Are you mad?' she stormed, shoving the door back until it was virtually closed. 'What time is it? I was fast asleep. And what is it you want to show me? Can't it wait? If it's the sunrise over the house, I've already seen it.'

'Sorry. How soon can you be ready?'

He didn't sound at all sorry and Flora saw him grin before she slammed the door properly. Having to deal with the reality of him outside her bedroom door seemed a bit much when she had been dreaming of him half the night. 'Ten minutes.'

By the time she opened the door to him again, nine minutes later, her senses were wide awake, even if her eyes weren't. She had brushed her teeth, splashed cold water on her face and quickly wound her hair into a plait, but that was about it. She was cross at being dragged from her bed after a late night, looking worse than dishevelled, for some crazy, unknown scheme of Mac's. She wondered if anyone had seen him hovering outside her room and glared at him again for good measure, as he leant idly against the wall, hands in pockets. But as she stepped into the corridor, she couldn't deny the excitement of an adventure with him.

'You won't need those,' Mac said, pointing to her ever-present camera and notebook as he hurried her down the staircase, passing a couple of curious guests no doubt on their way to breakfast. The handsome young receptionist stared at them as they passed through the hall, and Flora tried and failed to summon a casual smile to suggest that everything was quite normal. Then they were outside and moments later were heading down the hotel drive in Mac's car.

'I'm better when I've had coffee,' she grumped, bending down awkwardly to lace her boots. It was still cool at this hour and she zipped up her jacket, trying to ward off the chilly air as it wound itself around her body. She had assumed that their journey had something to do with Róisín and so she had dressed as usual in her practical working clothes.

'I've got some with me.' Mac laughed at her cranky gaze. He pointed at the two travel mugs in the drinks holder and she took one gratefully, sipping it and enjoying the smooth taste as her mind began to wake up properly. Any pretence of professionalism seemed to have disintegrated after last night, and she hoped he wasn't able to fathom all she was feeling. 'Anyway, you're a morning person, Flora, just like me.'

'How do you know that?'

'You told me, at Mel's wedding,' he answered easily, checking for the unlikely prospect of traffic as they left the hotel grounds and putting his foot down on the accelerator. 'In between dances.'

'Oh.' She didn't want to be reminded of what else she might have said at the wedding, when she had been feeling elated and sexy and beautiful, until he had kissed her and disappeared into the night. 'Where are we going?'

'To see a cottage.'

'What? Why? Where is it?'

'Because I think you might like it and it will suit you.'

She fell silent, holding the cup between her hands as she wondered why he would possibly want to show her a cottage, wherever it was. Sheep straying onto the stony road leapt for their lives back into the safety of the heather as the car flew past, and she giggled at the madness of it all. Time was edging towards seven and very soon they were dipping down towards the sea. She knew from the position of the climbing sun behind them that they were near the north-western tip of the island, and she saw the brilliant blue water sparkling in the clear morning light.

Mac turned off the road, such as it was, and then they were bumping along a rough track, all the time dropping down a hill. At the end of the track they reached a farm gate, and he stopped the car and they jumped out. Mac pushed the gate to one side and leaving it propped against a slope as he called back to her.

'We'll have to walk from here; I can't take the car any lower. It's not far.'

The track softened to a grassy path and she could see the roofs of a pair of cottages below, perched in front of the sea. She heard gulls swooping and calling, and the muttered hiss of water hitting rock; in the distance a ship was ferrying passengers from island to island, a shrinking speck on the horizon. At the water's edge a narrow wooden pier ran out to sea, sheltering a dinghy and a yacht rising slowly as the tide approached.

'Where are we?' The early-morning start was already forgotten as Flora looked around with delight, breathing in the fresh salty air. 'This is completely stunning. Almost worth being dragged out of bed for.'

Mac laughed as he leant forwards to push open a small wooden gate leading to the pair of stone cottages. 'I hope you will think it was worth it.'

Immediately, Flora was drawn to the gardens, planted as one and rising to a narrow point where a seat was perched above the top of the houses, offering a glorious view. The gardens were full of weeds and overgrown shrubs, and she spotted a raised vegetable bed surrounded by rotting sleepers and a stunted pine tree.

'Don't look at the garden,' he said sheepishly, reaching out and playfully covering her eyes. Then his hands fell away and he said, 'Róisín isn't the only one that needs your help.'

She followed Mac around to the front of the buildings, a smile already lighting up her face. A path from the cottages led down to a tiny and deserted golden beach tucked amongst the cliffs, completely private and hidden from the road above. Mac came to a halt beside her and she turned to look at him, hardly bothering to conceal her exhilaration. 'Mac, this is absolutely incredible!'

'Isn't it? I never get tired of the view. No matter how often I come here, I always stop and stare before I do anything else. Come and see the cottage.'

He took a key from his pocket and they walked up to the first entrance. Long, narrow and single storey, with a window painted a bright, sky blue on either side of the front door, the stone cottages were whitewashed. He unlocked the door, pushed it aside and stepped back to let Flora enter first. Inside, the kitchen and living room were open-plan and small, with one blue wall surrounding a wood-burning stove and three white walls to brighten the effect. Rugs covered the wooden floor and a basket of logs nestled against a striped armchair pushed close to the fireplace. Through an open door, Flora could see a bedroom with a double bed and a pile of artists' canvases propped against a wall.

'Do you like it?' Mac asked, his voice gentle through the quietness.

She turned to look at him, her face shining with pleasure. He was propped against the small square table squashed between the few kitchen cupboards and tiny stove. It was smaller than even her little cottage, but she loved it anyway, as she was sure he had known she would.

'It's perfect,' she told him, diverting her gaze to the deep window overlooking the beach so that he could have noticed only the briefest moment of pleasure. Thoughts of last night and what she might have unknowingly revealed were still tumbling through her mind.

'Well, it's extremely basic but it's yours for the rest of the week, if you want it?'

'Are you serious? I can stay here?'

'Of course I am. I know it's going from the sublime to the ridiculous but if you think you would feel more at home here, then please do consider it. Sorry, I feel I ought to have offered it to you sooner.'

Flora took a few steps from the window into the bedroom and glanced around, excited by the idea of the cottage and being so close to the water. 'Please, don't apologise, it's really kind of you. How soon can I move in?'

'Now, if you like. I'll have the hotel pack for you and bring everything here.'

Flora dismissed his suggestion with politeness. 'Thanks for the offer but I can take care of it myself.'

'I thought you might say that. Help yourself to whatever you need; the kitchen is quite well equipped, and you can order whatever you like from the hotel and they'll bring it down.' He paused, and their eyes met again in the brief silence that stretched across the room, memories of last night hovering between them. 'But you won't, will you?'

'No. But I do appreciate the offer.'

'I'd bring some basic provisions back at least. It's a long way to the mainland for a pint of milk if the shop is closed.'

Flora laughed. 'I think we both know I could knock on a neighbour's door and they'd give me some.'

'Good luck with that.' Mac grinned as they slowly drifted towards the door, drawn outside to the glorious little beach beyond the cottage. 'The nearest house is about a mile away, so I'd still go to the shop, if I were you.'

Flora was still smiling, the salty tang in the air hitting her senses immediately, and she instinctively bent down, unlaced her boots and took them off. They were far too heavy to wear on a beach and she stuffed her socks inside, loving the feel of the sand between her toes. The tide had risen higher even in the short time they had been here; she straightened up and glanced across at him.

'Couldn't help it,' she said happily, tracing a pattern in the sand with her toes, and she recognised the amusement in his gaze. It was the same look she had seen at the wedding and then again last night, when his reticence had seemed to diminish and been replaced with teasing gentleness. But she heard his quiet sigh and realised then he was dressed for the office; he didn't have any more time for this silly diversion.

'Sorry, Flora, to rush you but something has come up with a client and I have to go to Edinburgh to meet with them. I ought to be going.'

'Of course.' She grabbed her boots and turned back towards the car. The sand scraped against her skin, as she set off up the hill to the gate, mingling with the damp grass soaking her feet. 'Please will you give me a lift back to the hotel so I can collect my stuff?'

'Absolutely,' he said immediately, falling into step alongside her and making Flora wish he didn't have to leave. She knew she must be more careful; she mustn't allow absurd impulses to interfere with her usual wisdom or hard-won resistance, as they had last night. Mac reached the little gate before she did and pulled it open for her to pass through.

Once he had returned her to the formality of the hotel, she immediately set about packing to leave. Within an hour she was back at the cottage after a trip to the shop, key in hand, and let herself in, thrilled with her new, albeit still temporary, home. She knew Sophie would not approve of her leaving the spa behind, and Flora had no intention of confessing that she hadn't been near it for any of the delectable treatments on offer. She dragged her suitcase into the bedroom and swung it on the thick, obviously home-made, patchwork quilt. The sun was already brightening the white walls and she headed to the window and opened it, smiling at the sound of the sea lapping at the beach just a few yards away. Grabbing what she would need for work, Flora left the cottage, locked it behind her and set off on foot.

When the evening drew near, it was a pleasure for her to leave the garden at Róisín and head back to the beachside cottage instead of the hotel. She took her time on the way, familiarising herself with the northern part of the island, and it was almost thirty minutes later when she arrived. She opened the door again to the lovely little house and sank into the armchair next to the fireside, closing her eyes to enjoy the solitude and rest her weary muscles after a day spent mostly digging. There was no Wi-Fi and absolutely no suggestion of 4G – or even 3G – and so she left her phone beside the bed, unperturbed by the lack of signal. Her handset was unreliable at the best of times and her brother Charlie was always trying to persuade her to upgrade it, but Flora didn't see the point when it was often dropped in soil or falling out of her pockets at work.

A bath was out of the question when she saw the tiny cubicle that housed a shower, so she undressed quickly, shivering in the cool air as she stepped inside. Once the hot water had done its best with her aches, she brushed her wet hair, scooping it into a high ponytail, and slipped on pink shorts and a simple vest top over her underwear. It was still warm outside, and she opened the door and strolled down to the beach.

She dropped down onto the sand, amongst crushed shells and bits of dried seaweed, idly watching the glint of small fish in the clear water and the bob of seals near the rocks on the opposite side of the hidden cove. It was beautiful and silent, and she loved it. She tilted her head back, soaking up the evening sun on her skin, and stretched out her legs, allowing her toes to wriggle in the sea warmed by the Gulf Stream. She would swim in the morning – it was all far too inviting to miss the opportunity. But the persistent rumbling in her stomach reminded her that room service was no longer available, and she stood up, resolving to come back outdoors the moment she had rummaged in the fridge and produced something for supper.

Sand clung to her damp feet as she strolled back up to the cottage, and she was lost in thoughts of Tamsin and the garden when she heard the unmistakeable sound of a car in the lane above her. Surprised, she lifted a hand to shield her eyes as she squinted through the light. She saw the gate above the cottages swing open and Mac heading rapidly down the path. It was too late to dash inside without being seen and he spoke, cutting through the sound of the sea as he neared her.

'Hey.' He was still wearing the shirt and trousers from this morning, crumpled now, and she noticed tiredness as a quick hand moved to disguise a yawn. 'Sorry, long drive. Hope I'm not disturbing you.'

His eyes dropped to take in her simple clothes and long legs in shorts, and desire danced through her all over again. Pinned by the sudden heat in his look, Flora tore her glance away first. She had not expected to see him again today and her voice was a scratched murmur that betrayed the response she had hoped to conceal. 'No, of course not. I was just going inside to make something to eat.'

'Sounds good,' he said idly. She wished she could smooth away the tiredness evident on his face with her touch and then sent the thought away; it was not her place. 'Well, see you later. I think I'll go and change.' He gave her a final nod as he moved towards the cottages and she watched, puzzled.

'Back at Róisín?'

Mac paused, almost at the second cottage, and when he turned around, she saw the surprise in his expression. 'No. Didn't I tell you? I'm living in the cottage beside yours when I'm here, until I can move into the house.'

'What? You're staying next door?' Flora had no chance to keep the alarmed squeak from her voice as she realised what he was telling her. She stuffed her hands into her pockets and faced him, the delectable thought of having him so close hurrying through her mind. She had assumed that he was either living in the hotel or camping at Róisín whenever he was on the island.

'Yes. Cassie – my sister – and I have been coming here since we were small. She usually stays in your cottage to paint; I think she left some canvasses here last time. Is it a problem?'

'No, of course not. I was just surprised, that's all. I'd assumed both the cottages were empty. Mac, are you sure I won't be in your way?'

'No.' His smile was patient and Flora tried to ignore the softness in his narrowed gaze. She swallowed when she noticed him tugging the shirt from the waistband of his chinos, freeing it to drift around his hips, and he casually undid a couple of buttons. 'Not at all.'

'Well then, I think I'll head inside and leave you to it.' She was feigning brightness and hoped it wasn't too obvious. 'Good night.'

She spun away from him and stepped inside her cottage, banging the door and making sure it was locked, even though she was certain he'd have a spare key. She knew it was going to be difficult to pretend that everything was fine when he would be sleeping just the other side of the wall – even if it was two feet thick. For an irrational few seconds, she longed again for the impersonal space of the hotel, where she could more easily ignore him and not have to think about his proximity. Unwelcome reminders of Mel's wedding and the amazing kiss with Mac raced into her head as she rummaged distractedly through the kitchen cupboards, leaving her longing for the intimacy they had shared then.

Her search revealed eggs and bread, and from the fridge she collected butter and cheese, and set about making herself an omelette. She had barely begun, when there was a rap on the door and she jumped, dropping the wooden spoon she was holding. Of course, she knew who it would be as she unlocked the door and faced Mac. He had changed into shorts and a dark blue T-shirt, the tiredness already gone.

'I'm going to throw some fish on the barbeque, if you'd like to join me? It won't be as good as the hotel, but it seems a bit silly to eat on my own when you're just next door.'

'Oh.' Eat on her own was exactly what Flora was planning to do and she felt a bit mean as she considered his offer. She dithered for a minute, rubbing one foot against the back of her leg. She still hadn't let go of the door. 'That's kind of you, but no, thanks.'

'Why not?'

'Excuse me?'

'Why not, Flora?' Mac asked patiently, dipping his head to one side at her confusion. 'We're the only two people here, and what possible sense does it make to sit inside on our own and not share? And it's the most perfect evening.'

Put like that, there wasn't a good reason to refuse – not one she could reveal anyway – and Flora blew out a breath, only too aware that she was getting caught up in something she would not be able to easily evade. 'Okay. Thank you. But let me help – what can I do?'

'Salad,' he answered, as she finally let go of the door. She stepped outside and he reached behind her to leave the door on its latch, passing her the key and she slipped it into a pocket. 'Are you any good at chopping?'

'Just branches,' she retorted, and he laughed. He pointed to a folding table and the barbeque set up beside it on the beach, near the water, already smoking as the coals became hotter. 'I'll be back in a minute – make yourself at home.'

Flora strolled down to the water and set to work on the salad as Mac disappeared into his cottage, returning a few minutes later with a tray loaded with food. She tried not to stare; it all looked so much more delicious than the simple supper she had been planning.

'Do you like prawns and scallops?'

'Love them.' Her mouth began to water at the thought of such a meal.

'And salmon?'

'Of course.'

She watched as he expertly threaded skewers with pineapple, prawns, scallops, cherry tomatoes and baby onions, dipping the kebabs in a thick, gooey sauce and placing them on the grill. The barbeque hissed immediately, and the salty smell of seafood cooking drifted across to her as the smoke rose to the sky. She tried not to be too impressed with his skill and concentrated instead on slicing cucumber, pears and crisp green lettuce, dropping everything into a bowl. He was turning the kebabs with one hand, while dusting the salmon with seasoning with the other, and she thought it really wasn't fair that he looked so good in shorts.

'Where did you learn to cook like this?' she asked, bending to retrieve a scrap of pear that had missed the bowl. She carefully wiped off the sand and chucked it in. 'Or is all of this something you had the hotel chef whip up for you? No offence.'

'That's okay, none taken,' he replied, flicking a stray tomato at her. She laughed as she hurriedly ducked out of the way and it shot past her head. 'This is all my own work. After travelling the best part of a year in South America and living off street food, once I got to university, I didn't want to go hungry so I learned a few basics, nothing that would take me very far. When I'm in Edinburgh I tend to eat out more; I suppose I only really enjoy cooking when I'm here, on the island. How about you?'

'Me? Do I cook?' Flora paused, holding the knife steady in her hand as she considered his question. What she did in her own kitchen didn't exactly match up to this unexpected feast on the beach. 'Sometimes, mostly if I have friends around for dinner. I get by, but the microwave is used more often than the oven.'

It wasn't quite the same, cooking for one, but she didn't tell him that. Her ex-boyfriend David had been careful about his diet and she had quickly given up trying to find dishes he would deem acceptable. They had almost always eaten in restaurants when they had been together.

'Beer?'

'Thank you.' She reached across to take the bottle Mac had offered, enjoying the taste of the cool drink on her tongue. She found a jar of home-made dressing on the table and dribbled it over the salad, hoping she hadn't smothered it.

Mac had been right; it was the most beautiful evening. The sun was setting somewhere far in front of them, sliding gently into the sea, and the water was calm. The ferry service had ended for the day and only the little dot of a yacht sailing miles away was visible on the horizon.

'Grab a plate, these are ready.'

She thanked Mac as he dropped a perfectly cooked kebab onto the plate she had picked up, and she took some salad from the bowl. She watched as he lowered the salmon onto the grill, smiling easily at her while he loaded his own plate. He helped himself to a beer and stuffed a tomato in his mouth.

'Not bad.' He peered into the salad bowl to check her work. 'I never saw cucumber cut that way before.'

'You're so rude,' she exclaimed, starting to laugh at his impish expression. 'You can do it yourself next time, chef.'

'Next time?' He paused and the look he gave her with his questioning grey eyes was amused, challenging her.

'You know what I mean.' Flora hadn't intended to sound flustered and she lowered her voice. 'Speaking figuratively.'

'Then it's your turn to cook tomorrow.'

'Won't you be back in Edinburgh?' She kept the question casual, as though his reply would not matter.

He shook his head. 'Not if there's a chance of a decent meal here.'

She laughed again, loving the feel of the sand between her bare toes and the gentle swish of the water lapping nearby. 'You'd do better at the hotel; you've set the bar pretty high with all this. I'm not known for my skill in the kitchen.'

'We'll see,' he said, giving her a quick grin. They wandered along the beach with their plates, stepping over shells and clumps of dried seaweed stranded on the sand. He pointed to some rocks, their backs worn smooth by years of high tides splashing over them. 'Shall we sit here?' They settled down, facing the sea, and Flora realised that she was starving, as she began to eat, tugging the food from the skewer with her fingers.

'This is fantastic, Mac, thank you,' she said appreciatively, as she devoured another kebab. 'Much better than the omelette I was planning to have.'

'You're very welcome. So, what will you cook for me tomorrow night?'

Flora hoped he was joking. But he seemed quite serious, even if the smile was still playing around his lips. She realised then how easily he had changed from the well-dressed businessman into this laid-back figure, sprawling beside her and hungrily eating the food he had prepared for them.

'I have absolutely no idea,' she replied smoothly, inching her foot away from the tempting nearness of his bare leg. Tomorrow was Thursday and it would be her last evening on the island. Leaving so soon filled her with dismay. The days had easily sped by, becoming memories she would never forget, and Tamsin's face danced in her mind again. 'It will be a surprise to both of us. But beans on toast is looking good right now. I found a couple of cans in the kitchen earlier.'

He laughed at that as he jumped up and took her plate, and she watched lazily as he returned to the barbeque for the salmon and shared the last of the salad between them. The blackened fish smelled amazing and they were silent as they ate.

'You mentioned South America earlier.' Flora moved her empty plate from her knees to the sand. 'What did you do out there?'

'The usual: travel, teaching, volunteering. Angus and I spent six months in Argentina, which was incredible, just the most amazing and stunning country. We taught English for a while then travelled around Patagonia and finished off volunteering with street kids, before we came home. I'd love to go back.' He sounded wistful, his gaze on the water. 'It was just a simpler time, when decisions didn't really come any bigger than where we would sleep and how to get to the next town.'

'You sound as though you miss it.'

He shrugged. 'Not really. I'm a romantic and I loved it. But it's never the same when you go back, is it? Proper life comes and finds you eventually. Responsibility, work, all that stuff, I suppose. And worse.'

Flora knew he was referring to the loss of Angus and Rachael, and there was a pause before he spoke again. His question took her by surprise.

'Have you heard from David since the wedding?'

She shook her head fiercely; her hair swinging down her back and his eyes followed the movement. It was a reminder of last night she didn't want, and she pushed away the thought. 'Absolutely not. He seems happy and settled with his new girlfriend. Why do you ask?'

'I just wondered, that's all.' Mac stretched out distractingly long and suntanned legs. 'I thought that after seeing you again, he might have changed his mind about the two of you breaking up.'

Surprised, Flora stared at Mac. 'I wouldn't expect him to. And if he did, well, there would be no point in going back. It's definitely over.'

'Did you meet him through Harry? They seemed quite different; I heard they'd been friends for years.'

'Since school. David was a bit of a swot and Harry was always in trouble. And, somehow, they became friends; David helped Harry with his work and calmed him down, and Harry dragged David along to everything, made him part of the group everyone else wanted to be in.'

'There's always one,' Mac answered, sounding sleepy, as the sun did its best to keep on warming them into the evening. His eyes had closed, and he looked boyish and peaceful – and utterly tempting.

'Yep. And I bet you were it.' His silence told Flora she had been right. 'I'd known David for years, too,' she admitted, trying and failing to remember the actual moment she and David had met. 'Harry and Mel were always together, and David kept in touch, met them regularly, even after he went to university. Once we'd all settled down and started working properly, somebody suggested that David and I should get together. We couldn't think of a good enough reason not to, so we spent the next couple of years pretending to one another that it was the real thing, when of course it wasn't.'

'And the real thing? Have you ever had it?'

'Well, there was that abseiling instructor…' she retorted, desperate to keep the moment light and not betray that she felt awfully close to it. 'I'm sure that counts.'

'Seriously? Nobody else?'

'Just the one,' she replied quietly, remembering when she had been nineteen and travelling, before everything had changed and she had decided that trusting her future to one person was not for her. 'But he was in Australia and it was never going to work out. What about you?'

'Once or twice,' he admitted lightly. The sudden reminder of his relationship with Chloe was startling and Flora fell silent, unwilling to prolong a conversation in which she would have to confront the reality of his absent girlfriend.

Chapter Seventeen

Supper was over, the sun had almost slid completely into the sea and they were silent as they finished the last of their beer. Flora was feeling sleepy and she lifted her face to the diminishing light, trying to catch the last of the day's warmth on her skin. It seemed so easy and right, sitting here with Mac, and she wished she could cling onto this borrowed time forever. Eating supper together at sunset on a deserted beach seemed far from the professional relationship he had promised her, and she had no idea how the evening would end. She just didn't want it to end, not yet.

'I saw your sister's canvasses in the cottage. I didn't mean to pry, but they're beautiful.' Flora hadn't been able to resist looking at them when she had noticed the first, a breathtaking oil of a beach and turbulent, stormy sky. 'She's very talented. Does she show often?'

'Occasionally, through a gallery in London. She's going to America with her partner next month; it seems likely that he's about to become more collectable. A gallerist from New York spotted his work in Paris and has put together a small exhibition through a museum.' Mac had moved to stretch out on the sand, and he swivelled around to look up at her. He, too, seemed in no hurry to leave and bring about an end to their evening, and she was content to listen to him talk of his family.

'How brilliant, they must be so excited.'

Mac reached for a pebble to lob at a couple of gulls picking around the remains of their meal, near the barbeque. 'I think they are when they're not rowing.'

Flora laughed, trying to picture Cassie in her mind. 'It all sounds very volatile; it must be a very expressive household.'

'It definitely is. He used to make ceramics and Cassie's reducing his collection every time they fall out, usually over his ex-wife or teenage daughter turning up unannounced and demanding money or shelter, or both.'

'You don't sound very alike,' Flora said thoughtfully. 'I can't imagine you throwing things in a temper.'

'We're not, really. I'm more like my dad, quieter and quite shy. I'm not usually as impulsive as Cassie; I like to think things through. I guess she wouldn't paint as beautifully as she does if she didn't capture the inspiration when it strikes.'

'Shy?' Flora quirked a brow, as images from Mel's wedding sprang to mind. She remembered how much fun they'd had together and how easily he had become part of a special day, even whilst amongst strangers. 'You're not at all shy, how can you say that! I saw you dancing at the wedding and then at the ceilidh, remember?'

'But I am, Flora. I'm quite reserved and my two closest friends are both people I met when I was at school, and you know about Angus. I travel regularly and the practice keeps me busy. I don't tend to socialise much when I'm free, beyond the people I already know.'

'But you're so good with people,' she blurted out. There was something about the hidden beach that seemed to separate them from reality; for now, Flora could pretend that there was nothing else, as they shared their history with one another. No job in Yorkshire, no girlfriend far away, no heartbroken little girl wanting Flora to stay. 'With everyone here and my friends, at least.'

'It doesn't come naturally with strangers,' he admitted, scraping a pattern in the sand with his toes. 'I have to work at it, and I know I can be a bit distant sometimes. And your friends are great, I liked them very much. That part was easy.'

A picture of the bright and lively Chloe shot into Flora's mind, and she couldn't help wondering when she and Mac ever managed to meet, and how two such apparently different people maintained a relationship in those circumstances. But then Flora shoved the thought away, changed the subject back to his friend and hoped he would not mind her asking.

'Did you meet Angus here or at school?'

'Here, on the island. My parents fell in love with it when we were tiny, and they rented the cottages so we could spend most of our holidays here. They both travelled but usually managed to avoid doing it at the same time, so we would be here for weeks on end in the summer. Angus and I were at different schools, but there was only a year or so between us and we became mates from the start. We both loved mucking about in boats, swimming and camping and stuff. When the island came up for sale, my parents bought the cottages, converted the hotel and moved here to run it for a few years. Then they found another place in Seville and they mostly live there now.'

'It sounds like you and Angus had a lot of fun together.'

Mac's fingers were in the sand, idly tracing a pattern, and he picked up a handful of golden grains, watching as they trickled to the ground once again. He raised a shoulder in silent agreement. 'We really did. I was so angry, after the shock from the accident had worn off. I couldn't believe he'd gone, that he or Rachael wouldn't see Tamsin flourish, watch her grow. I took some time off work, and everyone here just came together, closed around us. Food arrived and we had no idea who'd brought it. Animals were fed, shopping fetched, decisions made. I really struggled when I had to go back to Edinburgh. I hated Angus not being here, but I couldn't stand being anywhere else without him either. At least when I'm here, I can still feel him around me. Everyone on the island understands. He and Rachael are still a part of this place and I want Tamsin to feel that, too, when she's old enough. To know how much we loved them and that we'll always remember them.' Mac paused for a moment before turning to look at her. 'But you know what it's like, Flora. I can't imagine your dad would've wanted any of you to be hurt so badly.'

Mac had summed it up perfectly; there was nothing else she could add other than a pursing of her lips that just about passed for a smile. She didn't quite recognise the sense of community he spoke of. Her own hometown had been small but still too large to completely close around a grieving family.

'No, I don't suppose he did. Strangely, Mum eventually met with his other partner and they've become friends, sort of. In the end they were the only two people who understood how the other felt. Charlie and I had each other and we're still close. Mum was adamant that there was another child who had lost his father, too, and he shouldn't suffer any more than anyone else, because of everything that had happened. So Charlie and I have a half-brother, Liam, who was just as devastated as us. Even though we don't see a lot of him, we do keep in touch, mainly thanks to Charlie. In my more accepting moments, I can understand that my dad must have loved us all and just didn't know how to proceed. In the less kind ones, I can't stand to think of him, because I feel now that half of our childhood was a lie. I was only twelve and Charlie fifteen when Liam was born.'

Flora fell silent. She noticed the stubble on Mac's skin and the long, fair lashes surrounding the blue-grey eyes that were watching her. He moved, and she felt the shift of his weight, his arm brushing her leg until he settled again, still on the sand just below her.

'What does your brother do?' Mac's tone was lighter and Flora was glad he had changed the subject to something easier. They had both revealed perhaps more than they meant to, and she was happy to talk of other things.

'He's a vicar.' She heard Mac's laughter and she smiled, wriggling on the sand to get comfortable again, as she stretched her legs. 'I know. Charlie was a really talented rugby player, and his wife Sam was already a Christian when they met, so he started going to church with her. They'd been together for about a year when Charlie felt certain he'd been called to ministry, which was a big surprise. Eventually he left the club and married Sam, so they could be together whilst she was at university and Charlie was studying, too.'

'That's quite a story. Not many people would give up a sporting career, or the prospect of one, for the Church.'

'No. But Charlie's amazing with his parishioners and the communities around them, and there's no doubt whenever I see him that he's doing exactly what he was meant to do. Their faith has certainly sustained them through difficult times. He and Sam care for and make themselves available to others in ways that not many people can.'

'You have a gift, too, Flora.' Mac's voice was soft, caressing her as night fell, carrying them away somewhere where ordinary life would not find them. 'Being able to love your work is one thing, but it's obvious that you put your heart into everything you do and I'm sure the results are amazing because of it. I feel very thankful to have found you.' Flora stared at him as he hurried on, quickly clarifying his comment. 'For Róisín, I mean. I'm so glad you decided to come back.'

Thrilled by his words, Flora tipped her head forwards, allowing her long hair to cover her suddenly warm skin. 'Thank you for asking me,' she answered gently, still glowing from his compliment. 'Róisín is incredibly special; I feel so privileged to have had the opportunity to discover its stories and learn about the family.'

'Do you really think a garden could make a difference to Tamsin?'

She understood the seriousness of his question and could only offer him the truth she believed with all her heart. 'I do, yes. Obviously, I don't know Tamsin very well at all, but creating a garden at home or working on the school one could really help her. Her grandparents, too, if they felt able to become involved. I realise it can't in any way give them back what they've lost, but it might give them something special to focus on. I'd love to be able to support them.'

'But you won't be here.'

'No,' Flora admitted, hoping she had concealed her sadness at his matter of fact comment. 'But there might be other ways I can help. If Doug and Moira think it would be appropriate, of course, and wouldn't negatively affect Tamsin.'

Mac sighed, picking up his bottle, only to toss it on the sand again when he realised it was empty. 'I'm sorry I said what I did last night, Flora, about you upsetting Tamsin. It was very unfair of me and I know everything you've done for her is from your heart.'

'You were only trying to protect her. I understand.'

'I still shouldn't have said what I did.' He looked at her curiously, furrowed brow smoothing. 'What did you mean last night in the car, when you said that everything was my fault?'

Horrified that he had remembered her half-tipsy confession, Flora tried to distance herself from her real meaning. 'Nothing!'

'Really? I think you meant something.'

'How can you expect me to remember anything from last night, after that damson gin?' Flora's tone was light, and she hoped her words would convince him. But just the memory of the look in his eyes when he had been about to touch her, before Tamsin had stirred, ignited that same desire once again. Silence fell over them until Mac nodded, accepting her explanation. He changed the subject, drawing them away from the intimacy of that moment in the bedroom.

'Let's go for a walk,' he said suddenly, jumping to his feet and holding out his hand. 'Come on, I'll show you what I plan to do when I'm not working on the house.'

She slid her hand into his and gave him an answering smile as he pulled her upright. Mac led her down the narrow pier towards the boats. When they reached the end, he leapt easily onto the small yacht and Flora followed more cautiously, as he held out his arms to catch her. Once on board, he let go of her and she saw that the yacht was in a poor state, its white paint chipped and dull, and without most of its fenders. A torn and mouldy hood was pushed down to the bottom of a rusty and cracked frame, and he unlocked a wooden door and dropped into the cabin below. She followed him down a couple of steps, this time ignoring his outstretched hand as she reached the bottom, steadying herself on the wall.

It felt damp inside but not as dark as she had expected, her eyes rapidly adjusting to the dim light. Most of the curtains were missing, and the only remaining ones, on the starboard side, were torn and very dirty. They were in a small galley with the main cabin beyond and Flora was surprised by the space inside. A foldaway table that would easily seat six stood in the centre of the cabin, half-tipped towards the port side.

'What do you think?'

She heard the note of pride in Mac's voice. He was standing in the galley opposite the navigation station on the port side, casually leaning against an old-fashioned stove. She noticed a fire extinguisher dumped in the sink and, above it, three mismatched plates stacked on a damp shelf.

'I don't know anything about boats,' she confessed, betraying her enthusiasm for his project. 'But it's lovely. What is it?'

'She's a Westerly Fulmar – quite rare in their day because they're fast and still easy to handle under sail as well as power. But this poor girl has lost her way; she'd been abandoned in a marina for quite a few years until I brought her up here. I'm hoping to spend a bit of time over the summer restoring her.'

'And then what will you do with it?'

'Sail her around the islands, to begin with,' he replied promptly, swatting at a couple of flies buzzing noisily on the glass behind him. 'And then maybe around the coast, if time allows.' He tilted his head to glance outside and then looked at Flora again, an impish smile lighting up his face. 'It's the most glorious evening. Let's go for a swim.'

Flora's eyes widened in astonishment as he darted past her and back up the steps onto the deck. Alarm was already beating a rapid tattoo through her body, as she realised that he was completely serious. He winked at her, reaching for his T-shirt and pulling it quickly over his head.

'What are you doing?' The question was a strangled mutter that she knew sounded ridiculous, as her feet remained planted to the ground inside the galley. Words no longer came when he casually tossed the shirt onto a seat and faced her, ready to drop into the turquoise water below. The sudden glimpse of a muscular, golden chest covered with dark blonde hairs was delightful, and her heart began to race in shocked anticipation, as she wondered frantically how she might escape back to the safety of the cottage. She watched open-mouthed as she saw him dive effortlessly into the water with barely a splash, only to emerge moments later, shaking seawater from his face.

'Come on,' he called, treading water as he gave her a cheeky grin. 'Your turn.'

Flora squirmed nervously as she backed away, glancing around wildly for an escape route. 'No! You're crazy, it's freezing! I'm not going in there.'

'Oh yes, you are,' he shouted back, raising his voice above the waves swirling around him. She saw him swimming expertly back to the yacht. 'It's not that cold.'

'No! I haven't got anything to wear.' Real panic was beginning to replace silliness, as she recognised his determination.

'Doesn't matter,' she heard him say, and then the yacht was swaying in the water as he hauled himself back on board. 'You don't need anything. Do I have to come and get you?'

'No! Don't you dare!'

'Are you daring me?' he asked wickedly, and she drew in a breath as he dropped down the steps into the galley, where she'd retreated. Soaking wet, he was leaving salty water in his wake as he slowly walked towards her. 'Could be dangerous, Flora. You already know that I don't like to pass on a dare.'

Flora recognised the implacability in his look and she made a dash for the door, not really expecting him to follow.

'You wouldn't,' she called over her shoulder. But Mac was quicker, and she squealed as he easily caught her, pulling her against his wet body. His arms went around her waist and he tugged her backwards until they were on the deck again and laughing madly.

'Okay,' she gasped, every sense shrieking in delight as his damp skin pressed against her, and she reluctantly stepped out of his embrace. 'You win.' She climbed carefully over the rail and stared down at the water.

Mac quickly hopped up beside her, grabbing her hand and tugging her into the sea with him. Flora was still screaming as she hit the water and disappeared underneath. Spluttering from the shock of the sudden chill hitting her body, she quickly swam back up to the surface, trying to grab her wet hair and tug it into submission as it fanned out around her.

'You're mad, it's freezing!' she yelled at him as he emerged once again, shaking his head and still laughing. She scooped water into her hands and flung it into his face as a punishment, and he dived back beneath the water, reaching out to grab her again. But this time she was ready, and she swam away quickly, hoping to warm herself, as well as putting some distance between them. But good swimmer though she was, she was no match for Mac, who powered easily after her.

Flora was too cold and far too aware of him to remain in the water for long. She swam back to the pier, reaching for the ladder submerged in the water and hauled herself up onto the rickety wooden planks. Mac followed and she felt his eyes on her, suddenly very conscious of her wet shorts and white vest top, outlining every curve and concealing almost nothing. She knew that the light-hearted playfulness between them had been replaced by something much more serious.

Water streamed down from her hair onto her back and the sand on the wood was soft beneath her feet. Flora wanted to cling to this moment and never let it go. She wanted always to remember the expression in his eyes as they gazed at each other, and she shivered, entirely aware of every sensation he was arousing. But with every minute that hurried away into tomorrow, the end of the unexpected evening with him drew nearer.

'I'm sorry, I've made you cold.' Mac closed the distance between them with one small step. 'Come here.' His hands were on her shoulders, smoothing her skin until heat was blazing through her body and the trembling was no longer because of the sea. He pulled her against his bare chest, spreading his fingers across her back and lifting her wet hair with his free hand. His chin was against her temple, the imprint of his stubble rough against her soft skin.

She lifted her hand, about to touch his face, when a sudden awareness rose inside her and was enough to banish the perfect pleasure she found in his company. In less than two days she would have to leave the island. She would return to her real job and single life at Middlebrook, not this pretend thing – this foolish attempt at offering advice on a forgotten garden and trying to remain professional as her feelings for him grew day by day. Hovering unseen between them was Chloe, and Flora felt shaky as she tried to understand what all of this meant to Mac. He was not free to play these games and she was determined to take no further part. She stepped back abruptly, and he stared at her as his hands fell away.

Chapter Eighteen

'I'm sorry,' Mac muttered, and Flora could not offer a response, as she continued to back away from him. With every reluctant step she took towards the relative privacy of her cottage, the separation became more real as she left him behind, where he belonged.

'What about Chloe?' she asked him tightly, trying to contain her shivering now that he was no longer preventing the cold from claiming her body. 'Don't you think she would mind, about all of this, tonight? When did we forget that I'm only here because of the garden?'

'Chloe and I, we aren't really...' He paused, an awkward lull in his explanation, but Flora was in no mood to be helpful. He swiped at the water still trickling down his face and added, 'It's not what you think.'

'You've said that before. You're either in a relationship with her or you're not, Mac. And if it were me, I'd definitely like to believe that you wouldn't be doing this with someone else whenever I wasn't there.'

'What is *this*, then, Flora? What would you call it?'

'I know exactly what it is,' she said hotly. She lifted her chin to glare at him furiously, fighting to contain the way her body still wanted to be gathered against his. 'It's *nothing*.'

She spun around and walked away from him. All she could hear was the noise of the waves lapping onto the beach, as the tide continued to rise behind her and swirl around the boats at the pier. Lifting the latch on the front door, it took her a moment to recognise the sound of Mac's hurried steps as he tried to catch up with her. She paused on the threshold, her heart slamming in her chest as she looked at him over her shoulder, through the darkening night. The low rasp of his voice and the words he spoke shocked her.

'Actually, Flora, it isn't nothing. It's so much more and we both know it. But you're going to have to trust me.'

She was motionless for a few seconds, unable to break the tension. Trusting him was a step too far, and she only needed to recall the images of him with Chloe to remember the shock she had felt when Sophie had called her, the hurt and horror that Mac had deceived her and she had not seen it coming. Refusing to trust him, to give even more of herself beyond everything she already felt, would be her salvation in the days and weeks to come, when they'd be apart for good. She would cling to the knowledge that he couldn't give her the one thing she needed above all else – and it would help, eventually. She offered no answer as she entered the cottage and banged the door shut.

She couldn't settle once she was alone inside the little house, and she strode from kitchen to bedroom and back again. Finally, she huddled in a chair beside the unlit fireplace, staring into the empty grate, only too aware that all attempts at professionalism between them had finally disintegrated. Shaken by how easily her body responded to him, she was finding it impossible now to pretend that everything they had shared meant nothing to her. She couldn't be around him, couldn't keep on hoping, when her ordinary life was waiting, far from here. The dare, the wedding, their kiss, this night, the island, seeing him with Tamsin – all of it had only made her fall more deeply in love with him. Eventually, an uneasy sleep claimed her, still folded awkwardly into the chair. When she awoke in the night, still in her damp clothes – another unwelcome reminder of Mac – she quickly changed into pyjamas and crawled into her comfortable bed.

The morning sky had already been light for hours when she woke again, exhausted, at seven thirty. Her first thoughts, as she unwound herself from the bed, were of what had passed between her and Mac last night. She remembered their shared supper on the beach and their long, intimate conversation, but then came the memory of the end of the evening. She drew in a breath as she recalled his final words and the undeniable truth in them that she'd chosen to ignore. She would be leaving tomorrow, and she didn't want to go whilst everything was so unsettled between them, didn't want to picture the shape of the coming days at Middlebrook when spending time with him would no longer be her reality. She had told Mel and Sophie that her silly crush, as she had once referred to it, would pass but now she knew that it had not and would not.

She showered quickly, washing her hair twice to remove the sand and salt still tangled in it. She wasn't hungry and just coffee served as breakfast, sitting at the small table and with only her thoughts chasing one another through her mind for company. The coffee brought an energy she really needed, and she gathered her things to leave for the day. She couldn't find the key to the cottage and, after a few minutes of searching, it dawned on her that it had been in the pocket of her shorts last night. She found them on the back of a chair, with the rest of her damp clothes, and checked. The key was gone, and she sighed impatiently. She considered checking the beach, but the key was far more likely to be at the bottom of the sea after the swim with Mac.

She went to look anyway, but the key had disappeared, as she had feared. She glanced at Mac's cottage. The curtains were still drawn, and she hoped she wouldn't have to wake him. It was an inconvenience and one she could do without. She also hoped he wouldn't be angry about the key; after all, the cottages were pretty isolated and didn't seem to present much of a security risk.

The weather had changed from the glorious, late-spring sunshine of yesterday into cool grey clouds that blew crossly through the sky, threatening to keep the sun at bay and send rain to soak everything beneath them. Flora knocked on the door of Mac's cottage, quietly at first, and then louder when he did not immediately respond. After a couple of minutes spent hovering outside, she was beginning to think that he had already left, as she couldn't see the lane or his car from where she stood. Finally, she heard the door being unlocked and cautiously opened a few inches. Flora rolled her eyes, thinking his gesture a bit dramatic. What did he expect her to do? Crash in and leap on top of him? The thought was an unwelcome distraction and she rushed out a greeting to remove it from her mind.

'Morning! Sorry to bother you so early. Really sorry, again, but I can't find my key for the cottage. I think I lost it, in the sea.' She swallowed, remembering their swim, his arms, that look, his words. 'Do you have a spare I can borrow, please?'

The door swung back to reveal the sitting room and her smile faltered, as her gaze took in Chloe Berkeley standing inside the cottage, looking impossibly stunning for such an early hour. Flora's mouth fell open in shock and she felt a swift blush burn across her cheeks.

'Oh!' Chloe smiled, her eyes darting over Flora's shoulder to check the beach. Flora saw her visibly relax, her shoulders dropping slightly. 'Are you Flora?'

Words hadn't come to Flora yet and it was another few moments before she found some. 'Yes, I'm the gardener, at Róisín. You must be Chloe.'

None of the photographs she had seen of Chloe had done her any kind of justice. Chloe was smaller in person and much prettier, even when sleepy and dishevelled. Dark smudges beneath her eyes only emphasised the smoky-blue irises, and her hair was softer, less sharply cut and falling across one side of her lovely face. Smooth tanned legs made Flora feel even more faded and untidy, and she couldn't help noticing how Chloe was completely unselfconscious, even in nothing more than a skimpy vest and shorts.

'Yes, I'm so pleased to meet you. I've heard a lot about you.'

'Oh!' That was another surprise and Flora saw Chloe glance back over her shoulder towards the bedroom.

'Did you want Mac? He's in the shower, I'll call him.'

'No!' Flora's tone was sharp, dreading the thought of seeing him now. She cleared her throat, trying to soften her abrupt response. 'I just need to borrow his key for the other cottage, I can't find mine. I'm meeting Maggie at the school soon and I wanted to lock up before I leave.'

'Oh, here he is,' Chloe said cheerfully, as a door was opened somewhere behind her. 'Ready at last. I'm sorry, I don't know where he keeps the spare key and I'm sure he'll want to see you before you go.'

Over Chloe's shoulder, Flora was aghast to see Mac emerge into the sitting room, wearing jeans and pulling a T-shirt over his head. He looked uncomfortable as he approached the door.

'Flora needs the spare key, Mac. She can't find hers.'

He quickly reached into a drawer in the kitchen and lifted out a bunch of keys. Flora saw him separate one and return the rest.

'Well, I'll leave you two alone,' Chloe said, turning away. 'You probably have things to discuss.'

Flora could have laughed at the truth of Chloe's comment, but Mac seemed distracted, and every suggestion of the warmth and closeness they had shared was gone. She was instantly reminded of their first meeting at the hotel and it hurt to think that they were back to being strangers. Nothing could have chilled her heart more quickly than seeing him with Chloe as she moved gracefully around the cottage, slipping in and out of view and yawning, covering her mouth with a beautifully manicured hand.

'I'm just going.' Flora backed hastily onto the path, desperate not to be left alone with Mac. 'It was nice to meet you, Chloe.'

She saw Chloe raise her hand to say goodbye. 'You too, Flora. Good luck with the garden! I hear it's practically a jungle.'

'Flora?' Mac ignored Chloe, lowering his voice as he stepped outside and pulled the door shut behind him. 'I'm really sorry. I had no idea this was going to happen; I wasn't expecting Chloe to turn up. Here.' He ran a weary hand over his tired face as he passed her the key, and Flora noticed the shadows beneath his eyes. It wasn't much comfort to know that he looked as distracted as she did. 'Are you all right?'

Flora's composure was slowly returning, and it was easier, with Chloe there, to remain professional. She had no intention of letting him glimpse any of the love she had finally admitted to herself last night. She thought instead of the weeks ahead trying to forget him, realising that all they had shared on this magical island would be nothing more than conversations consigned to their past.

'I'm fine,' she assured him coolly. 'I'm going to see Maggie before I go to Róisín and then I'll keep out of your way when I come back. You and Chloe obviously don't need me hanging around when you'll want to be together.'

'That doesn't matter,' he told her impatiently, quickly reaching out to take her hand. Flora pulled free just as swiftly. Touching him was not going to help with the process of forgetting him. 'We still need to talk. There's something you need to know.'

'Just forget it,' she snapped, tired of the constant battle to restrain her own body around him, to always want what he could not give her. Her gaze was scornful as she glared at him. 'The only discussions we need to have concern the garden. Beyond that, whatever you say or do has nothing to do with me. You really ought to be with your girlfriend now, Mac, not me. And don't worry, I have no intention of telling her anything about your behaviour, which she might find… unfortunate, shall we say? But maybe you should.'

Flora strode away from him and didn't look back to see if he was still watching. Last night, her final day could not have come slowly enough, but now that Chloe was here with Mac, Flora suddenly couldn't wait to escape the island. She grabbed her things from the cottage and locked it, stuffing the key into her bag as she strode up the hill to her car.

Maggie was pleased to see her when she reached the school, and Flora spent a couple of hours with her, walking around the work in progress and helping to draw up plans and ideas for it. She was sorry she would not be here to help in the future, especially since the garden reminded her of Tamsin. Flora's unhappiness grew when she thought of the little girl trying to find a way to make a garden without any of the help that she could have given her. She refused Maggie's offer of an early lunch and excused herself to return to Róisín for her final visit.

When she arrived, the builders were banging in the house and Flora let herself into the peacefulness of the garden. It was so familiar to her now and she made her way down to a narrow gap in an overgrown hedge, where once had stood wrought-iron gates leading to a thin strip of shell-covered beach and, beyond it, the turquoise sea. The tide was rising fast and she stepped over the rough shoreline, turning to photograph the house and garden from the lowest point of the landscape. When she had finished, she sank down onto a dry patch of sand and powered up her laptop to make notes. Downloading the photographs she had taken would have to wait for Wi-Fi when she returned home.

Oblivious of the approaching water, she sat for a while, lost in unwelcome thoughts of leaving this extraordinary place – the beauty of the island and its people – and returning to Middlebrook. In the end it was Mel who had been proved right, not Sophie; it would have been better for her if she hadn't come back to Alana. Flora realised that much as she loved the garden and had wanted to learn its secrets, she had done it partly to test her feelings for Mac and his for her. She knew she had allowed herself to believe that perhaps everything between them could have been different, that all she had glimpsed in his eyes really was true.

Until this morning. Now Chloe was settled in his cottage and their relationship felt horribly real, no longer confined to online images. Flora could make up the headlines herself – she didn't need a magazine to do it for her: the beautiful, successful actress and her adoring architect boyfriend, pictured together playing in the surf on the secluded island he called home. Just the thought of such images stung. She snapped the laptop shut and stood up decisively. Tomorrow wouldn't do – she would leave today.

Flora returned to the beachside cottages but there was no sign of either Mac or Chloe, and she was relieved. She let herself into Cassie's cottage and dumped her things, suddenly feeling tired. She started to pack, folding her clothes neatly and sliding them into her case. The bed looked very inviting, but she knew it would take more than sleep to relieve the ache pounding through her head. She looked around one last time and then walked out with her belongings, locking the cottage and placing the key under a blue-and-white pot beside the door.

She needed to try to see Tamsin before she left the island. They had made no further plans to meet, but Flora couldn't go without offering a goodbye and whatever hope she could, so she drove to the B&B. A fine, misty rain was drizzling and disguising the views as she approached the headland; the stone house was surrounded by clouds that seemed to dangle almost within reach. Flora got out of the car, a sudden anxiety at the thought of a final goodbye spinning in her stomach, as she approached the house. Her knock was soon answered by Moira, who smiled when she saw it was Flora.

'Flora! How lovely, come in.' Moira pulled the door back. 'I hope you were all right after supper the other night. I know the damson gin can be a bit strong and Doug's very generous with it. I think he forgets that not everyone has an island constitution! What can I do for you?'

Flora's answering smile was wry as she followed Moira into the sitting room. 'Let's just say it was delicious and my head certainly knew that I'd tried it!' They drew to a halt beside the sofa and Flora's gaze went naturally to the view. She listened out for little footsteps but there were none, and she looked at Moira, swallowing down her feelings. 'I was hoping to see Tamsin to say goodbye. Something has come up and I'm leaving today. Now, actually.' Her voice was strained, and she smiled, trying to relieve the tension. 'Is she here?'

'I'm sorry, Flora, she's not.' Moira explained. 'She's gone over to the mainland with Doug; it's market day and she loves to see the animals. She wasn't feeling too well this morning and I kept her off school but as she perked up, I thought it wouldn't do her any harm to have a bit of fresh air. I'm not expecting them back before teatime.' Moira's hands were twisting together, and Flora noticed the questions written across the older woman's face. 'Can you wait and have a cup of tea and some cake? There's a lemon drizzle just out of the oven.' Moira paused. 'I know she'd love to see you. She's asked Doug to take her to Róisín again tomorrow after school. I think she was hoping to see you there, before you go.'

Flora shook her head slowly after a glance at her watch. It was almost four o'clock already and she knew the ferry to the mainland would be leaving at five. If she didn't make it, she would be forced to stay another night on the island. She couldn't go back to the hotel and she certainly didn't want to hang around the cottages, with Mac and Chloe next door. 'I'm so sorry, I can't. I need to make the ferry. I really am sorry to miss her.' She thought about what to do, how best to say goodbye to the little girl who had so touched her heart. 'I'll write her a note, if that's okay with you?'

'I think that would be very nice and I'm sure she'll love it.'

Flora didn't have anything in her bag that would do, so Moira brought her a notecard and envelope, and Flora thought for a few moments about what to say. In the end she wrote of how much she had enjoyed getting to know Tamsin, and her hope that she and her grandparents would be able to make a garden at home, and that her sweet pea seedlings would be beautiful and very pink. She promised to email and apologised for not being able to share a hug goodbye. She folded the piece of paper into its envelope and handed it to Moira with a sad smile. Their eyes met, as some form of understanding passed between them, and Flora made her way back to the front door. She had her hand on the latch when Moira spoke again.

'Flora? I've no idea why you've suddenly got to go, and I know it's none of my business, but I hope it's not something to do with Mac.'

Flora froze, her heart skidding in her chest as she slowly turned around. Moira's expression had softened, and her hand reached out, quickly touching Flora's arm with cool fingers, before slipping away.

'Doug and I have known him most of his life and he's like another son to us, especially after what happened.' Moira swallowed and then smiled brightly as she continued, using the gesture to disguise her sadness. 'He's only ever brought one or two girls here before and I know you'll tell me your being here is all to do with the garden. That might've been the start of it but, TV girlfriend or not, I've never seen him look at anyone like he looks at you. He's a very good man. The best, really, and we think the world of him. Don't dash off without sorting out what's happening between you both. You could start by asking him why he wanted us to make up a room for you here and keep it on standby, just in case.'

Chapter Nineteen

With every mile, it seemed to Flora that the real world was beckoning, dragging her back to normality, as the romanticism of the island dimmed with each grey cloud in the sky, reflecting her mood. Her phone was still dead; she'd forgotten to charge it before she had left the cottage in such a hurry and it was stuffed somewhere in her handbag.

She was supposed to be going home to Middlebrook and wanted nothing more than the long journey to be over. But soon after ten p.m., just as it was turning dark, she changed her mind and drove to Thorndale instead. When she finally pulled up outside the vicarage, she was exhausted and suffering from a terrible headache. She had hardly stopped, and the busyness of the roads as people hurtled from place to place on the mainland, after the peace of the island, had left her drained. She was extremely glad that the journey was finally over. She wanted to see Charlie, not the silent shadows in her cottage, to feel the peace and sense of home she always found with her brother and his little family.

She dragged her case up the steps to the front door and knocked, hoping they would not mind her late arrival, and give her a bed for the night. Their baby daughter, Esther, would hopefully be sleeping peacefully, and Flora was just about to knock again when the door was opened and her brother appeared, a welcome smile already lighting up his face as he spotted Flora.

'Hey, sis, what are you doing here?' he said, keeping his voice low. He immediately reached for her case and lifted it easily into the hall. 'We were expecting you first thing on Saturday. Have we got it wrong?'

'I'll go then, shall I?' Flora retorted as she followed him inside. Her emotions were very close to the surface and she resorted to irritation in an attempt to disguise her sadness.

'Don't be silly,' Charlie told her, as he dumped her stuff on the floor. He was a couple of inches taller than Flora but broader, the professional rugby player's physique still retained. His dark, curly hair was slightly longer than the last time she had seen him, and it made him look more boyish. A door opened along the hall and Flora saw Sam, her sister-in-law, emerge. Her small round face broke into a grin when she realised who it was.

'Flora!' she exclaimed quietly, dashing down the hallway to envelop Flora in a tight hug and trying not to spill the glass she was holding at the same time. 'Urgh, sorry, I think I've just sloshed some wine down your back! Never mind, it was white – it'll wash out! How lovely you came early; Esther will be ecstatic to see you.'

Despite her headache, Flora giggled as she pulled back and then Charlie dragged her into his embrace, too, tipping his head back to peer at her critically. 'You look tired.'

'So would you if you'd just taken a ferry and driven for five hours to get here.' Flora shoved him away. She saw the glance that passed between Charlie and Sam, and took a deep breath. 'I'm fine, it's just the drive. Any chance of a cup of tea and a bed for the night?'

'You go on up and I'll bring you one,' Sam said gently. 'Charlie will carry your case to the room. We can catch up properly tomorrow.'

Flora thanked her gratefully and trudged upstairs after Charlie. She managed to brush her teeth and change into pyjamas, before she slid into the cool bed in the big, high-ceilinged room. She could barely believe it was only twenty-four hours since she had been sharing supper on the beach with Mac, and memories of seclusion, sunshine and swimming tumbled into her mind. She snuggled under the covers and was asleep long before Sam crept in with a cup of tea.

Several hours later, Flora stumbled groggily out of bed, pulled the curtains back and blinked in the bright sunlight that met her. Windows on the south and east walls gave the room a lovely view of the garden and the village just beyond the trees. After a quick shower, she unpacked and discovered her phone still in her bag. She plugged it in to charge and went downstairs, making her way to the warmth and welcome of the kitchen. Sam was up already, busy unloading the dishwasher while also setting the huge oak table. She noticed Flora at the same moment as the baby sitting in her highchair squealed in delight.

Flora grinned and heard Sam's chuckle as she hurried over to Esther. She knew she was biased, but Esther really was the most beautiful baby. She had inherited her mother's large brown eyes and pink cheeks, and her growing hair resembled her father's dark curls. Esther offered Flora a heart-melting smile, and grasped a clump of her aunt's hair as she bent down for a kiss.

'Ow!' Flora said laughingly, as she carefully disentangled herself from her niece's chubby fingers. 'Come and give your Auntie Flora a cuddle, you gorgeous girl. She looks more like Charlie every time I see her, Sam.'

Sam was watching Flora lifting Esther from the highchair. 'I know. Thank goodness he's so handsome, otherwise it might've been a disaster! Watch she doesn't transfer soggy Weetabix onto your top.'

'I don't need to ask how you are,' Flora said, reaching for a wipe to clean Esther's sticky fingers. 'You look amazing, Sam.'

Motherhood clearly suited her sister-in-law. Flora had first met her more than ten years ago and she had always been cheerful and merry, able to see the best in everything and just about everyone. Flora noticed two new rings high in one ear lobe to compliment her other piercings, and pink and green highlights in her short blonde hair. Sam suited her role as Charlie's wife perfectly, and together they made a whole that was enriching to be around.

'Thank you. You look great, too, Flora. Your summer glow is coming along well. I can't wait to hear all about your time on the island – the garden sounds amazing. Did you fall in love?'

Startled, Flora's eyes shot up from Esther wriggling on her knee to find Sam's gaze casually waiting as she pushed a cup of coffee across the table to her.

'What do you mean?'

Sam looked puzzled, her hand hovering somewhere above the table. 'The garden? I bet you fell in love with it, didn't you?'

'Oh, well, maybe a little. But you know how it is, you always have to go home.' Flora fell silent, her mind suddenly full of Mac and the memories linked to him. She busied herself with Esther, lifting her up and pulling her against one shoulder to chatter nonsense, hiding her eyes from Sam.

'Do you?'

Before Flora could reply, the door opened and Charlie stepped into the kitchen. Flora knew at once from his expression that something was wrong, and she felt nerves spike in her stomach. Was it her mum? Or something else? She watched as he absently reached out to take Esther from her, his expression tense.

'What's wrong?' It was Sam who had spoken, and she pulled out a chair, sitting opposite him. 'I heard your phone before and I thought it was early. Is it family?'

Charlie shook his head slowly, expelling a long breath, and then his look settled on Flora.

'Just say it,' she blurted out. 'You're really worrying me.'

'Sophie called me,' Charlie told her quietly. Flora's mouth opened immediately to ask what was wrong but he held up a hand. 'She's fine; they all are, Flora, don't worry. She's been trying to get hold of you since yesterday afternoon but apparently your phone is switched off and she tried me because she knew you were coming here at some point. She really wanted to be the one to speak with you.'

'Why?' Dread had reduced Flora's voice to a whisper and Charlie sighed again.

'Mac, is it? The guy you were advising on the island? Apparently, he has a rather high-profile girlfriend, and it seems she's having a thing with a Hollywood actor that's now splashed all over the internet. Sophie said there's going to be pictures in the press, too, any day now. The girlfriend's apparently done a runner from the show she's filming and disappeared, presumably to wait for the fuss to die down.'

Flora knew exactly where she was, understanding now why Chloe had appeared on Alana so suddenly. Was that what Mac had meant when he'd said that things with Chloe were not as they seemed? Was it over? A flicker of hope flared in her mind before she registered that Charlie still looked serious and his hand reached out to hers, squeezing it tightly.

'That's not quite everything,' he told her gently, and her stomach lurched at the sympathy she read in his face. 'It seems you're involved, too, Flora.'

'Me? But how?' Her voice had risen to a shocked screech and Charlie clung to her fingers, while Sam bustled over to take Esther from him. 'I've only clapped eyes on Chloe for about two minutes and I know next to nothing about her! How the hell am I involved?'

'There's a couple of pictures of you and Mac online, too, from Mel's wedding. The gossip sites are suggesting he won't be too cut-up about Chloe, because you're comforting him. Somebody must have made the connection and leaked them. I'm so sorry. Sophie's been trying to track you down to tell you, before you found it somewhere.'

Flora's eyes widened in horror as a wave of nausea rushed into her mouth. She stood up quickly, staring from Charlie to Sam, as though they might suddenly laugh and tell her it was all a joke.

'If they go looking for me, then they'll find Dad,' she whispered brokenly, staring at Charlie again. 'Then Mum and Liam, and they'll have to go through the gossip and speculation all over again. It'll be even worse this time, if it gets in the media because of me.'

Her chair fell back as she pushed it away and hurried from the room. She raced upstairs, just making it to the bathroom in time before she retched, and hot flashes of shame shot through her body, feeling responsible for dragging her family into the public glare, however unwittingly she had done so. She crept back to her room and switched on her phone, now fully charged. There were five missed calls from Sophie and seven from Mac, as well as more than a dozen voicemails. She began to play the ones from Sophie. Each had urged her to call as soon as she could but not to worry.

She leant back on her bed as she looked at the calls from Mac. The first had been at ten thirty yesterday morning, when she had still been at the island school with Maggie. Then the calls had followed at twelve thirty, two fifteen, three p.m., three forty-five, five twenty and finally seven fifty, before he had given up. Her finger hovered over the list of voice messages and she selected his first.

> 'Flora, it's Mac. Call me as soon as you get this, okay? I'm guessing you're still at the school, and I know the signal's not great. I need to see you.'

She deleted it. She pressed play on the second one, the third, and so on, until she had heard, and deleted, all but the last one.

> 'So, I know you've left, and I can't say I blame you. I'm so sorry about last night and Chloe turning up. Look, Flora, if you

> haven't already heard, there's some stuff about Chloe and her co-star on social media, and it includes pictures of us, too. I can't tell you how sorry I am that you've been brought into this. I wish I could just make it all go away. I didn't want to have to discuss it over the phone and I'm hoping you've gone home, as you're not here. I'll try you again tomorrow. Call me, please. There's so much I have to tell you.'

He hadn't called this morning yet and Flora replayed the last message again, thinking about what might happen next and how much scrutiny she and her family might be subjected to. There was a tap on her door, and Charlie's head peeped around it, holding a tray. He carried it over and settled on the other side of her bed, the mattress shifting under his weight.

'You should eat,' he said, sliding the tray onto her lap and offering her a plate of toast. She shook her head with a shrug.

'I'm not hungry.' She stared at him quizzically. 'Have you seen the photos?'

'I looked them up. I thought I should see them.'

'And?'

Charlie sighed, as Flora replaced the toast on the tray. 'Anyone can capture a moment in a picture and make it seem like it's something it's not. You and Mac look very close, and I can see why people believe that there's something going on. I don't think we should call Mum yet, in case the story just disappears, but we'll have to if it looks like it's going to keep on running.'

Her phone rang then, making her jump, and Charlie stood up, dropping a kiss on her head as he left the room. Flora stared at the screen, her finger trembling anxiously over Mac's name, and she stared until the ringing stopped. A moment later the voicemail icon popped up and she deleted his message without listening to it. She typed a quick text to Sophie to let her know she was fine and would call later, and then tossed the phone onto her bedside table. Anxiety and fear were churning in her stomach. She knew there was only one place where she would be able to leave her thoughts behind: in a garden. She stood up and crossed to her case, angrily pulling out her work clothes as she hunted for a clean set. Soon she was ready; she left the phone in her room and carried the tray, the food uneaten, back to the kitchen.

Charlie and Sam were talking quietly and they both looked up as Flora entered. She gave them a wan smile, bending down to kiss Esther, who squealed, raising her arms to be lifted up. Flora obliged, snuggling the tiny girl's plump body against hers. For some reason, the gesture reminded her of Tamsin, and she wondered how she had reacted to her note and whether she would still go to Róisín today.

'I'm going to Annie's cottage,' Flora said, filling a glass with water whilst still holding Esther. 'I know I'm a day early, but everything should be ready, and it would be good to make a start on the planting before Annie and Jon get back.'

'Flora, are you sure you're all right? What's happened must have been a nasty shock.'

Flora tried to bat away Sam's concern. 'Well, it's not our first, is it?' She sighed as she handed the baby over to her sister-in-law. 'Sorry, Sam, that wasn't fair. I know you're concerned but I am okay, honestly. I just need to be working.' Silence drifted over them whilst Sam threw together a packed lunch and then Flora was outside, rummaging in the boot of her car for her trusty work boots and gloves. She found her plans for the garden and set off on foot.

Still only a small village, its origins rooted firmly in farming, Thorndale was popular with tourists, who arrived every day to wander around its craft courtyard and art gallery, and eat in the pub that offered locally brewed beer and home-made food. The only shop, no longer just the post office, had diversified with a deli counter, ice cream from a local dairy farm and excellent cheese. Flora was impatient to begin work and she hurried past the shallow, bustling river along the high street without pausing to appreciate her surroundings. Thoughts of the pictures of her and Mac – that people had seen and were no doubt gossiping over – churned through her mind and she prayed that her family's past would not be dredged up again.

Willow Cottage was at the far end of a lane leading from the high street; only a high farm gate separated it from the fields and moorland beyond. When she reached the gate leading to the front garden, she finally paused her furious march and smiled with a genuine pleasure that eased the tension in her temples. When Annie Armstrong had married Jon Beresford in December last year, they had established an education trust through the Thorndale estate to provide sponsorship for two pupils to study at agricultural college.

Annie's godmother, who had bequeathed her Willow Cottage, had been an Oxford professor until early retirement, and the principle of education for all had always been of great importance to her. Rather than sell the cottage or turn it into a holiday let, following her marriage, Annie had donated it to the trust to ensure it would always be a rent-free home for the students supported by the estate, and so it was occupied in its new capacity by two young people. Flora was thrilled to see that the garden was being carefully transformed, exactly as she had hoped, and knew that the weekend was going to be non-stop.

The plants had been delivered on time and she separated them into groups for the different borders, thankful for the opportunity of working alone, allowing her mind gradually to settle. But after lunch, Charlie and Sam arrived – wheeling a pushchair containing a sleeping Esther – and were quickly followed by Nathan and Ally, the two students who lived in the cottage. Nathan had arrived in Thorndale last summer, under difficult circumstances. He was quiet, polite and wary of making new friends, and a few of the villagers hadn't immediately taken to him. But despite all that, he had gradually settled in, worked hard and was thrilled to have been offered one of the first places at college through the new education trust.

There was much to do in the garden and Flora was grateful for their help, as she directed her little team of volunteers. By late afternoon, they were much further on than Flora had hoped, and she was delighted with the results. They were sitting on the lawn, taking a break whilst they waited for Ally to return from the village with ice cream. Esther was playing on the grass, crawling between the plants and shrieking as Charlie slowly followed her. Flora smiled at them, appreciating once again her brother's complete happiness in his marriage and family. She was drained but knew it to be more than the tiredness that came with physical exertion; sleep would be hard to come by when she eventually crashed into bed. The day in the garden had busied her mind, but it couldn't free her from the scrutiny of the online world lurking somewhere beyond the cottage.

They heard Ally return, as the garden gate creaked, and Flora looked up in expectation of a refreshing ice cream to cool her after a day of physical work. But it wasn't Ally who appeared in the garden, and Flora's eyes widened in amazement as her heart fluttered in shock. Mac's gaze swept over the group, before coming to rest easily on her, and Flora hurried to her feet, the bottle of water she held falling to the ground.

'You followed me.' Flora's whispered words weren't a question, merely a statement, as she took a step towards him and then halted suddenly. Charlie made his way to stand beside her, his squirming daughter held firmly under one arm, offering his support, as Nathan disappeared into the house. There was a challenge, too, in Charlie's gesture and Flora appreciated it, even though she knew she didn't need it. 'How did you know where I was?'

'The vicarage wasn't hard to find, and I asked at the shop for the cottage. I've already been to Middlebrook and they said you weren't back yet.' Mac was still staring at her, exhausted and pale, and it was little consolation to know he was troubled, too. 'Flora, I had to come and find you because you didn't return my calls and there are things I have to say.' He hesitated, his glance flicking to

Charlie for a second, before returning to Flora. 'Could we go somewhere?'

Strangely, Flora didn't want to. They had created their own version of a secluded reality whenever they were together on the island, and now she just wanted to remain in the real world. 'Whatever you need to say, you can say it here. This is my family.'

'Okay. If that's what you want.' She nodded and Mac took a couple of strides forward, until he was near enough for her to touch. Her fingers trembled, remembering only too easily the shape of his shoulders and the feel of his bare skin against hers. She became aware of Sam, still sitting behind her, trying to yank Charlie back. It worked; he glanced down and then stepped away to join Sam, as they busied themselves amusing Esther, who was crawling amongst the pots on the lawn.

Mac began to speak. 'I'm sorrier than I know how to say about everything that's happened. I wish I could change it and spare you whatever you and your family are going through just now.' He sighed, running a hand over his face.

Flora waited, wanting desperately to close the gap between them, to hold him and be held in all the ways she had been imagining for weeks. She scrunched her hands into tight fists, unable to escape his solemn blue-grey gaze, as her feet remained planted to the ground.

'You should know that the pictures of Chloe and me in Ibiza were a set-up, Flora. They were only taken to imply something that's not real. There was nothing in them that couldn't be passed off as mates, old friends meeting up. I made sure of that.'

'What?' Flora felt shock, a moment of relief and then resentment chasing one another through her mind, as she tried to make sense of his words. 'But why?'

'Chloe and I ended our relationship a few months ago, but then she called out of the blue on the day of Mel's wedding to ask me for help.' Mac rubbed his neck with an agitated hand. 'She's seriously involved with someone she works with, and they were desperate to keep it out of the press until filming's over and they could announce it.'

'But why you?' Flora whispered, a shred of hope growing into something more. 'What does that have to do with you?'

'She knew it was a big ask but she wanted something to divert attention should anyone be looking – she thought that a couple of pictures of me and her in a magazine would do the job. No one would be very interested in her getting back with an ex who isn't part of her world.' Mac was staring at Flora, his gaze pleading with her to understand. 'I agreed, eventually, with a couple of conditions. The first was that the pictures would only run if she had no other choice and the second was that our agreement expired after four weeks, when she was due to finish filming. If they appeared after that, then I would say that she and I were still over and always had been. No one knew about it, other than her best friend, who was in Ibiza that weekend to take the shots. Not her agent, publicist – no one.'

He paused for a moment, before continuing. 'The only reason I did it, Flora, was because Chloe had been there for me last year when Angus and Rachael died. She dropped everything to support me through those first weeks, when I couldn't think straight. I wasn't sleeping or eating properly, and I couldn't work for a time. I knew she wouldn't have asked me to do this unless she was desperate.'

Mac's smile was wry, rueful. 'But I'd just met you and we'd shared that amazing kiss at the wedding – and, quite honestly, I haven't stopped thinking about you since. I knew that if you were angry with me, then at least one of us would be trying to keep their distance. So I didn't contact you, didn't do anything that might attract attention to us, still hoping that the images wouldn't run, and it would all go away and you'd forgive me once I'd explained everything. Then Chloe texted to say someone was onto them, and the pictures were out. I wasn't happy and realised then how complicated I'd let things get. I drove straight to Middlebrook to tell you myself.'

'But I already knew.' Flora knew she had assumed what everyone else had, she hadn't tried to trust him or ask for the truth.

'Yes. I was too late. And I was going to tell you, but you made it clear that everything that happened between us at the wedding was over and you weren't interested. I'm so sorry that I hurt you, Flora. But I still wanted to protect you as much as possible until the final two weeks were up and Chloe could release her statement.'

'What do you mean?' Her voice was low, finally pressing him for the truth.

He paused and his gaze became gentler still. 'The garden was the perfect excuse to bring you to the island and keep you safe there. But it wasn't just that. I'd barely looked twice at it before I met you and, for me at least, everything changed when I found you there amongst the madness of it all that first morning. You looked like you'd come home and now there isn't anyone else I would trust with its future, however you feel about me.'

Esther was crying now, and Flora wanted to join her. Tears pressed at her eyes and she swallowed down her desire to tell him it was how she had felt that morning too, and her elation that he had recognised it. Moira's final words before Flora had left raced into her mind and she blurted out her next question. 'The room at the B&B? I thought you'd done that just to keep me out of your way.'

Mac nodded wryly. 'So Moira told you? I did want you out of the way but not for the reason you think. If Chloe's story went public before she'd finished filming, any reporter looking for me as the ex she'd cheated on would go to the hotel and find you. The cottages are pretty isolated, but I knew they could still be found, as everyone knows they're mine. I asked Doug and Moira to be ready to take care of you if needed, but even they didn't know why. With the B&B closed, I didn't think anyone would come looking for you there. And every moment on the island with you, Flora, just made me realise how much I wanted you to stay and how it was beginning to feel like home again, after Angus and Rachael. I felt we were safe there and I was struggling to pretend, to stay away from you. And then Tamsin and how everything is between you both. I didn't see that coming.'

Tears shone in his eyes and Flora rushed forward, wrapping her arms around him. She held him, feeling his tension dissolve, relief coursing through her. 'I didn't trust you,' she muttered sadly. 'I should've done, when you asked me to give you time, after the ceilidh.'

Mac pulled his head back to look at her, and she nearly gasped at the tenderness, the new openness, she saw there.

'You had no reason,' he said softly. 'It was a lot to ask, given what happened before, with your dad, and how I left you after the wedding. And then Chloe's story broke and everything changed again. She only came to apologise; she's already left to sort out what happens next. Flora, I'm sorry I've made such a mess of things.' He touched a hand to her cheek, stroking her face gently. 'So, really, what I'm trying to say is that I love you. I have done probably since that first weekend after you marched up to me with your crazy dare and made it impossible for me to forget you. It wasn't until the evening at Doug and Moira's that I began to think you might feel the same.'

She gasped at his words, as she began to accept the truth of his feelings. Everything around them melted away and even the sound of the birds in the trees seemed silenced, as she listened.

'I can't fast-forward forty years and show you our history, Flora. But I want to spend my life creating it with you and showing you all the ways you can trust me.'

'How do I know that I can?' She whispered the words, hardly able to think of anything other than the fact that he loved her, as his hand continued to stroke hers.

'You don't,' he told her simply. 'But if you love me too, and I'm praying that you do, then you're going to have to try to let me show you the rest.'

He let go of her hand to draw her into his arms, pulling her against him. She could feel his heart racing, as they held one another again, until he placed his lips against her temple and kissed her lightly. He drew back to look at her. 'Doug and Moira send their love,' he said gently. 'And Tamsin asked me to tell you that her plants have grown, and she liked your note but still wants her hug.'

Flora did cry then at his words, tears skittering down her face as she thought of Tamsin, far away on the island. Mac leant forward and lightly kissed her lips, before he spoke again. 'I have to go home now, Flora. I've got to make the last ferry. And I'll be there if you decide to come back and give me another chance. It's up to you.'

Chapter Twenty

Flora returned to Middlebrook on Sunday, her time off at an end. She had finished the garden at Willow Cottage, and Annie and Jon were thrilled with the results. Champagne had been opened and a party spontaneously started, but she had pleaded a headache and slipped away. She loaded her car and returned home that same evening, despite Charlie and Sam's pleading to stay for another day or two. She was still stunned by Mac's declaration of love and, much as she knew that she loved him, too, she needed some perspective to decide what should happen next.

Back in her cottage, she had a long chat with Sophie, and they went over the stories in the press. To Flora's relief, even though she had eventually been identified as the woman in the pictures, Chloe's sudden appearance at a movie premiere with Noah Maguire was the only story everyone wanted, and she and Mac had gratefully faded into the background. Noah was a recently divorced American actor, seventeen years Chloe's senior, who had just played her stepfather in their TV drama. The two actors were pictured with their arms firmly wrapped around one another, their respective social media accounts full of 'it's early days but we're madly in love' photos.

Sophie had raved about Flora's appearance in the pictures that had been leaked from the wedding, teasing her that it was a good thing they hadn't tried to pap Flora at work in muddy jeans and her beloved steel toe-capped boots. Flora had laughed, eventually, and looked at the photographs. There were just two and, although they had caught only a small moment in time, she knew that they undoubtedly revealed the truth of their growing feelings. In one she and Mac were standing at the bar while Flora was talking with someone, her hand tightly wrapped in his and her head turned away from him. He was looking at her in an unguarded moment, his gaze fixed adoringly on her face. In the second they were dancing and, from the way one of his hands was placed on her back while the other stroked her hair, she knew immediately that it was their first time. Her hands were on his shoulders and they were gazing at one another with an unspoken desire needing no words to reveal it.

Three days after returning to work, Flora let herself into her cottage after a long day spent training a couple of volunteers new to the team. She was finding work more of a challenge now that her thoughts constantly strayed to Mac, Tamsin and the island, and she knew she had a serious decision to make. Her heart knew what it wanted, and it was only her head that was still advising caution. She collected her post and dumped it on the table without looking at it, desperate for a shower to sluice away the tiredness that seemed to seep into her limbs. Twenty minutes later, feeling refreshed and with her hair piled on top of her head, she flopped on the sofa to go through the post. None of it was interesting, until she found a thick, white envelope; the writing scrawled across it unfamiliar. She turned it over and ripped it open, impatient to discover what was inside. She read it incredulously and then again, just to be sure.

Dr and Mrs David McDonald invite you to join them to celebrate the marriage of their daughter Amanda Grace to Mr Rory Alexander MacKay

On the island of Alana, Argyll

And so it went on. Her eyes raced through the details a second time, and she discovered that the wedding was to be held this coming weekend in Mac's hotel. But it didn't make any sense. Flora had never heard of these people and she puzzled for a moment, trying to imagine how the invitation could possibly have made its way to her. Perhaps it had been sent by mistake from the hotel? She held it in her hand and then slowly turned it over. On the back, that same black handwriting was scrawled across the centre of the blank, white card.

I dare you

And then she knew, her tiredness evaporating, as joy and a surprising certainty replaced confusion and doubt. The laugh that followed the realisation was jubilant and she immediately reached for her phone, discarded nearby. For once it worked and the message sailed away.

I haven't got anything to wear…

The answer came in a moment, as though Mac had been waiting for her response to his invitation.

> Doesn't matter. Wear your jeans, I love the way your legs look in them. Just come. There's a flight on Saturday morning and a ticket waiting for you.

Sophie almost exploded with excitement when Flora rang to give her the news. There was nothing Flora could do to prevent Sophie from calling her parents for emergency childcare, leaping into her car and hurrying all the way to Yorkshire. She dragged Flora into Leeds to get her hair cut and help her choose a wardrobe deemed suitable for the approaching weekend. Much to her delight, Sophie even managed to convince Flora to get a manicure and pedicure.

It was a scramble to get time off again after two weeks' holiday, but Flora managed it by begging and issuing mad promises to reciprocate for those who promised to stand in for her. Sophie was still so wild with euphoria that she offered to abandon her family for a bit longer and stay on at Middlebrook to volunteer to do some gardening on the estate. Flora had laughed so much at the thought of her stylish and organised friend trying to command the weather and cope with the mud that she had almost been tempted to accept. The hours seemed to crawl by as Flora hurried around in her spare moments to get everything sorted and ready.

Her flight on Saturday was due to land at Glasgow around ten a.m., and Flora was expecting Mac to meet her there. Relieved that it wasn't delayed, she collected her case and dived into the ladies to freshen up before she saw him. Anticipation danced through her, as she remembered his words at the cottage a few days ago and the adoring expression in his eyes. She slid lip gloss across her mouth, already imagining kissing him hello, the thought enough to make her hurry. She touched up her mascara and added a little more of her perfume that he had so loved at the wedding. Desire hummed in her veins as she remembered again the sensation of his lips very close to her neck when he had breathed it in and told her how much it suited her.

She glanced in the small mirror, pleased with the floral ivory shift dress she was wearing, sleeveless and sitting just above her knees. It suited her perfectly, a new confidence spilling through her. Her hair was piled into a casual bun on the top of her head and she remembered Mac's eyes roving across her whenever it had fallen loose.

She hurried out into the arrivals hall, nervousness suddenly bringing doubts as she glanced across the people bustling past her, heading for friends and families waiting to meet them. There was no banner, no sign displaying her name, and she thought that perhaps she had misread his plans and she was supposed to find a taxi to take her to the island. She hovered for a few moments more, as disappointment began to replace elation. She fumbled in her bag for her phone, thankfully still working, and checked for messages.

'Flora!'

Her head snapped up and she felt her heart soar. Mac was running impatiently through the hall, trying to pass the people in front of him, all heading in the opposite direction, without pushing them aside. He skidded to a halt in front of her, shoving his keys and phone into his jeans pocket, and she dropped her case with a clatter. His eyes were on her face, and then he stepped forward and she was in his arms, feeling the taut strength of his body against hers as she clung to him. He lifted her easily and swung her around as they both laughed, before he reluctantly set her down again.

'I'm sorry I was late,' Mac said, gripping her hand and Flora was already lost in the love shining from his face. 'There were roadworks, and I was held up.' His eyes became more thoughtful then, roaming over her with a longing she had sensed before but had never seen, not like this. 'I'm so glad you're here. I wasn't sure you would come.'

'You dared me,' Flora said, exhilaration and confidence adding a teasing note to her voice. 'What did you expect?'

He grinned, tracing a pattern across her fingers. 'Is that it?' His voice was low, and she was aware of people staring curiously as they edged past them. 'Or is there more?'

'Are you asking me if I love you?'

He nodded slowly and she smiled, wanting – no, needing – to tell him what she had been holding back for weeks.

'Yes, I love you. You've turned my world upside down and I never imagined feeling for anyone what I feel for you. I even spend more time thinking about you than I do about gardens. Will that do?'

She saw wonder and relief racing across his face and he reached for her, pulling her quickly back into his embrace. A searing heat lit up her senses as he kissed her, oblivious to everyone around them, and she curved towards him as one hand tantalisingly explored her back. This new intimacy between them was startling and blissful. His other hand went to her hair and pulled away the pins holding it, so that it tumbled into loose waves that he gathered between his fingers.

'I wanted to do that every time I saw you,' he said huskily, sending her pulse galloping to a new rhythm. 'We really ought to go.' There was reluctance in his voice, and she could feel his smile against her cheek, now that the kiss had ended. 'It's not very private and we're attracting attention.'

She giggled, her hand firmly in his, as he scooped up her case and they quickly crossed the hall to the exit. Once they were in the car and speeding away from the airport, Mac began to speak.

'I can't stand gardening,' he told her with a grin. Flora felt laughter bubbling up as she listened to his confession. 'I've thought of almost nothing but you since we met. I've been hopelessly distracted and it's all your fault. Driving to the island from Edinburgh after work just so I could be near you when I was supposed to have been staying out of your way… Taking a week off work when I couldn't really spare the time because I couldn't bear not to be on the island if you were… Trying to pretend I didn't want to dance with you at the ceilidh when I really wanted to carry you away to somewhere we could be alone… Encouraging you to help at the school because I thought it might be another reason for you to come back… Shall I go on?'

'Oh, Mac,' she said softly, finally understanding that the last few weeks had been no easier for him and that, like her, he had struggled to constantly hide his feelings. The realisation left her elated and she reached across to smooth the small frown on his face with her fingers. He smiled, trapping her hand against his cheek for a moment, as they waited in a queue at a set of traffic lights. 'I thought the school might be a reason to come back, too.' She paused, and felt him looking at her. 'How's Tamsin doing?'

'Truthfully? Not as well as when you were there,' he said quietly. 'But it's only been a few days and I know you can't promise her what you can't give, Flora. She's not your responsibility.'

Flora knew he was right and, although she was certain now of how she and Mac felt about one another, the future was still far from certain. She was silent as she thought of Tamsin and how she might be able to help her; eventually, her thoughts brought her back to his garden.

'Have you done anything with the garden since I left?' She had finished compiling her report and had emailed it to him. It was probably too soon for anything to have changed but she wanted to know.

He looked at her, snatching his attention from the road for a moment. 'Nothing, Flora. It's waiting for you. It's always been waiting for you. Just like me.'

She smiled but still, niggling at her, was the thought of her job hundreds of miles away. She tried to blank their inevitable parting from her mind, content for now to cling to these moments with Mac. The wedding was taking place at four o'clock, and they arrived at the hotel in time to deposit Flora's luggage and share a late lunch together, before she reluctantly chased him away so she could get ready for the ceremony. He'd teased her again about wearing jeans, and she wanted some time alone to dress up.

Thanks to Sophie, she now possessed a selection of gorgeous underwear and, after a shower, Flora chose some pink-and-cream satin lingerie that made her feel deliciously sexy. She reached for her dress and stepped into it, twisting around to do up the zip on her side and smiling as she imagined asking Mac to do it for her. She scooped up her hair again and twisted it into an elaborate updo that left her neck bare and emphasised the elegance of the strapless dress. She crossed to the mirror, hardly able to recognise her own reflection. The pale lilac silk dress, with its fitted bodice, floated down to gather in simple pleats above her knees and Flora loved how it fluttered against her skin. She spritzed more perfume on her neck and wrists, put on nude high heels, and reached for a clutch bag, before walking to the door and finally emerging on the landing.

Mac was waiting for her, leaning casually against the wall, changed into a beautifully tailored navy suit. He had seen her only once before dressed like this, and he didn't bother to hide the leap of approval and interest in his eyes as he walked over to meet her. His hand went around to her back and he pulled her towards him for a kiss. He was still smiling as he lowered his face to breathe in the scent on her neck.

'We ought to go,' he said reluctantly, stepping back. 'You look so beautiful, Flora, but then you always do. I almost didn't recognise you without the baseball cap. Have you brought that too?'

She laughed, shaking her head and thanking him for the compliment, and then his arm was around her waist, keeping her close as they walked together down the wide staircase to the main hall. Flora felt nerves spinning in her stomach, as people eyed them curiously, and she glanced at Mac. Suddenly, the reality of attending this event with him seemed too much after the very recent revelations about Chloe, and she reached for his hand.

'Mac? Maybe it's too soon, all of this,' Flora said anxiously, seeing all the other guests spilling into the building and gathering in the sunlit garden. She noticed more glances being thrown their way as people huddled in groups, and she hoped that the talk would not be about them. 'Perhaps we should just keep things casual today, not rush?'

He stopped and stepped closer, his hand warm on the thin silk nestling against her back. 'I'm crazily, madly in love with you,' he said simply. 'And if you're okay with that, then I don't want to hide it any longer or pretend it's not true, no matter what people think. I'm done with all that – this is our reality.'

'I love you, too,' she whispered, and all thoughts of keeping their relationship private disappeared as she kissed him. His hand was still on her back as they reached the hall and they paused to smile at the staff, who eyed them discreetly. Mac nodded at a few guests he recognised, and then they found seats in the drawing room and settled down.

Flora already knew the wedding about to take place was between Amanda McDonald – one of Mac's colleagues at the practice in Edinburgh – and her fiancé, Rory MacKay, a professional golfer. He looked like a sportsman, Flora thought, as she watched him hovering at the front of the room with his best man, both looking fit and lithe in their kilts. The registrar with them waited patiently, and as the moment approached when Amanda would make her entrance, the guests murmured quietly, glancing behind them for that first glimpse of the bride. Never before had Flora attended a wedding where she had not known a single person, but her nerves were held at bay by the soothing, yet entirely intoxicating presence of Mac at her side.

After the ceremony there was to be dinner and dancing later, and fireworks into the evening. Mac introduced her to the people he knew, whilst champagne and canapés were served. Each time, she was elated to be presented as his girlfriend, and she forgot about the obvious questions about Chloe that people must have been dying to ask. Once they had done their bit and made lots of new acquaintances, Mac drew Flora into a quiet corner in the main hall, away from the efficient presence of the bustling staff.

'Let's disappear for a bit.' He gave her a look that would have had Flora willingly following him anywhere. 'We can be back before they notice we've even gone.'

He led her out to his car and she wondered where he was taking her, as he drove away from the hotel. But very soon she knew, and she smiled happily, her hand resting on top of his, as he headed along the hidden lane to Róisín.

The house was still swathed in plastic and poles, and yet Flora noticed changes. She saw that the roof repairs had finished, the weeds had been cleared from the windows, and the dull walls were gradually being repainted in a soft cream that drew the extraordinary light to the building. Mac opened the car door for her, and they made their way along the drive. But he didn't take her to the house.

The old green door leading to the garden that she had first seen all those weeks ago had not changed and Mac shoved it open, kicking away weeds and nettles with his feet to make a path for them. But it wasn't enough, so he lifted her into his arms and carried her through into the silent garden. He didn't set her down again until he was standing on the terrace outside the drawing room.

'Do you remember that first morning here?' he asked her, suddenly serious again, and Flora felt a flare of worry. 'When you first discovered the garden and fell in love with it?'

'Yes, of course I do.'

'I know you have a job, Flora, and it's hundreds of miles away.' Mac paused and ran a hand through his hair distractedly. He reached up to loosen his tie and shrugged out of his jacket, tossing it idly onto the rusty old bench behind them.

She held her breath as she waited for whatever was coming next.

'I just want to say that you can have this garden,' he said, holding out his arm and sweeping it across the view all around them. 'All of it, every part of it is yours – if you want it.'

'Are you offering me a job?' she whispered, half-afraid of the answer. Not that, surely? A professional role here when all she wanted was him. Mac grinned as he shook his head, and his arm dropped back to his side as his gaze clung onto hers. 'No. The thing is, the garden comes with a house, too. And me.'

Flora was utterly lost for words as she stared at him, thoughts of the garden vanishing at once. She stepped backwards, suddenly lightheaded, and he dashed forwards to grab her hands.

'I know how much you love your job, and I don't want you to have to give up anything to be with me. I'm hoping we can work all that out somehow, if we were to live here together,' he said earnestly, his gorgeous eyes alight with exhilaration. 'I'm hoping the garden might be an incentive.'

'You are all the incentive I need,' she told him, trying not to laugh and cry at the same time. 'I don't need a garden as well. You know I'll come, how could I not?'

'There's Tamsin, too,' he said, more uncertainly. 'Do you think you—'

'I want to help take care of her, too,' Flora said unwaveringly. 'I can't explain it; I just know that I love her, and I want to share whatever we can do for her with you.'

His reply came as he wrapped her in his arms. He held her for a long moment, until she impatiently tilted her head and lifted her mouth to kiss him, loving the feel of his hand in her hair and his heart slamming against her. She recognised once more the wonderful feeling she had experienced on that very first day, when he had found her in the garden, and they had fallen in love amongst the chaos and beauty of it all.

'Mac,' she said eventually, smiling into his shoulder and still distracted by his hands caressing her neck and sliding down to explore her back. 'Can I ask you something?'

'Of course.'

'Are you any good at weeding?'

Epilogue

Hogmanay

Gradually, the house was brought back to life as Flora and Mac set about making it their home. The months since the renovations began had seen careful and thoughtful changes brought about. The principal rooms downstairs were restored first, each leading to the garden, offering glorious views of the south and the sea. Heating was installed, wiring replaced, and bathrooms created to improve the running and efficiency of the house. Everything that could be saved was stored away until it could be used again and brought back where it belonged once more.

But the Arts and Crafts principles had not been lost or sacrificed. Everything possible was done to ensure that the house remained faithful to its history and the original design. They were still discovering its secrets: cupboards that had not been emptied, tools littering the garden, books lost on shelves and smothered in dust. And in every forgotten corner, stories from the past made themselves known with every object found and everything that grew outside.

By far the most extraordinary surprise they had come across was two paintings, unframed, hidden at the back of a wardrobe. One was of the herbaceous border below the terrace, painted at eye level – as though the viewer were sitting amongst the plants themselves and immersed in their beauty – with a suggestion, an outline, of the house beyond. The second depicted a blonde and handsome boy, laughing over his shoulder outside the summerhouse, as he looked back at the artist with a glimmer of mischief in his eye. Thrilled with the discovery, Mac and Flora had arranged for Rose's paintings to be cleaned and framed, and they now hung in the drawing room, where they were seen and appreciated every day.

In the hall, the oak panelling on the walls and wooden floor had been carefully repaired, and huge windows peeped out from between heavy scarlet curtains. The table in the centre held only winter flowers in an antique vase, filling the air with the scent of pink-flowering virburnum. The alcoves tucked into the walls were still empty, waiting to be filled with the things they would gradually collect together. The fire laid in the hearth was already lit, and it burned merrily, sending a bright glow over the walls. The huge Christmas tree, found at the top of the north garden, glittered far away from the open fire, adorned with the old and simple decorations they had discovered in the attic.

Everything was ready for the party. The table was laid in the dining room and drinks piled in the courtyard to chill in the icy temperature outside. They would begin with cock-a-leekie soup, followed by haggis, venison pie, and tatties and neeps. The cheese would be served with shortbread, and three big Tipsy Laird trifles would be enough to feed everybody, even if they wanted seconds.

It was freezing outside, and Flora dashed indoors from the garden, stamping her feet to try to get the blood flowing again. She dropped her coat in the utility room and tugged her boots off, crossing into the kitchen in her stockinged feet. In here all was warmth and comfort. The room that Mac had created from the old kitchen, pantry and larder was full of natural light, leading onto a private courtyard on the west side of the house. He had designed the kitchen to be a functional space as well as somewhere to relax – a place for entertaining their friends but also somewhere to enjoy intimate suppers for just the two of them – and it worked perfectly.

As there was no sign of him, she ran through to the hall and his office on the south side of the house. The door was open, and she peeped inside; his laptop was on his desk, but he had disappeared, and Flora carried on to the staircase, reaching the gallery moments later and finding it empty. The space was still waiting for new paintings and furniture to fill it, but for this evening the carpet had been rolled back and there would be games, as there had been before, another detail revealed in Rose's journals. Flora checked Tamsin's room, decorated in pink and purple, making sure that everything was ready for when she would arrive with her grandparents later.

Tamsin had quickly made herself at home in the house, soon after they had moved in, and she loved to spend time in the garden with Flora, helping her or racing around and having fun with the friends who came over to play. Flora and Mac both adored her, and they had talked early on about her future and what they could offer. When Doug and Moira had suggested that they become Tamsin's legal guardians, they had immediately accepted. During the process, an idea had come to them which, eventually, tentatively, they had discussed with Tamsin's grandparents, and the possibility of adoption was mentioned.

After much thought, discussion and with tears on both sides, it had been agreed. Doug and Moira were concerned about Tamsin's future, given their age, and they wanted above all else for her to have a secure and loving family long after they were gone. It also meant they would be able to return to their role as grandparents and, once they got used to the idea, there was a great deal of relief.

Tamsin's delight and excitement at the idea of living with them at Róisín had thrilled Mac and Flora; they had explained that they would become her new parents and it would make them a family of three. So sometime in the New Year, hopefully not too far away, Tamsin would join them permanently at Róisín as their daughter. There would be challenges ahead and a period of adjustment needed, given the changes over the past year, but Flora and Mac were prepared to do whatever necessary to begin their new lives together as a family.

Satisfied that Tamsin's room was ready, Flora crossed the gallery to her and Mac's bedroom. It was such a beautiful room and she loved it. Windows on the west wall and the huge, curved bay overlooking the south garden and the sea leant it masses of natural light. She could never enter it without being drawn to the view and staring outside. The pale walls, almost white, reflected the ever-changing landscape outside and she was glad that the fire was lit, adding to the beauty and comfort of the large room. There had been so much to do in the house; Flora was kept incredibly busy overseeing the renovations and working in the garden every spare minute she had.

She had left her job at Middlebrook and next year they were planning to renovate the outbuildings to offer working holidays, where she could teach garden history and restoration, as well as provide opportunities for students to begin their careers in the garden that Rose Campbell had loved so long ago. Rose and Archie's story had also attracted the interest of a writer who was planning to produce a biography, and Flora and Mac were keen to explore the idea of an artist in residence, who would teach and encourage other young painters just starting out.

Flora looked out to the garden, hoping fervently that the weather would not worsen and prevent their guests from completing their journeys, some from many miles away. The door to their bathroom opened and she whirled around to see Mac emerge. Her heart flipped over; she was still hardly able to believe that it had already been over a month since they had got engaged.

He had surprised her one cold November evening, insisting that they sit outside on the terrace to watch a display of the Northern Lights. Flora had been enthralled: they'd wrapped up warm to huddle around a firepit, eating hot dogs and watching the night sky flashing above them. Before the display was over, he'd astonished her by going down on one knee and asking her to marry him. He had produced an exquisite sapphire and diamond ring that, he smilingly explained, he'd chosen because it reminded him of her eyes. Flora had accepted, laughing and crying all at once, and they'd opened a bottle of champagne, drinking it on the terrace where she had first seen the garden.

So Flora would have the wedding she had never expected, and her half-brother Liam would walk her down the aisle, so that Charlie could marry her and Mac.

Liam and her mum had spent time at Róisín since Flora had moved here, and the idea had formed soon after she and Mac had got engaged. She was closer now to her younger brother and, in some strange way, she felt that the wedding would help to lay to rest all of the heartache of the past. Mac had approved, and she knew Charlie was pleased. Tamsin was ecstatic about the wedding and they had already chosen a lilac dress for her to wear as bridesmaid, along with one for Sam and a miniature one for Esther. Her two best friends were to be bridesmaids, too, and Sophie was helping Flora with the planning, applying her usual efficiency to every detail, for which Flora was grateful.

Mac had a towel around his waist and was using another to rub his hair, and his face lit up when he saw Flora. She still couldn't look at him without a rush of delight and she hurried over, curling her cold body around his.

'Have you been outside again?' he asked her, amused, sliding the towel in his hand around her neck and holding her close. Flora laughed, her lips tantalisingly brushing his cheek as she spoke.

'Just to check that the heaters in the greenhouse haven't switched off. I'm back now; I must have a shower, Annie and Jon are—'

But she couldn't finish her reply, as he lowered his head to kiss her, and her shower was very rushed indeed, when she eventually managed to take it. They darted downstairs together, barely five minutes before their first guests, Annie and Jon Beresford, arrived. They were shaking the snow from their hair as they stomped inside, bearing gifts and compliments about the house, and were quickly followed by Doug and Moira, with Tamsin. The first party in this home for many, many years was about to begin, and Hogmanay was the perfect day to celebrate their engagement and bring the house and its lost garden back to life.

Acknowledgements

This book was a joy to write, not least because Flora and I share a passion for plants and a belief that gardens are good for you. Researching the Arts & Crafts period and its properties has made such places a favourite and I hope to visit more in the future. I stand in awe of those whose skill and vision first brought these gardens to life. Thank you to all horticulturists who continue to care for gardens both past and present, and ensure that they reflect their history whilst looking to the future.

Thank you to Audrey and Andrea, good friends and writers, who are always there to offer encouragement, support and much laughter. Zoom is brilliant but bring on the champagne in the garden!

Thank you to Susan Yearwood, Emily Bedford and the team at Canelo, and Katrina Power. Your insight, support and guidance makes all the difference. Everything that looks beautiful on my website and social media was designed by Katie Birks; thank you for your vision, creativity and skill, I so appreciate the work you do. Anna Caig has taught me much and is a brilliant advocate for writers. Thank you, I can't wait to read your book!

Thank you to Irene, Becca and Jen, wonderful betas once again, for being so enthusiastic about this book and Mac especially! Having readers who enjoy my characters and their stories is such a pleasure, and I'm thankful for each one.

So many thanks to Clare, who increased my plant knowledge considerably and shared your own so readily. For every garden you designed, there are more plants and trees in the world and that's a wonderful legacy. To Kev and Dave, whose different skills are renowned and complement one another brilliantly. Thank you both, you quite literally made my job so much easier and a whole lot funnier. Flora would love to have you on her team!

To my mum Irene, a gardener for as long as I can remember. Wherever we went, you were always able to create a garden, however unpromising the plot, and I appreciated even then the pleasure to be found amongst it. More than I realised has filtered down over the years!

To Stewart and Fin, thank you both, as ever. To Stewart especially for that wonderful, surprise, 600-mile round trip to Scotland. I loved every moment and the insight it brought to my research, as well as the understanding of two very special properties and their period of design.

To paraphrase Flora in the book, it doesn't matter about the size of the space you have to grow plants or create a garden. Whether it's a balcony or a courtyard, a windowsill or a wall, a huge plot or something in between. What really matters is what you do with it and how it makes you feel to be amongst it. Setting out on a journey with plants and a garden is a wonderful thing, and I hope that doing so may bring you much pleasure and peace.